dare me
once

OTHER TITLES BY SHELLY ALEXANDER

The Angel Fire Falls Novels

Dare Me Once

The Red River Valley Novels

It's in His Heart
It's in His Touch
It's in His Smile
It's in His Arms

The Checkmate, Inc. Novels

Foreplay
Rookie Moves
Get Wild

dare me *once*

An Angel Fire Falls Novel

SHELLY ALEXANDER

This is a work of fiction. Names, characters, organizations, places, events, and incidents are either products of the author's imagination or are used fictitiously.

Published by Montlake Romance, Seattle

www.apub.com

Amazon, the Amazon logo, and Montlake Romance are trademarks of Amazon.com, Inc., or its affiliates.

ISBN-13: 9781503901766
ISBN-10: 1503901769

Cover design by Erin Dameron-Hill

Printed in the United States of America

*For all the parents of special-needs kids out there
who get up every day and choose to love. Because love
definitely is a choice. Sometimes it's an easy choice,
and sometimes it's the most difficult choice of all.*

*And as always, for my husband. A wonderful man.
A loving partner. A great father. And the one person in
the world I know I can always count on to be there,
no matter what.*

Chapter One

LILY'S LIFE LESSON #1

Never date a man who can't make you moan louder than your masseuse can.

"I don't need to get laid," Trace Remington said in response to his two younger brothers' smart-ass remarks about his love life. Getting laid was the last thing on Trace's priority list.

Trace chalked his pool cue and waited patiently for Spence, the youngest, to get too cocky and miss a shot. Always did.

"Might do you some good." Elliott, the middle brother, chuckled as he lounged on the old orange sofa in the game room of the Remington—the family-owned resort where they'd grown up. Even with the shades up, the dark paneling, dim light from the stained-glass light fixtures, and giant old-fashioned video game machines blocking the back windows made the room look dank.

Spence studied every possible shot on the table. "It might make you more pleasant to be around, big brother."

"I'm pleasant enough, and you two need to mind your own business."

"Like hooking up is even an option for him," Elliott said, as though Trace weren't standing right there.

Trace flipped off both his siblings, who were only sixteen months apart in age and could pass as twins with their tall, powerful builds, green eyes, and light-brown hair—with just enough curl and length to give them that bad-boy look. Trace, on the other hand, favored their mother. She'd had dark-brown hair that matched the color of her eyes and a smile that had made Trace trust her when she said she'd always be there for them.

He wasn't a naive eleven-year-old anymore.

"And you two wonder why I don't want you around my son." Trace knew that would get a rise. He leaned on his pool stick as Spence cracked a shot that banked left and dropped into the side pocket.

"You love that Ben is around his uncles, who can do everything bigger and better than his dad can." From the sofa, Elliott tried to poke Trace with a pool stick.

Trace knew it was coming and stepped out of the way just before the tip connected with his ribs. "You do realize you two act like obnoxious teenagers whenever we spend time together, right?"

"We're a helluva lot more fun than you," Spence said.

That warranted another flip off, and Trace added, "I can't wait until you two have kids. I'm going to laugh when a screaming toddler brings your player lifestyles to a grinding halt. Not to mention when the mothers of those children—whoever the unlucky ladies may be—bring you to your knees."

"I'm not a player, bro." Spence bent over to look down the barrel of his cue.

Elliott coughed *bullshit* behind his hand.

Spence ignored him and circled the table like he was on a reconnaissance mission. "I just don't do long-term relationships, but I always tell them straight up that I'm a commitmentphobe."

Growing up without a mother did that. All three Remington brothers sucked at relationships. Unlike Trace, at least his two siblings hadn't been stupid enough to knock up a woman with zero maternal instincts.

A tremor of guilt slid through Trace.

Ben was the best thing to ever happen to him, but being a single father of a special-needs kid required every minute of Trace's time, every ounce of his energy, every bit of his focus.

Precisely what had caused him to mess up so badly as a pilot in Los Angeles and forced him to make the decision to move back to Angel Fire Falls where he had a support network. Flying vacationers from Cape Celeste to the island in his eight-seater floatplane and giving aerial tours was a lot less demanding.

It was also a lot less stressful leaving Ben with family.

"Seriously, bro"—Spence walked around to the other side of the table—"now that we're all living on the island again, you can at least go out on a date once in a while. Between Elliott, Dad, and me, we've got Ben taken care of. You don't have to live like a monk just because you're a father."

"Women are distracting." Trace's tone went flat. "My son has been through enough." For Ben's sake, Trace couldn't screw up again. And since Ben's mother offered no help whatsoever, Trace couldn't get sidetracked by a woman.

"Relationships are distracting, not women," Elliott said. "Big difference."

Trace shook his head. "Both are complications I don't need. End of discussion." He pulled over a barstool and perched on the edge.

Spence's next shot hit a small wrinkle in the worn felt that covered the old pool table and missed the pocket. "The table needs to be re-covered."

"No kidding." Trace got up and looked for the cleanest shot. "The entire place needs an overhaul." Which was why their dad had hired some hotel executive as the Remington's new hospitality manager—to bring a fresh face and a new breed of clientele to the place.

Someone who might transform the Remington into a place they no longer recognized. *That* had Trace's fatherly instincts rattled.

Trace leaned over and lined up his shot. He'd been back in Angel Fire Falls longer than his siblings—two and a half years, as opposed to Spence's six months and Elliott's nine weeks—and had learned to play pool around the wrinkles, memorizing every bump and snag in the felt, just like flying around severe weather and turbulence.

Ben's Asperger's syndrome might prevent him from picking up on social cues or tolerating change without having a meltdown, but the boy could rack 'em and stack 'em. So Trace had played a million and one games of pool. Pool seemed to be one of the activities Ben zeroed in on like a laser beam.

"Dad's convinced the new manager will have the know-how to breathe life into this place again. I guess we'll see, because she's flying in this afternoon. Dad said she's catching the ferry to the island, but I've got to take a few guests who are checking out to Cape Celeste, so I'll bring her back with me." Trace let his stick fly, and the cue ball cracked against the solid red number three. It disappeared into a corner pocket, Trace already taking aim on the purple number four.

"Dad asked me to generate a budget so the new employee has something to work with," Elliott said. Graduating at the top of his class at Wharton, he'd practically set San Francisco's financial district on fire. After six years of working 24-7, he'd finally burned out and showed up on the Remington's doorstep for Christmas. No warning. No explanation. Just a suitcase full of expensive suits he'd never bothered to unpack. "I don't know what changes she has in mind, but they'll have to be implemented over time. The resort's bank account isn't empty, but it's not overflowing either."

Spence rubbed the scruff on his jaw. "Dad's let the place decline the past few years. I've already got a list of repairs as long as the island." As a builder, Spence had a talent for land development and had built quite a reputation throughout the Pacific Northwest—until something had gone terribly wrong with one of his partners and Spence had shown up at the Remington for a visit and never left. "Our guests are mostly older folks. Where did all the family vacationers go? And I can't help but wonder why a big-city hotel exec would want to live on this little vacation island and work for the Remington."

Trace shrugged. "Dad said she was looking for a slower-paced work environment. Sounds like she might be past her prime and looking for a less stressful job."

"She's coming to the right place." His head leaning back against the sofa, Elliott pointed to the solid yellow ball. "Left corner."

Trace sent a blur of yellow flying. It disappeared right where Elliott had pointed.

"So back to you getting laid," Spence said, just as Trace got off another shot.

The tip of his cue skimmed the side of the ball and sent it rolling in the wrong direction.

"Works every time." Spence laughed and slowly circled the table, looking for his next shot.

Trace sat on the edge of the stool again. "Funny you have to use cheap tricks to try to beat me."

"All's fair in love and pool, especially between brothers," Spence said, hunching over the table. "Elliott and I can give you some pointers since your game with women doesn't even register in the positive numbers."

Trace's eye twitched.

Elliott laughed and propped one hand behind his head. "This is gonna be good."

"I don't need pointers. Especially from you two horndogs."

Spence straightened. Wrapped both hands around the top of his stick. "Really? Then how long has it been since you scored with someone in the bedroom other than yourself?"

"You're an asshole." Trace twirled his cue like a baton.

"Yes, I am." Spence drew out each word like the smart aleck he was. "I'm guessing if you won't answer the question, it's been much longer than you want to admit."

Trace's leg started to bounce because his gut told him where this was going.

"Dare you to go out on a date." Elliott flashed his boyish grin. "We'll babysit."

"Not gonna happen. Ben needs all my attention."

Spence lined up another shot. "Ben probably needs a break from you more than you need one from him. You're overprotective. Let him skin a knee. Break an arm. Girls love casts. They'll be all over him."

"He's eight," Trace deadpanned.

Spence dropped another stripe. "I'll just bet"—he bent to set up his next shot—"you couldn't get a date if you tried, because it's been so long you don't remember how." The cue ball cracked against another stripe.

Here it came.

"Forget getting laid," Spence taunted. "I dare you to get a woman's phone number by the end of the day."

"Is that so?" As immature as it was, Trace found himself taking the bait just as if they were teenagers again. He never could resist throwing down with his little brothers. Showing them who was boss was just too much damn fun.

Elliott rubbed his hands together, enjoying the show.

Spence scratched his chin. "One phone number by midnight tonight." He gave Trace a cocky stare.

"That's it?" Trace smirked and checked his watch. "I'm heading over to the Cape in thirty minutes. I'll have the number within an hour." He winked. "All I have to do is tell 'em I'm a pilot, and they'll practically throw their panties at me."

Which was why he rarely talked to women about his profession. Doing that had gotten him rushed down the aisle with a starry-eyed aspiring actress who realized she didn't love him about thirty seconds after the "I dos" were exchanged.

Regret washed through him. He hadn't been in love with Megan either. His willingness to do right by her hadn't been enough to keep her from ditching both him and their son when the first signs of Ben's autism surfaced.

"The number has to be in your phone." Elliott scratched his chin thoughtfully. "And you have to call her with us in the room as proof you didn't take the cheap way out by hitting on Old Lady McGill at the ferry crossing ticket window."

All three of them shuddered. Mabel McGill had a thing for Remington men. Any one of them, including their father.

"This is juvenile," Trace complained. "But I'll agree, just to remind you two who's still boss around here."

His two annoying siblings, whom he preferred to call Thing One and Thing Two, both flicked the tips of their thumbs across the ends of their noses—the Remington brothers' code for *It's a go*.

Trace shook his head at the secret communication system they'd created as boys. "There's no one here but us. Is code really necessary?"

Elliott ignored him. "It'll be a pleasure hearing how humiliated you are after you ask a dozen women for their numbers and still show up here tonight empty-handed."

They were already acting like adolescent boys, so why not go all in? Trace brushed the pad of his thumb across his nose and sank the last two solids to win the game. He tossed his stick onto the table. "And that's how it's done, little brothers."

"*Ooooh God.*" The moan of utter ecstasy Lily Barns let out was far more sensual than it should've been in a public place. For a small commuter airport, the masseuses who had their chairs set up in the middle of the terminal sure knew how to treat a gal right. A quick neck massage was just what she needed after flying halfway across the continent, changing planes three times, missing her last connection from Portland to Cape Celeste, and having to pay double to hop a later flight. The trip had been hell on heels, and her Jimmy Choos weren't made for traveling.

A massage might also work out the tension that had her shoulders balled into knots. She'd best be ready to meet her new employer before catching the ferry at Cape Celeste that would take her across the narrow channel to her final destination—Angel Fire Falls.

"Ahhhh," she moaned again as the small woman, who had *Yin* embroidered on her uniform, worked out a spasm in Lily's neck. Her face was planted in the round headrest of one of the portable upright massage chairs when a pair of swollen ankles attached to pale white legs and a swishing floral skirt came to an abrupt stop next to her.

"I think I need what she's getting," Ankles said.

Obviously Ankles's male companion disagreed because all Lily heard was a grunt of disapproval before the two walked off, their suitcases thumping behind them.

Poor Ankles. That caveman grunt was probably why she wanted a massage. Probably why she needed *something* that would make her moan. Maybe Mr. Grunt wasn't getting the job done.

Lily could relate.

Her ex-fiancé, Andrew, hadn't exactly rocked her world. Oh, in the beginning, he'd been affectionate and attentive. Everything Lily thought she wanted in a man because the attention he'd lavished on her made up for her father's indifference. But the two-carat engagement ring, the expensive condo, and the gigantic wedding Andrew had insisted they start planning to impress nine hundred and ninety-eight thousand of their closest friends and family had been for show—*not* because he was crazy in love with Lily.

Apparently, he loved his reputation as the CEO of one of the most prestigious hotel chains on the Gulf Coast more. The depths of her father's thievery headlining the news every day hadn't boosted Andrew's support or brought out his protective instincts for her either.

He'd broken up with her. Over the phone. And fired her to boot.

She let out a heavy sigh, which made a whistling noise through the headrest as the masseuse went to work on her lower back.

Lily made a mental note to add *Never date a man who can't make you moan louder than your masseuse can* to the top of her new list of life lessons. Lessons she'd learned the hard way since her father had gone to prison for embezzlement. Since all her so-called friends had turned their backs on her. Since the death threats had started.

The masseuse dug the base of one palm into a knot between Lily's shoulder blades. She almost howled from the shock of it, but then the pain melted away along with the knot in her aching muscles, and she relaxed. Good thing she'd paid in advance, because her mind was relaxing as fast as her muscles, and she might not be able to count out money once Yin was done.

"You tight," said Yin. "Lot of stress."

She had no idea.

"Need vacation."

Did Lily ever.

The job she'd taken using her new name was perfect. A secluded resort on an island off the coast of southern Washington State was as far removed from New Orleans's French Quarter as she could get without moving to another country. The Remington wouldn't be in the same league as managing the exclusive hotel she was used to working for. The pay wouldn't be in the same solar system. But less money and blending into a new location with new people *would* be like a vacation compared to the harassment Lily had been forced to live with since her father's fall from grace.

So what if she'd left some key work experience off her résumé so she wouldn't seem overqualified? So what if she'd written her own letter of reference and signed her old name to it? Everything in the letter was true, even if Andrew couldn't admit to it after firing her.

Her old life had crumbled around her, leaving her with nothing but a few degrees and an in-box full of hate mail. Her new life was a blank canvas, and Lily was ready to paint a beautiful, fresh masterpiece onto it.

She could get on with her work-vacation as soon as Yin finished turning Lily's muscles into limp noodles. As soon as she had time to slip into the ladies' room to ditch the trendy clothes meant to pacify her mother, who still hadn't accepted that the Devereaux family was broke.

Mom had dropped Lily at the airport thinking her baby girl, Scarlett Lily Devereaux, was going on an indefinite secluded retreat in Vermont to relax and escape the headlines. Little did her mother know, Scarlett had adopted her maternal grandmother's name, Lily Barns, and her destination was a tiny little town named Angel Fire Falls where galoshes were likely more socially acceptable than designer shoes. Where no one would know who she was, where she came from, or what her father had done.

She'd have to tell her mother the truth sooner or later. Lily preferred later. Much, much later. After she had time to legally change her name, was settled into her new life, and there was no coaxing her back to New Orleans.

Her phone, still lying on the airport floor next to her purse, dinged with a text. Lily ignored it. Yin was sending her to a happy place, and Lily didn't want to leave it.

Yin pressed both magical thumbs into Lily's tense shoulders, and she moaned again. Loud.

"That feels better than—"

A pair of large leather work boots appeared on the floor directly under her headrest.

"I'll pay double for whatever she's getting," a deep masculine voice said. The fluid tenor of that voice slid through her like a drink of her mother's favorite fine scotch, warming her insides as it flowed to her fingertips, her toes. Her . . .

She crossed her feet at the ankles and clenched.

Because she was *done* with smooth-talking men who possessed voices that could make a woman believe anything. *Done* with relying on a man the way she'd relied on her father and then Andrew. *Done* with men who said the right words but couldn't back them up with real heart.

Done, done, and done.

The work boots disappeared, and Lily uncrossed her ankles, letting her body relax again.

Until she heard the massage chair next to hers creak under the weight of a new customer, and that same low, velvety voice rumbled through her again.

"Make that triple," the Voice said. "She looks pretty relaxed."

She had been until now.

The other masseuse must've gone to work on the Voice, because he let out a deep, sexy groan that had heat spiraling through Lily in the most inappropriate way.

Good God.

"First time to the Cape?" the Voice asked.

Was he talking to her? Because she certainly didn't want to talk to him.

She lifted her head just enough to get a peek at him. A masseuse was already working on his shoulders. Very, very broad shoulders. His face was planted in the headrest, but everything else Lily could see was as attractive as his voice. Dark-chestnut hair with a slight wave, broken-in jeans, an indigo-blue polo.

Big and built.

His arms . . . nice muscular arms . . . circled around the front of the chair and leaned on the armrests.

Meow.

She might be off the market where men were concerned, but she wasn't dead.

A stylish yet masculine watch was strapped on his right wrist, which meant he must be left-handed.

Her father was left-handed.

Andrew had been left-handed.

A surge of anger hit her like a wave crashing against a rocky coastline, shocking her back to her senses.

She plunged her face back into the headrest and tried to find that happy place she'd been in before the Voice had interrupted.

Her phone dinged with another text. She knew without looking that it was her mother, because none of her "friends" contacted her anymore.

Still ignoring it.

She let out a sigh while Yin worked on her lower back.

Her cell vibrated and belted out the Cajun tune "Jambalaya (On the Bayou)." The music from Bourbon Street was one of the few things she'd miss from her hometown. That and beignets with extra powdered sugar. Nothing beat a French gourmet doughnut.

"Sounds like someone really wants to get ahold of you," the Voice said.

"It can wait." Lily didn't lift her head. No need to give the guy any encouragement.

"Do you come to the Cape a lot?" he asked her for the second time.

She sighed. "No. First time."

"You must be a tourist on vacation?"

"Um, something like that," she mumbled through the opening in the headrest, hoping he'd go away.

He went quiet.

Thank God.

"I'm a pilot, and I do private aerial tours. Once you see Cape Celeste and Angel Fire Falls from the sky, I guarantee this won't be the last time you vacation here. How about I get your phone number and call you after I check my availability?"

"Thanks, bu—"

"I'll give you and whoever you want to bring with you a nice discount."

This guy wasn't taking a hint. He didn't seem to be going away either. And he was using his slick, sexy voice to drum up business and make a sale.

Lily wasn't buying. And she was done with slick businessmen.

"No." Her tone was flat. Rudeness wasn't built into her southern DNA, but he wasn't giving her much choice.

Blessed silence stretched between them, and the tension in her shoulders slowly evaporated.

"Hey, would you mind if I used your phone?" asked the Voice. "I guess I left mine at home."

Her shoulders knotted into granite.

"Relax," Yin scolded her.

Self Defense 101 had taught Lily never to let a stranger use her phone. She weighed that wisdom against her desire for *this* stranger to leave her alone. Without looking up, she slid her phone across the floor to the Voice.

In a few seconds, he slid it back. "Thanks. I appreciate it."

She didn't respond. Quietly, she lifted her head so the paper on the headrest wouldn't crinkle. The Voice was still facedown while the masseuse went to town on his shoulders. Silently, Lily motioned for Yin to stop. She eased out of her chair and picked up her purse and phone. On tiptoes so her heels wouldn't click against the cement floor, she slipped away.

To go start her new life where her new all-weather hiking boots would be perfectly acceptable. Where ordering fruity drinks with umbrellas instead of fine scotch would go unnoticed. Where the Prius she planned to buy as soon as she'd satisfied her employer's probationary period and saved up a down payment would be considered smart and environmentally conscious.

Where slick businessmen with ulterior motives would be part of her long-forgotten past.

Chapter Two

LILY'S LIFE LESSON #2
When the words *how hard can it be* cross your mind, it's time for
happy hour so the alcohol can restore your judgment.

Louis Vuitton luggage didn't exactly reinforce Lily's plan to stay incognito, especially since she was the sole passenger on a ferryboat the size of a canoe.

Her suitcases thumped down the narrow ramp toward the open-air terminal where her ride to the Remington Resort should be waiting. A sign over the entryway said WELCOME TO ANGEL FIRE FALLS.

Exactly the kind of place she needed to hide in plain sight from the media.

When she stepped inside, she stopped cold. *Terminal* was a generous description. There were a few benches covered by a roof with no walls except around the one-window ticket booth where a clerk shuffled a deck of cards.

No one was there to welcome her. No one held a sign with her name on it. Best of all, no reporters crowded her—asking questions about her father—and no haters yelled insults, which usually included phrases like *rot in hell*. That kind of greeting she could live without, but no greeting at all on a vacation island she'd never been to might be a slight problem.

She pulled her phone out of her purse and double-checked her messages. Several more calls from her mother, which was why Lily had silenced the ringer, but no reply from her new employer. The text she'd sent Mr. Remington about her new arrival time had gone unanswered, and that didn't make her feel warm and fuzzy.

Lily glanced around the deserted terminal. Her new boss wasn't kidding when he said she'd have plenty of time to get the resort in shape before the summer tourist season started, because there wasn't a single tourist in sight.

Her gaze slid along the rocky island shoreline to the south, the cliffs rising above the channel she'd just crossed. Just north of the terminal was a country road leading inland, and to the left of that, the shoreline was a gorgeous sandy beach with boulders dotting the water.

She drew in a breath and let the cool misty air fill her lungs, then rolled her conspicuous luggage over to the small ticket booth.

She should've ditched the French designer bags along with the Choos when she'd changed in the airport bathroom before leaving the mainland. She'd had no choice, though, but to use the expensive status symbol for traveling since her mother had brought her to the airport. Less than haute couture *anything* would've put her mother on alert, and the prying questions would've started to flow. Smelling less-than-the-best merchandise like a bloodhound on the trail of a hunted animal was her mother's superpower.

Never mind that her mother would soon have to start donating blood just to pay her bills.

A wave of guilt rippled through Lily.

Leaving her mother behind hadn't been easy, but Lily couldn't take the drinking or the denial anymore. At least she'd cleaned out her modest savings and left the cash in a safe hiding place, so her mother would have *something* once she finally hit rock bottom.

Lily should feel ashamed that she wouldn't be around to see it. Instead she felt relieved.

Just because her mother chose to cling to the past didn't mean Lily had to. She desperately needed to get on with her life. Which was why she was stranded at a ferry crossing in the middle of nowhere, staring at a woman behind the ticket counter whose back-combed hairdo could house a flock of geese.

The ticket clerk's name tag said Mabel McGill. Her coral lipstick that bled into the wrinkles around her mouth said she'd spent a lifetime working hard for the money. Her sparkling blue eyes said despite her lack of skills with coiffeur and cosmetics, she was as friendly as the cawing seagulls that hovered around the terminal looking for scraps of food.

Mabel lifted a calloused hand to slide open the scratched acrylic window. "Can I help you, hon?"

Lily wasn't sure where to begin. Because that was exactly what this was—a new beginning. In every way. "I just arrived from Cape Celeste."

They were on a small island with not even a causeway connecting them to the coast. Where else would she have come from? Lily fought off a self-deprecating eye roll.

Mabel leaned forward just enough to note Lily's designer luggage over the counter. Her eyes gleamed with amusement when they skimmed across the purse slung over Lily's shoulder. It was made from supple alligator and was also straight from the Parisian fashion scene. *Thank you, Mom.*

"Tourist?" Mable asked.

"Not exactly." Lily stepped in front of her luggage and let her purse slide to the ground, out of sight. This was her chance to start over. Damned if she'd let the French take her down now. She might be from New Orleans with Cajun French running through her veins, but she was a scrappy red-blooded American girl, and Louis Vuitton could take a hike.

She bit her lip. She was keeping the purse, though, because the purse-whore in her had to draw the line somewhere. "I'm the new hospitality manager at the Remington Resort. I guess I missed my ride because I had to take a later flight." She wrinkled her nose. "Maybe I should call an Uber."

Mabel's penciled brow disappeared into her hairline. "This is Angel Fire Falls. We don't *Uber*." She said it like it was a dirty word.

A gust of misty spring air blew Lily's long brown hair across her face, and she hooked a finger around it to push it out of the way. She rubbed the arms of her white cotton button-up shirt. "Is there a cab company on the island?"

Mabel snorted. "We have a shuttle." She pointed to the exit behind Lily.

"Great." Lily flashed a relieved smile. She was beginning to think she'd have to walk to the Remington.

"It only runs twice a day during the off-season, and it just left ten minutes ago." Mabel shrugged. "Won't be back for several hours, but you're welcome to wait here. There's hot coffee, if you'd like a cup."

Lily looked down at her new hiking boots and turned one on its side. "How far is the Remington?"

Mabel pointed to the road that meandered over a bluff and disappeared behind a lush green landscape. "Up the road a piece. The road forks a few miles in. Left takes you into town. Stay right and you'll run smack into the resort. I can try to call and see if one of those handsome Remington men will come get you." Her eyes gleamed, and she licked her painted lips.

Lily had already been left stranded once today. This new job wasn't off to the greatest start, but it was all she had at the moment. No way would she sit around waiting. Depending on someone else. Lily Barns could take care of herself.

Her gaze wandered to a sign pasted to the right side of the window that said BIKE, TRIKE, & SCOOTER RENTALS. She glanced over her shoulder at the beach, the waves crashing against the white sand. A long row of rentable bikes was lined up and chained to a bike rack, each with a tall yellow-and-blue flag attached to its back. The flags waved in the wind. Her stare snagged on the giant tricycles at the end of the row. There was a basket between the back wheels.

How hard could it be? Just like riding a bike, only with an extra wheel for balance.

Lily pulled out a wallet that matched her purse. "How much to rent one of your adult tricycles?" Not words she'd ever expected to say. Her new life was shaping up to be an adventure already.

"Hon, if you're brave enough to ride that thing all the way to the Remington with your suitcases strapped to the back, you can use it for free." Mabel reached under the counter and produced a bungee cord and a key. "This unlocks the trike on the end." She pushed the key across the counter. "I'll throw in the bungee cord for the luggage just because you're my kind of gal." Mabel winked. "Return both at your earliest convenience."

Lily stared at the key and bungee, then swung her gaze back to the road. Her earliest convenience? None of this was convenient. But she'd come this far, and she wasn't about to give up easily.

Her hand closed around the key and bungee. "Thanks, Mabel. I owe you one."

Mabel shrugged again. "You may not think so after cycling all the way to the Remington." She hooked a thumb over her shoulder, and Lily leaned to the side to peek around the booth toward the ferry ramp. An angry black cloud hung over the mainland and crept toward the island. "A storm's rolling in, so you better hurry."

It was late afternoon by the time Trace banked left by dipping the wing of his floatplane to the port side so he could circle behind the resort and land into the wind.

He'd flown to the Cape a few hours earlier with two assignments: show his annoying brothers he still had some skill with women and deliver the new employee—a Ms. Barns—to the resort.

The first was *won and done* thanks to the pretty tourist getting worked over by an airport masseuse. Sure, she hadn't given out her number willingly, so he'd had to resort to asking to use her phone so he could call himself from it. Still, he *did* get her number. Thing One and Thing Two could suck it.

Because the Remington brothers were so damn mature.

Unfortunately, Ms. Barns was a no-show, a fact Trace was about to discuss with his dad because that was a red flag.

He set the plane down in the inlet behind the Remington, the water a little choppy because of the storm brewing on the mainland. The plane skipped across the water before settling to a glide. He maneuvered it toward the dock, slid out of the cockpit onto one of the floaters, and then hopped onto the wooden dock.

He moored the plane, checked the cockpit one last time, and grabbed his jacket before starting up the trail that led to the family's back entrance to the resort. It was still early spring, and the storm had caused the temperature to drop, so Trace pulled on his jacket.

As he walked up the path, he found himself whistling the catchy tune that had been Sexy Airport Girl's ringtone. It must've been the best massage of her life by the way she'd moaned. That moan had stirred something inside Trace that had no business stirring because he wasn't in the market for a relationship. Not even a temporary hookup with a babe who lived somewhere else.

She obviously wasn't from Angel Fire Falls or Cape Celeste because her trendy clothes screamed *tourist*. But that body . . . even lying face-down couldn't hide the fact that she was a knockout.

It had been a long time since a woman caused a chain reaction that started with a double take the moment he laid eyes on her, then tightened his chest into a knot, and ended somewhere south of the border—a sensation that would likely keep him awake most of the night.

The trail veered left around a grouping of giant pampas grass, then opened onto a playground for their family vacationers. Since it was still preseason and school wasn't out for summer yet, the few guests staying at the Remington were older and kid-free. Only Ben and his cousin Charley's six-year-old daughter, Sophie, were making use of the large jungle gym.

"Dad!" Ben leaped over the side of the slide instead of sliding to the bottom. He barreled toward Trace. "Dad!"

"Hey, buddy." Trace hugged his son as the boy threw his arms around Trace's waist. "How was school?"

Ben let go and toed the ground. "I got in trouble for telling Miss Etheridge her new haircut was ugly."

Oh no. Trace could feel another parent-teacher conference coming on. They'd already had so many with Miss Etheridge, who insisted Ben would be a better fit in special ed. Yes, Ben had special needs, but he could do the work. He just got frustrated easily when he didn't understand something. Miss Etheridge was twenty-five and straight out of graduate school. Trace wasn't going to let Ben miss out on the education he deserved because his teacher didn't have experience dealing with Asperger's.

"Ben, we've talked about this." Trace tried to be gentle. Harsh words only heightened Ben's responses and caused more outbursts. Something his ex could never seem to grasp.

"But it's true," Ben insisted. "Her hair used to be long and pretty, and now it's short and blue at the bottom." He held out both palms as if he were incensed. *"All the way around."*

Trace chuckled. "Instead of focusing on what you *don't* like about her hair, try to find something kind to say about it. Like maybe it's a nice shade of blue. You like blue, right?"

Ben nodded, still not convinced this was good advice.

"Say *that*, and don't mention the negative stuff that might hurt her feelings, even if it's true."

Little Sophie slowed her swing and hopped off, skipping over to them wearing a tiara and a princess costume with a skirt made of hot-pink netting.

"Hello, Princess Sophie," Trace said, all serious and refined. He even threw in a bow.

She scrunched up her shoulders and batted big round eyes at him without saying a word.

"Miss Etheridge says I have to pick the topic for my science project soon or I'll get behind schedule." Ben toed the ground some more. "I want to build a remote-controlled plane like yours. One that really flies."

"I think we need to pick something easier." Ben might have a meltdown over such a difficult project if it didn't turn out the way he expected.

Ben started to rub his hands against his thighs in a distressed rhythm. "We always pick easy projects." His voice rose. "And the other kids make fun of me like I'm a baby."

Trace sighed and ruffled his son's hair. "That's because the other parents do the projects *for* their kids. I want you to do the project yourself. We'll give it some thought this week, okay?"

Ben grabbed Trace's right arm. "Can I wear your watch?" The rubbing stopped, and his voice returned to a normal volume.

Trace unstrapped his Garmin D2 Pilot watch and put it on his son's wrist.

"And your sunglasses?" The excitement in Ben's voice rose. "Then I can pretend to be a pilot."

Trace pulled his aviators from his inside pocket and slid them onto Ben's nose.

Sophie grabbed Ben's hand and tugged him back to the playground, skipping all the way.

Ben glanced over his shoulder at Trace with a look that said *Help!*

Trace shrugged. "Get used to it, buddy. The pilot thing gets 'em every time." He studied the churning sky for a moment. "It's going to rain soon," he called out to the kids. "Come inside as soon as it starts."

He made his way through the back entrance, stomped his feet on the mat, and walked into the resort's kitchen. His cousin, Charley, was hard at work on a fresh batch of her famous gourmet doughnuts. She had retreated to the island to lick her wounds after the sudden breakup of her marriage had been publicized in every foodie magazine and gossip column up and down the coast. Coming from the branch of the family who'd made their mark as coffee tycoons, she'd taken charge of desserts and coffee at the resort to feel useful and hadn't seen fit to move on. Yet.

"Hey, Charley." Trace set his phone on the counter.

"Hey." She didn't look up. Bent over the counter, she decorated each doughnut like it was a masterpiece. "Did you happen to see my daughter on your way in?"

"Yep. She's in full-on princess mode, commanding her subject around the playground." Trace's mouth watered as he stared at the tray of doughnuts.

"Poor Ben." Charley kept decorating.

"He'll get through it. At least she's not trying to dress him up like a girl."

Charley looked up with a twinkle in her eye because, yes, she'd tried the same thing on him and his two brothers when they were kids. Trace and Elliott had run like hell. Spence, being the youngest, got caught up in Charley's diabolical plan. The pictures were priceless and had been fun to leave lying around when Spence brought his dates home in high school.

Trace couldn't resist the temptation any longer and reached for a cinnamon-sprinkled doughnut.

Charley's twinkle turned to a glare. "Don't you dare. I've been working on these all afternoon. They're for Ben's teacher. She *loves* my doughnuts."

"Ah, you heard about Ben's critique of her new hairstyle." Trace braced both elbows against the counter.

Charley nodded. "The minute I pulled into the school parking lot to pick them up."

He had to hand it to his cousin. She knew the hardships of being a single parent, and it was nice that family had his back. "Thanks for smoothing things over. I owe you."

Not only was she an incredible pastry chef, but she was also an even better cousin for keeping so many of the Remington brothers' secrets. Plus, she had one mean left hook, which Trace had experienced a time or two while they were growing up.

So he let his hand fall to the counter. "Just one?" He tried to pout. Hell, he'd already borrowed a woman's phone and called himself from it to get her number just to win a bet. Pouting was the least of his transgressions today.

Although, he would've been happy to follow through on his offer to give the pretty tourist an aerial tour, and he'd have done it for free after the way she'd moaned. If she hadn't disappeared without a word.

Charley slid a doughnut onto a saucer for him, and he poured himself a cup of coffee. He took a big bite and washed it down, growling in pain as he swallowed the scalding coffee. When he could finally speak again, his voice was hoarse from the burn, and he couldn't feel his tongue. *"Jesus,"* he wheezed and rubbed his throat.

"Are you okay?" Charley got him a glass of water.

"The coffee's hotter than usual," Trace croaked, wondering if his voice would ever be the same again.

"The burner's been acting up. It wasn't hot enough earlier," Charley said.

"Well now it's surface-of-the-sun hot," Trace managed to choke out. "I may have to eat intravenously from now on because my windpipe disintegrated."

Elliott blew through the door. "Hey, asshat. Back to admit defeat?"

Trace pulled up Sexy Airport Girl's number and shoved his phone into his brother's chest. "Read it and weep." Still in pain, he kept his voice low.

Elliott stared at the screen and leaned against the wall next to the phone that was anchored there for the staff's convenience. "No way. You either paid her, or it's a fake number. Still have to call her with us in the room to prove it or you lose."

Which could be a problem since Trace had gotten her number without her knowledge. He snatched the phone from his brother.

His dad came in through the dining room entrance. His age was showing now that his hair had gone from salt-and-pepper to solid white, but his stature was still tall and strong. He loved his family and the resort he'd spent his life building. "Is Ms. Barns getting settled into her cottage?" His dad's stare landed on Trace.

"She never showed up." Trace broke the bad news.

His dad rubbed his chin. "Maybe she's stuck somewhere because of the storm."

"You haven't heard from her?" Not showing up for the first day of work was bad enough. Not even calling was grounds for termination. Better they discovered her irresponsibility now before she started making changes to the resort. Changes that Ben might not handle well.

His dad shook his head, a worried look in his eye.

"Look, Dad"—Trace softened his voice to ease the blow—"maybe she changed her mind. It wouldn't be the first time we've hired the wrong person. We'll find someone else."

"What's wrong with your voice?" Elliott asked.

"Burned my throat with the coffee," Trace said, rubbing his neck.

One of the resort lines started to ring, and Elliott grabbed the handset from its cradle. "Wuss," he said to Trace as he balanced the receiver between his ear and his shoulder. "Yeeel-low," he said like the smartass he was. He listened for a second, then pushed off the wall and shoved the handset into Trace's chest. "It's for you. Old Lady McGill."

Trace put a palm over the receiver. "Who's the asshat now?" he whisper-yelled at his younger brother.

Elliott shot him the bird over his shoulder. "Gotta go organize a movie night for our guests since they have to stay indoors with a storm coming."

Trace put the phone to his ear. "Ms. McGill?"

"Hello. Which Remington fella is this?"

"It's Trace."

"Is Lawrence there?" she cooed.

Trace glanced at his father, who shook his head as if he knew exactly what Ms. McGill was asking.

Trace exhaled long and hard. "Can I help?"

She sighed into the phone, clearly disappointed that she wasn't going to speak to Trace's dad. "I just wanted to check to see if your new employee arrived yet. She left the terminal some time ago, and the storm is about to unleash on the island."

Hell.. "Uh, Ms. Barns arrived on the ferry?"

His dad perked up.

"I don't know her name, hon. Just that she's a young, pretty little thing. Spunky too. Reminds me of myself back in the day." Ms. McGill kept rambling. "Said she had to take a different flight than planned, and no one was here to pick her up."

Trace put his hand over the receiver and whispered, "Ms. Barns is on the island. Are you sure she hasn't called?"

"Not on the landline," his dad said.

"Nope. I'd have heard the phone ring," Charley confirmed.

"Could she have called your cell?" His dad came from the generation that didn't keep their cells attached at the hip, and text messaging was as painful for him as a root canal without anesthetic.

His dad's expression blanked. "I did give her my cell in case of emergency." His tone told Trace he probably hadn't checked it in days.

"Ms. McGill?" Trace removed his hand from the receiver. "If she left the terminal a while ago, who picked her up?"

A chafing laugh from years of cigarettes and ferry exhaust coursed through the phone. "No one, hon. She insisted on getting there on her own."

"She's *walking* to the Remington?" With a storm coming their way? What kind of person had his father hired?

Ms. McGill laughed again. "Of course not," she said, like Trace was the foolish one. "She's on a tricycle."

Trace's jaw went slack. Because that wasn't the least bit insane. Traveling by trike, probably with a suitcase, while a raging storm bore down on them was completely understandable.

"Thanks for the call, Ms. McGill." Trace hung up. "Gotta go." He snatched his cell off the counter.

"I'll come with you," his dad said.

"No. You make sure the heat is on in her cottage." Trace swung into captain's mode, like he used to when he piloted private jets. "Charley, can you brew some hot coffee that won't send Ms. Barns to the burn unit? If the storm opens up before I find her, she'll be freezing." And probably angry. Trace would be. Somehow Ms. Barns and his father had gotten their wires crossed, and she was left out in the cold rain.

"I'll get a tray ready. Ms. Barns can have a doughnut for her troubles." Charley poured beans into the coffee grinder. "Maybe she'll forgive you guys once she tastes it." She waggled her brows. "They're magical."

Trace grabbed a set of keys hanging by the back door. They belonged to one of the resort Jeeps. He ran toward the garage with Ms. McGill's words ringing in his ears. Apparently, Ms. Barns wasn't over the hill like Trace had assumed.

She was young. She was pretty. She was spunky.

In Trace's experience, that could be a lethal combination.

Chapter Three

Lily's Life Lesson #3
Karma can be a real motherducker.

Lily pedaled the giant tricycle faster in what she hoped was the direction of the Remington Resort just as the first big drops of rain pelted her face.

So what if no one had shown up at the ferry terminal to pick her up. The cross-country move was her way of taking control of her life. Lily Barns could find her own way. She would make her own destiny.

The rain fell harder, and she looked up at the growling thunderclouds.

She may have overcommitted.

Thunder crashed through the blackening sky so loud it shook the ground. She jumped and jerked the handlebars to one side. Her luggage tumbled off the back. The bungee cord Ms. McGill had loaned Lily at the ferry crossing was threaded through the suitcase handles and secured to the basket between the back wheels, so it dragged the bags along behind her.

Thump, thump, thump.

She kept pedaling but glanced over her shoulder at the suitcases. One problem solved. They wouldn't look like expensive designer luggage by the time she got to the Remington.

The road curved around a pond, a row of cedars separating the flinty water from the pavement. She thanked the Baby Jesus when a fork appeared up ahead.

Lily doubled down and pedaled harder.

Just as the sky opened up completely and dumped on her.

And not one vehicle had come along since she'd left the ferry crossing. Where *was* she?

The cold rain soaked through to her skin. She shivered and squinted against the heavy water shed. The purplish hue of dusk was settling over the landscape, so she set her sights on that fork and pedaled like her life depended on it. In a way, it did. The Remington shouldn't be much farther, and that's where her new life waited. She was almost home free.

Cheep.

Lily's brows pulled together, and she tried to listen above her chattering teeth and thumping luggage.

Cheep, cheep, cheep.

When she glanced over her shoulder to see where the noise came from, she slammed the pedals in reverse. The trike slid sideways, tilted, and sent Lily tumbling ass over elbow into the soggy ditch.

Cheep.

Lily sat up, pushed her sopping hair out of her face, and stared at the brood of baby ducklings that followed her. Small, brown, and fuzzy, they couldn't have been more than a few days old.

Cheep, cheep, cheep, cheep!

They scurried closer, and Lily counted them. Ten little motherless ducklings.

Cheep, cheep. They waddled to her, trying to snuggle into her leg for warmth.

"Get in line. I'm cold and alone too." She wrapped shivering arms around herself and took stock of her situation. Maybe New Orleans wasn't so bad after all. A new hair color to go with her new name— maybe a little plastic surgery to change her looks so the press and her father's enemies wouldn't recognize her—and she'd be golden.

The weather certainly wasn't any worse on the Gulf Coast. Just hotter. And she'd swear the mosquitos in Louisiana had teeth.

Lily mustered her courage as the rain kept falling. No, she was staying right there in Angel Fire Falls. This was the only job she'd ever landed on her own. The great job offer she'd gotten in the French Quarter was because of her father's connections. So she'd worked long hours and holidays with no complaint to be worthy of the position. With a father who'd siphoned off millions from FEMA and from investors who'd trusted him to rebuild the Gulf Coast after the last hurricane, she'd likely never get another job anywhere in that region. Stealing people's money and their dreams tended to make them see you as an employment risk, and Lily was guilty by association. So she wasn't giving up on the job at the Remington until she gave it her best shot.

Plus, it was the only prospect that hadn't required a thorough background check that would've revealed her true identity. Not to mention her father's transgressions.

More thunder growled, and the rain showed no sign of letting up.

Neither did the ducklings.

Cheep, cheep, cheep, cheep.

"All right, all right." Lily shook her head. "So demanding." She gently moved the ducklings aside and stood. "Here's what we're going to do." She pointed to the trike. "I'm going to keep riding that thing to the resort, and you're going to go back to the pond where you belong. Hopefully, your mom's okay, and she'll be back soon. Maybe she's getting a pedi or getting her feathers done."

Lily snorted. Because hell, it was either laugh or cry.

She was soaking wet and riding a giant tricycle, for God's sake. That was going to make a spectacular first impression on her new boss. She wasn't sure how long her probationary period would last, but she couldn't very well show up with a brood of baby ducks in tow on top of everything else. Lily straightened the big trike and swung a leg over. They'd just have to fend for themselves.

She pushed off and pedaled toward the fork, her luggage scraping along the road.

Cheep, cheep . . . cheep, cheep.

Lily's feet stopped pedaling, and her eyes slid shut.

Leaving those fuzzy little innocent things behind didn't seem right. It made her feel . . . well . . . like a big fat motherducker.

She drew in a breath that said *I surrender* and got off the trike. The ducklings all but stampeded her, gathering at her feet. Hands on her hips, she stared down at the chirping birds as the rain bit into her skin.

"Here's the deal"—Lily wagged a finger at the ducklings—"I'll take you with me, but you have to stay out of trouble once we get there." She stepped around the ducks and stooped over her luggage. The tiny birds followed her. "Lucky for you, I volunteered for a wildlife rescue after the last oil spill, so I know a thing or two about taking care of your kind." Which was how she knew ducklings bonded with the first living thing they saw after hatching, and she must be it.

She huffed as she unzipped her luggage and grabbed an armful of clothing to make a nest, most of which was lingerie.

Where was Mabel McGill's giant nest of hair when Lily needed it?

She layered the basket with a wool sweater, then fluffed the soft undergarments into a cozy home for her new wards.

Narrowing her eyes at the ducks, she said, "Happy now? My unmentionables are soaked."

At least her sexy, silky lingerie would finally be put to good use, since it had been wasted on Andrew.

Cheep, cheep.

"Okay, hop in." She lifted each one of them into the basket with no idea how she was going to explain this to her new boss.

Maybe she could find a place to stash the ducklings and the trike before she reported for work. Her own cottage on the resort grounds was part of the agreement, so she could move them in with her later that evening after her employer gave her a key.

If she was still employed by then.

No one had bothered to pick her up, and now she was showing up unannounced. On a tricycle, in the middle of a storm, carting a flock of birds.

Karma. Karma was catching up with her for lying to her mother. Lying about her name. Lying on her résumé. Her pants would probably detonate into a mushroom cloud if she weren't in the middle of a storm with raindrops the size of saucers and no shelter in sight.

If she did still have a job at the Remington Resort, her first priority would be to develop a method of communicating with new arrivals. If the management forgot their guests the way they'd forgotten Lily, no wonder the place was growing stagnant—as Mr. Remington had put it.

A bolt of lightning cracked open the dark sky, and Lily jumped.

She would not give up. She wouldn't.

Because of her father and her ex, she'd weathered worse than a thunderstorm. Been stalked by worse than a few harmless ducks. Had to explain worse to her employer than soaking wet clothes and her three-wheeled means of transportation. There was nothing left in her past to return to. Her only option was to keep pedaling forward. Take her chances with the Remington and see what happened.

And didn't that just suck like a motherducker?

Trace's Jeep splashed down the narrow road as he sped toward the ferry crossing, hoping to find . . .

Hell, he didn't know what he was hoping to find.

Other than a woman on a tricycle.

He wasn't sure why he hadn't mentioned the trike to his family. Maybe it was because he was thrown by Ms. McGill's appealing description of the new employee. Maybe it was because the Remingtons were at fault for leaving her stranded. Either way, a sense of protectiveness welled up in him once he found out she'd had the backbone to brave the storm on a trike instead of calling for help.

That was either mettle or madness, and for some reason, Trace wanted to see which before sharing details with his family.

The rain came down harder, so he flipped the wiper switch to high. The blades squeaked back and forth across the windshield as he rounded a densely wooded curve.

The image of a woman pedaling a huge trike like she was a NASCAR driver came into view, the blue-and-yellow flag on the back flapping wildly in the wind. Definitely not something he saw every day. It would've been funny except for the look of sheer hell-bent determination on her face.

She waved both hands in the air as though she was afraid he wouldn't stop.

He slowed the Jeep and pulled to the shoulder of the road opposite her. He slid from the truck and jogged across the asphalt.

She fanned long slender fingers over her chest. "You're the first vehicle to pass me on the road," she said through chattering teeth. "I was beginning to think the island was deserted."

Mabel McGill had described Ms. Barns as young, pretty, and spunky.

She was three for three.

"People stay holed up at home during a storm like this." He pulled off his jacket and handed it to her. "Put this on. I'm Trace Remington."

Something in her big brown eyes flashed. "You're my new boss?"

He could swear her teeth stopped chattering and started clenching.

He wasn't sure how to answer her question. Technically, his father was her boss, but Dad had insisted on signing over part ownership when Trace returned to the island for good. So a shrug was Trace's noncommittal way of responding without really giving Lily a straight answer. The parenting books called it *deflecting*. "My dad, Lawrence, hired you. Ms. McGill called from the ferry terminal. I figured you could use some help."

Ms. Barns gave him a blank stare, as though he must have the IQ of a rock. "Um, no." She waved a hand over two raggedy suitcases that were bungeed to the back of the trike. "I've totally got this."

Trace rubbed his aching throat and glanced over the luggage, which had a designer label but was in Goodwill condition. "Clearly."

She didn't break eye contact with him as she got off the trike and stood to face him.

Trace couldn't help it. He let his gaze slide over her because he was still stoked from Sexy Airport Girl's sensual moan. His stare traveled back up and snagged on Ms. Barns's dark-brown hair. There seemed to be a surplus of hot brunettes in his path today.

At most, Ms. Barns was a buck ten soaking wet. And oh yeah, she was definitely soaking wet. Strands of dark hair clung to her face and neck. Her muddy jeans and saturated shirt did some clinging too, and Trace swallowed hard because a) her shirt was white, and b) the spring storm had caused the temperature to drop lower than normal.

She either wasn't wearing a bra or wasn't wearing a very *good* bra, because her full breasts greeted him with much more enthusiasm than her expression, which had turned dark as the sky. She eyed him like she didn't trust him any more than she trusted the weather. He held the jacket out and returned her leveled stare until she slowly reached for it.

"Tell you what," Trace said. "Why don't you let me help . . . even though you obviously don't need it." He took a few strides toward her bags. "And I'll owe you one for humoring me." He stepped around to the back of the trike.

Cheep, cheep. Cheep, cheep.

Trace's lips parted as he stared down at the fuzzy ducks. He couldn't make this stuff up if he tried. "You brought your own ducks. How efficient," he smarted off. Because every hospitality manager should come equipped with her own set of ducks. Who knew when a good duck or two might come in handy?

"I found them . . . or they found me." She wiped the rain from her creamy cheeks. "They must've lost their mother."

Trace scrubbed a hand over his stubbled jaw.

"I'd like to bring them with us." She nibbled her bottom lip like she was nervous. "Just until I find someone to take care of them."

Trace unhooked the bungee cord and picked up the other suitcase. The last thing he needed was cute animals at the resort. Ben might get attached, but now wasn't the time to discuss the problems that would cause. Not with raindrops the size of golf balls pelting them. "Put 'em in the back seat. I'll get the rest." He loaded the bulging bag into the rear of the Jeep, while she transferred the ducklings to the floorboard behind the passenger seat. The trike wouldn't fit. He'd have to pick it up later when the weather cleared. He scooped up the clothes from the basket and turned to get in the truck.

"What are you doing?" She was in his path and glared at the wad of clothes in his hands.

"Getting your things." His stare followed hers to the fistful of panties in one of his hands to the purple lacy bra in the other.

Holy shit.

And one of the panties was a black thong.

Kill him now because not even the cold rain could cool the slow burn seeping to his core. His brothers might be right. If Trace was getting turned on by a few handfuls of wet lingerie, it had probably been way too long since he'd been naked with a woman.

His eye twitched. Now that he'd put the words *wet* and *lingerie* together in the same sentence, it was doing nothing to help the ache going on south of the border.

The sharp glint in her deep chocolaty eyes said she was irritated. The hard line of her perfectly shaped mouth said she was used to difficult situations. Only the sexy pink blush on her cheeks gave away the hint of vulnerability lurking beneath the surface.

She grabbed the lingerie from him, fumbled with it, and dropped the thong and the bra. A soft curse slipped through her ample lips, and the color on her cheeks deepened.

He stooped to pick it up, let the lacy purple number dangle from a finger, and gave her an innocent look. "I can put this in your suitcase if you'd like."

She snatched it away. "I can manage on my own, thanks."

He held out the thong. "I have no doubt you can." The corners of Trace's mouth hurt from suppressing a grin. "But thanks for letting me help anyway."

With no trust whatsoever in her eyes, she gave him a pasty smile. And Trace couldn't help but think how much her itty-bitty undies didn't match the size of her determination.

Chapter Four

Lily could swear there was something familiar about Trace Remington. She studied his profile from the passenger seat and hugged herself, trying to rub the chill out of her arms. His damp hair was just messy enough to look sexy, like he'd run fingers through it. It brushed the collar of his soaked shirt, and a single dark curl fell across his forehead. He possessed enough swagger to charm a girl right off her tricycle and into his Jeep.

His presence filled the vehicle, pressing her against the door with barely enough space to breathe. He was the full package as far as looks went. Add the soaking wet look and he could easily pass for a male supermodel. Or male dancer. Either way worked for her. He was so freakishly good-looking, she was sure she'd remember him if they'd met.

He maneuvered the Jeep around a deep puddle, then reached toward the dash to turn up the heat. "Getting warmer?"

Definitely. In all the wrong places.

When she didn't answer, he shot a glance her way.

Her stare flitted away from his strong jaw, the hint of stubble making him even more attractive. It was the kind of face that made a girl look twice. Made a girl sigh all over. Made a girl want to do stupid things . . . like search his body for tattoos, then outline them with her tongue.

Bad, Lily. Bad.

She refocused on why she'd come to Angel Fire Falls. A new job. A new beginning. A new life as an independent woman.

A new man wasn't part of her plan.

So she cleared her throat, determined to sound professional. Polished. Cool and collected. "Yeah." It came out as a croaky wheeze, as if a frog was blocking her windpipe. She clamped her mouth shut and counted the swipes of the squeaking wipers to get her mind off the awkward situation.

Then her stomach rumbled as loud as the storm clouds.

He chuckled. "Haven't eaten in a while?"

She shook her head. "It's been a long day."

Trace flipped on the headlights. "We've got hot coffee and home-made doughnuts at home." He rubbed his throat.

That word. *Home.* It took her by surprise, and she held her breath for a beat. A new home was what she'd wanted. Now that she had it. Fear tightened her chest until she was forced to draw fresh air into her lungs.

"Oh." She chewed her lip and finally blurted, "I love doughnuts."

She was such a conversationalist, it was almost scary.

Since her communication skills hadn't seen fit to arrive on the same flight she had, they were probably lost and circling a luggage carousel somewhere in Arizona. She clamped her mouth shut and stared at the road ahead. Lush green fields lined the road, and stands of trees stretched in the distance on both sides. The road meandered left, then back right until they turned into the resort entrance, which was framed with stone columns and a wrought iron arch that fashioned the words THE REMINGTON in artfully rugged letters.

The Jeep bounced through a dip in the long driveway, and the ducks turned up their volume, expressing their disapproval.

"The ducks can stay in my bathtub tonight. Tomorrow I'll look for a box or a container," she said.

He rubbed the back of his neck. "Yeah, about the ducks. The resort doesn't allow pets."

She couldn't hide her surprise. "Why? A family-friendly resort usually includes family pets, especially in this part of the country. Pet-friendly lodging is crazy-popular out here." Common knowledge within the world of hotel management. "The policy is likely costing you bookings." Another priority on her work list would be a new furry-friends-are-welcome strategy.

"I made that rule when I moved back here a few years ago." His tone wasn't so neighborly this time. "We don't want to deal with the liability if someone gets bitten."

Lily swallowed back an explanation of how business insurance dealt with liability because that probably wouldn't help win her ducks a stay of execution. "They'll die on their own. Give me a little time, and they'll be gone. Then I'll owe *you* one." She let a smile curl onto her lips. "And I'll make sure the ducklings don't peck a guest to death."

When the muscle in his jaw ticked, the tension in her shoulders dialed up a notch.

Who was she kidding? Her stress level had run full throttle for months, leaving her with the kind of bone-deep exhaustion that comes from too much anxiety and too little joy in life.

"All right, but keep them out of sight. I don't want my s—" His knuckles whitened against the black steering wheel.

Wow. Trace was uptight.

"People tend to get attached to animals. Letting them go is more difficult for some than others," he said.

"I'll make sure they're not a problem." Lily laced her fingers and rubbed one thumb against the other. "Thanks."

He shrugged. "Least I can do for leaving you at the ferry crossing." His tone was so serious, so sincere that Lily couldn't look away. "We usually take better care of people than that."

The point was for Lily to take care of herself, and she squared her shoulders. "You don't have to worry about me. I'm your employee, not your guest." Yes! She was the help, and Trace Remington was her boss. She'd be wise to remember that instead of focusing on his lovely cheekbones. His ridiculously muscular arms. His velvety voice that caused a flutter in her tummy and a tingle in her . . .

A twinge of recognition turned the fluttering to flailing.

Surely not.

Her gaze landed on his right wrist, and the butterflies in her stomach slipped away just as fast as they'd arrived. The Voice had been wearing a watch. Trace's wrist was bare.

Whew.

After the hellish day she'd had, after the horrible first impression she'd made, wouldn't it just suck if her new boss had turned out to be the Voice?

The universe couldn't be that cruel.

He slowed the Jeep as he maneuvered down the tree-lined drive.

"I'll need to return the tricycle." More stellar conversation from hers truly. She swiped a palm across her forehead. "I can't imagine how this must look. Or what Mr. Remington must think." With an elbow propped against the door, she rested her temple against her hand.

"I'll take care of the trike first thing tomorrow. I didn't mention it to anyone else," Trace said as they pulled through a circular drive and stopped in front of the resort under a covered portico. Floodlights lit the stone façade of the resort, and Lily watched an entire crew of men barrel toward the Jeep.

"And that would be the welcome wagon," Trace said. "Otherwise known as the Remington family."

Two younger guys and an older man, who were all just as big and built as Trace, swarmed the Jeep as soon as he pushed the gearshift into park. An awful lot of testosterone, and they obviously didn't know how intimidating they were as they pulled her suitcases from the back and opened her door, everyone shouting introductions as they moved.

"Ms. Barns! We finally meet in person." The silver-haired gentleman with a warm smile threw a blanket around her shoulders as soon as her feet touched the pavement. "I'm Lawrence."

"It's nice to meet you." She pulled the blanket closed in front to hide her muddy clothes. She ran a hand through her damp, disheveled hair and tried to smooth it. Her appearance was atrocious. She doubted she could make a worse first impression if she tried. Unless Trace decided to mention the tricycle. Or the ducks. Or the thong and the purple bra she'd used to make a bird's nest.

Good Lord.

Scalding heat crept up her neck. Today would go down in the record books as the most embarrassing first day of work ever.

"Can you take Ms. Barns's luggage to her cottage?" Trace said to his two brothers. He came around to the back door of the Jeep where the ducks were riding and leaned against it as if guarding her secret. She gave him an appreciative smile.

Elliott and Spence said their goodbyes and walked away, toting her luggage. They looked so much alike, Lily could barely tell them apart. But Trace, he was different. There was a family resemblance, but he stood out from the others.

Her mind raced, searching for the right description.

More handsome? More hot?

Her lips parted when he folded both arms across his broad chest and two incredibly formed biceps rippled.

Yes, yes. Definitely more hot.

"I'm so sorry about the mix up." Lawrence's gray hair was a surprise because his voice and enthusiasm during her telephone interviews had seemed much younger. "Let's get you inside where it's warm and give you the grand indoor tour." She could hear the same thread of excitement he'd used during their phone calls. "I can't wait to get started on this place." He rubbed both hands together. "It's going to be completely transformed back into what it used to be before I got old and lame."

She liked Lawrence already. He seemed approachable and genuinely concerned, unlike her own father, who still hadn't expressed an ounce of remorse for his crimes. Not an ounce of regret about the hell he'd put his wife and daughter through. Even from his prison cell, the only regret he expressed was that he'd gotten caught. So different from the father Lily remembered as a child. An invisible switch had flipped when Lily was a teenager, and her father had become distant and distracted, absorbed in work, work, and more work. Which had driven her mother to absorb far too much scotch on a daily basis. Eventually, Lily no longer recognized either of them.

"Dad, Ms. Barns had a rough day traveling." A corner of Trace's mouth turned up.

Her new name was going to take some getting used to. *Thanks, Dad.* How many kids needed an alias because of their father? "Please call me Lily."

Trace gave a quick nod. "I'm sure Lily would like to clean up and get settled in. Work can wait until tomorrow, can't it?"

"Oh, of course," Lawrence said, his expression apologetic. "I'll take you to your cottage."

"I'll take her." Trace pushed off the door. "I've got to put the Jeep away anyway."

A few minutes later, they were rolling down a wooded drive, past a large metal storage shed and a covered carport where several identical Jeeps were parked.

"Thanks for not mentioning . . ." *Anything. Everything.*

Trace responded with a nod.

41

The narrow road broke through a clearing where half a dozen white clapboard cottages of different sizes dotted the landscape. They each had a small yard and were far enough apart to offer privacy, but the grouping still gave off a quaint, neighborly appearance.

Trace pulled to a stop in front of cottage #3. "Family members who work at the resort live here. We never rent these to tourists. Dad assigned you one because you're a manager."

They got out and walked up the steps onto the front porch. As their footsteps echoed off the wood planks, Lily's chest tightened. That sound brought memories flooding back of rare visits to Grandma Barns's farmhouse, where they'd swing on the front porch. Lily had loved those visits. The home and the life Lily's parents had built in New Orleans were designed to mask the memories of their impoverished childhoods. But life at Grandma's had been real and simple, and Lily hadn't cared that the old house wasn't fancy or that her grandmother couldn't afford cable TV.

Just like Grandma Barns's house, the cottage was simple, warm, and welcoming. And all hers. Okay, not *hers* hers. But close enough.

Trace opened the front door, and Lily hesitated. Like walking through that door was a symbol, and there would be no turning back.

"Hey!" A pretty blonde about Lily's age appeared inside the doorway with a cherub-faced little girl clinging to her leg. "I'm Trace's cousin, Charlotte." She stroked the little girl's hair. "This is my daughter, Sophie. I brought you snacks to tide you over. We stocked your kitchen with a few necessities until you can go into town and do your own shopping."

Charley stepped back, and Lily took in the cottage. It was as cute inside as it was on the outside and in good shape. And if the steaming mug of coffee on the counter looked wonderful, the doughnuts sitting next to it looked divine. "Thank you."

Trace went to a broom closet in the hallway and rifled through it. "I need a box. And my cousin's name is Charley, by the way." Trace's voice was muffled, and the top half of his body disappeared into the closet as he searched.

"That's not my real name," Charlotte said.

Must be a thing. Because there was a lot of it going around. Lily took the mug and sipped to hide a shiver of guilt.

"My three irritating cousins gave me the nickname when we were kids, and it stuck. I don't get mad, though. I get even." Charlotte's lips turned up in a wicked smile. "I'm slowly poisoning their coffee."

Trace rubbed his throat and narrowed his eyes at his cousin. "So the coffee I had earlier that nearly made me spontaneously combust was on purpose?"

"You'll never know, will you?" She winked at Lily. "You can call me Charley too." She was pretty and well put together, even in a pair of skinny jeans, an oversize sweatshirt from the University of Washington, and a shimmery pair of Converse sneakers that looked just as functional as they were fashionable.

Trace pulled a cardboard box from the bottom of the closet. "Remind me again why we let you live and work here?"

"Because when you make coffee for the guests, it's so bad they riot." Charley pretended to crack her knuckles. "My job here is done. Here's the key, Lily." She pushed it across the bar and took her daughter's hand. "Let me know if you need anything," she said as she left.

The family's playfulness and the way they worked together suddenly made her feel more alone than ever.

The Remingtons were a close-knit family.

She fought off a heavy sigh. She'd come to Angel Fire Falls hoping to start over, but she was just as much an outsider here as she was in New Orleans.

"I'll be right back with your ducks." Trace headed to the door.

Lily wandered into the bedroom for a quick look around, then returned to the bar, where she propped a hip and sipped her coffee. She let out a soft moan as the robust flavor rolled over her tongue.

"Mmmmm." She let her eyes close for a beat. Only to find Trace standing in the doorway with the box in his hands, scrutinizing her in the most unnerving way when she opened them again.

Two wrinkles appeared across his forehead as he stared. Eyes cloudy. Stance wide. Body freaking gorgeous. He kept studying her as if seeing her for the first time.

A flush of heat surged through her at the attention. Attention from a man had been in short supply lately. God knew, once Andrew was done wooing her, his true colors had started to surface, and he'd shifted his focus back onto himself. Trace's steady stare made her squirm because attention from him wasn't a good thing. It was dangerous. Over six feet of dangerous because of the way his worn Levi's cupped and clung and made her thighs quiver.

Lily realized her stare had anchored to all that cupping and clinging, and she wanted to melt into the floor. "I'll take the ducks," she blurted and slammed her mug to the counter. Coffee sloshed over the side. She hurried over and took the box from him. "Thank you for everything. I can manage from here." She really needed to get Trace Remington and all his brooding hotness out of her cottage before she drooled all over him like a salivating dog. "The place is great. Really, you've been great. I'm exhausted, and I'd like to unpack," she rambled. When she stopped to take a breath, she glanced at the saucer of doughnuts. She should stuff one in her mouth to shut herself up.

Trace's ringtone went off, and he pulled his cell from his pocket. "Gotta take this," he grumbled under his breath and turned for the door.

He hesitated, like he was unsure about something. His phone quieted for a second, then blared to life again. "See you tomorrow," he finally said and closed the door behind him.

Lily planned to see as little of Trace Remington as possible. His ridiculous good looks would just distract her, and Lily didn't need distractions. Especially not the kind that could end with a pink slip that had her new name on it.

Lily looked down into her box of tiny birds.

"Well," she said. "Today sucked." But tomorrow didn't have to. She had six weeks before the summer vacation season officially started. Six weeks to prove her worth as the resort's new hospitality manager so she could build a new life for herself.

Six weeks to avoid Trace Remington so she wouldn't make the same mistake that had already cost her everything.

Trace stared at his ex-wife's number and pinched the bridge of his nose. He climbed behind the wheel of his Jeep and fired up the engine.

He took a deep breath before answering the call. "What's up, Megan?" He'd likely regret the question, but he had to at least communicate with Megan for Ben's sake. Their son was an eight-year-old boy who still held on to the hope that his mother would finally put him first.

"I was thinking maybe Ben should spend more time with me in Los Angeles." She cut right to the chase.

Trace bit down to hold back a curse. Megan couldn't bring herself to spend more than an hour with Ben, and that was with Trace present to run interference. No way would he allow Ben to stay with her alone in Los Angeles. "Beg your pardon?"

With the last remnants of daylight about to disappear, he eased the Jeep down the lane and parked in front of his cottage instead of storing the Jeep in the resort motor pool garage.

"I think he needs a mother"—she stumbled over the word—"in his life. I'd like to spend more time with him."

Trace hopped out of the Jeep and trotted onto the porch to get out of the pouring rain. "Since when?" He didn't try to hide the strain in his voice. Strain was unavoidable when dealing with her.

"I resent that." Her voice cracked on the last word.

Megan often played the crying card to get him to bend to her will. Guess she had learned something from the years she'd spent in acting classes. Otherwise, the classes hadn't done much for her career, unless he counted the commercial for a pharmaceutical product that cured constipation.

Ben had hardly lived the teasing down at school.

"You're welcome to visit Ben anytime, but I'm not going to ship him off to Los Angeles. He can't adjust to that kind of change, and you know it." Trace went inside and looked around for his son. Ben wasn't home.

His pulse kicked up a notch. With the storm still raging, Trace hoped Ben was at Charley's or in the game room. Or anywhere safe.

"I don't care for Angel Fire Falls," Megan clipped out.

It took nerves of steel to deal with her on a good day. Today it would take an act of God for Trace to keep his cool. After Sexy Airport Girl's sensual moan had made his pulse hum, then the surprise of finding Lily Barns on the road looking like she was ready to compete in a wet T-shirt contest, his nerves were already frayed. When Lily had tasted that doughnut, her moan had taken his nerves from frayed to shredded.

And don't even get him started on the ducks. The no-pets-allowed policy was to protect Ben. The kid had had a meltdown when his classroom's hermit crab died at school.

"Ben *does* like it here." He pulled off his wet shirt and put the phone back to his ear, digging through his closet for something dry to wear. He pulled on one sleeve of a button-up denim shirt and shifted the cell to his other ear to finish. "It's his home, and he's familiar with it. He wouldn't do well in a strange place."

"You used to come down on me for not spending enough time with Ben. Now that I want to, you're saying no. Shouldn't I get a say in raising him?"

Trace started buttoning the shirt from the bottom up. "Not since you signed over full custody to me." Five damn years ago.

"Yes, well about that . . . I was thinking . . ." She hesitated.

The hair at the back of Trace's neck prickled.

"Maybe Ben could spend the summer with me . . . alone." Megan didn't sound convinced that this was a good idea. Trace *knew* it wasn't.

"No," he blurted, and it made his throat ache worse.

"Just think about it, Trace. I've been interviewing special-ed teachers who have experience with autism. Working as a nanny is a great summer job for a teacher, and I'd have help, so we could take extra-good care of Ben."

His fingers stilled against the next shirt button, and he let a few beats of silence go by as though he really was thinking about it. "Hell no. No strangers, and that's final."

"You're the one who screwed up and trusted the wrong nanny service," Megan argued.

"Which is why I quit a high-paying job in LA and moved back here. If you'd been willing to come over and sit with him, I wouldn't have had to rely on a nanny service to begin with." Trace buttoned one more button, then ran his fingers through his soaking hair. Wanting to pull his hair out seemed to be the standard response when dealing with his ex-wife.

"Are we really going to rehash this again?" she asked.

"You brought it up." He drew air into his lungs to calm down. "Look, school will be out soon. You can visit Ben here this summer, several times if you want." There were enough Remingtons running around the place that someone could supervise Megan if she really did materialize. Which was unlikely, based on her track record. He started for the door again so he could find Ben. "Frankly, that's a generous offer, considering . . ."

He waited for her answer.

"We'll see about that," she finally huffed. "You can't keep me from my son." The line went dead.

He held out the phone and stared at it. Megan's sudden interest in spending time with Ben couldn't be a coincidence any more than it could be a sudden surge of maternal instinct.

An uncomfortable tingle shimmied down Trace's spine, and he shoved the phone into his shirt pocket. When it came to flying conditions, he had a gut instinct. That gut instinct told him a whole different kind of storm was brewing, and its name was Megan.

But why now?

Chapter Five

Lily pulled up a playlist on her phone and floated around the little cottage to get acquainted. It was the very first place she'd had all to herself. No parents. No Andrew.

She glanced toward the bathroom.

No one but her and an infestation of ducklings who had taken up residence in her tub.

When a soft tune came on, she twirled through the small den, running her fingers along the back of the leather sofa that was just scarred enough to give it character. The place was small but not cramped. Quaint and cozy. With rain pelting the cottage and thunderclaps echoing in the distance, it was exactly the type of place that made her want to curl up with a good book. She'd give the space her very own personal touch with a few throw pillows in her favorite colors, a pretty flower arrangement or two, and some new framed prints for the bare walls.

A catchier pop song came on, and Lily kicked off her hiking boots so her soft socks could slide across the knotty wood floor. She found a loaf of sliced bread in the pantry and danced her way into the bathroom. As soon as they saw her, the ducklings squawked.

She bounced to the music as she tossed bread crumbs into the claw-foot tub. "I hope you know, you're in the way of a seriously overdue hot shower." She put her hands on her hips and frowned at the shallow pan of water she'd given them. The water was already dirty with bird droppings. "Dudes, if this is going to work, you're going to have to get your *shit* together."

She snorted at her own joke.

Good Lord. With an eye roll, she carried the pan through the den so she could throw the dirty water outside. The next upbeat song had her humming and shimmying as she opened the door.

She nearly barreled into a little boy who stared up at her with big brown eyes.

She squeaked, stumbled back, and dumped the pan all over her feet. The metal clanked as it hit the floor and rolled away. With a hand fanned over her heart, she bent over to slow the thumping in her chest.

"You're weird," the little boy said and wrinkled a freckled nose. A hooded rain slicker framed full cheeks and the cutest face, which held an innocent expression that didn't match his rudeness.

"Well, you scared me," she said, her voice defensive at his lack of filter.

"You're pretty," he added.

So maybe the kid was more blunt than rude.

"My name's Ben. I'm eight." He rubbed his hands against his thighs like he was nervous. "I live here too. What's your name?"

"I'm Lily." She retrieved her phone from the counter. The second she turned off the music and Ben heard the ducks, his eyes rounded.

"What's that?" His voice was all awe and curiosity.

"Um." Her arrival had been strange enough without broadcasting that she'd brought along birds, but she looked down into those twinkling eyes, and they plucked a heartstring. "Baby ducks."

His face brightened. "Can I see?"

Lily stepped up to the doorframe and peered outside. Ben was alone. "Are you sure it's okay with your parents that you're here?"

He toed the ground. "Yeah."

Right. That was about as honest as her using her grandmother's name.

"Let's take a quick peek." She waved him in and retrieved the pan from the floor. "Watch your step." She directed him around the dirty puddle of water. "We'll leave the front door open just in case your parents don't like you visiting a stranger's house." She led him into the bathroom.

He ran to the tub and dropped to his knees. "Is this where they live?"

"For now." She washed out the pan in the sink. After she placed a fresh pan of water in the tub, she sat next to Ben. "They probably think I'm their mother."

"Why?" In his utter fascination with the ducks, he didn't look up, but stroked each one with a gentle touch.

"I guess I was the first living thing they saw after they hatched." Lily scooped up a duckling. "Hold out your hands." Gently, she placed it in the palms of his cupped hands.

"What're their names?" He cuddled the tiny bird like it was a treasure.

Lily gave him a thoughtful look. "How about we name them together?"

His face lit up like a Christmas tree. "This one can be Daisy." He lifted the duckling in his hands, and then he pointed to one of the birds who'd just snatched a bread crumb away from another duck. "Let's call that one Bandit."

They both giggled.

"Good one," said Lily. The kid was smart.

They made a game of it and took turns dubbing each with a funny name.

The tension in her shoulders released. Ben had managed to add a little unexpected fun to her crummy day. If she'd learned nothing else, it was to seize those moments that brought joy to her soul because she never knew when they'd slip away and be lost forever in the harsh reality of life.

When there was only one unnamed duckling left, she let Ben do the honors. With the gentleness of a grown-up, he set Daisy back in the tub and picked up the small duck that had strayed from the flock and sat alone in the corner of the tub. "Megan," he said, and a veil of sadness dropped over his angelic face. "This one is Megan."

"Ben?" A deep voice filtered in from the den.

An involuntary shiver licked over Lily's skin.

"Ben?"

"Dad! Come see!" Ben hollered.

Trace Remington appeared in the bathroom doorway just as Lily climbed to her feet. She shot a look between him and Ben.

Wait. Oh.

She drew in a breath. Karma, persistent little witch that she obviously was, must have a GPS lock on Lily.

Trace's brooding look hooked into her, but he spoke to his son. "What're you doing here? You know better." Then those cloudy eyes slid all the way down to the muddy hem of her jeans before he cleared his throat and looked away.

Lily shifted from one foot to the other. Since her verbal skills had been on vacation the entire day, she stayed silent.

His gentle but scolding tone seemed to go right over Ben's head. "Look, Dad! Baby ducks!" His body hummed with excitement. "I named them."

Trace's jaw ticked. "Naming them isn't a good idea. It'll make it even sadder when we have to say goodbye. Remember the hermit crab?"

Ben started to rock back and forth.

Trace's no-pets-allowed rule made more sense now. Naming a pet usually meant a connection. An attachment.

Well, didn't *she* feel like a slug. "I . . . I'm sorry. We were having so much fun. I didn't think it would be a problem."

Trace gave her a pointed look that said her entire existence was a problem.

Ben ticked off names as he pointed to each duck, even though there was no way to tell them apart. "Daisy, Sir Walter Raleigh—"

One of Trace's silky brows arched high, and his arms folded across that broad chest.

Lily bit her lip and shrugged.

"Roxy, Oscar, Squeaks, Bandit, Oreo, Scooter, and Belle." Ben named every duck except the one in his hand.

Lily gave it a stroke with the back of her finger. "This one's Megan."

The air in the room thickened with silence.

Ben rubbed his thigh with one hand the way he had when he first arrived. He looked down at Megan with so much love, it nearly melted Lily's heart.

Trace's stiff posture softened when he spoke to his son. "It's getting late." He gave Ben a reassuring look. "Go on home. I'll be right behind you."

Ben handed the bird to Lily and said his goodbyes.

"I'm sorry he bothered you." Raindrops starred Trace's long black lashes. Lashes so thick, they could make any woman drop her guard.

Trace equals boss. Boss equals threat of unemployment. Unemployment equals going back to a place filled with hatred for the Devereauxes. All Devereauxes, even though Lily had never committed a crime . . . unless her one-and-only parking ticket counted. Okay, two parking tickets.

"Oh, it was no bother." Lily cuddled the duck against her chest.

"It won't happen again."

"Really, it's fine. I don't mind."

"I do." He scrubbed a hand over that chiseled jaw, and Lily melted a little. The new shirt he was wearing dialed up the heat even more. It opened at the neck one button too low, and the phone in his pocket caused it to sag even farther, revealing a hard chest with a smattering of dark hair in the center.

The tip of Lily's tongue darted out and traced her bottom lip before she could stop it.

He pulled in a breath that said he was trying to be polite but was finding it difficult. "Look, I wasn't in favor of hiring you."

Obviously Ben got his bluntness from his father.

He glanced at the empty doorway where his son had just left. "Change complicates things." His gaze zeroed in on Megan, whom Lily was still holding at her chest. "Your presence here is already complicating things."

"I'm sorry you feel that way, but your dad *did* hire me, and I intend to do my job." She kept stroking the duck. "Change is growth." She repeated one of the mantras she'd been taught at every hotel management seminar she'd been required to attend at her old job.

It had sounded much less cheesy in her head.

"You seem like a decent person." His piercing eyes licked over her face and down her neck. "I don't mean to be rude."

"Oh, but you're so good at it." She lifted her chin.

"It's not like that." He swiped at the damp wavy locks, pushing them off his forehead. A few curls fell back into place just messy enough to look stylish. "It's just that I have to look out for my son." Trace hitched his chin toward Megan. "So do me a favor and rename that one. And the sooner they're gone, the better for Ben." He hooked both thumbs into his front belt loops. "I know you've had a long day." He didn't say *goodbye*. Or *see you around*. Or even *buzz off*. Instead, he simply walked out without a word.

Which probably meant *buzz off*.

The front door closed with a thud.

"Doesn't look like he wants either one of us around," Lily said to the duckling in her hands.

Megan squawked and spread her wings as if protesting the injustice.

"I'm right there with you, girlfriend." But out of respect for Trace's fatherly concern, she renamed the bird Molly. She returned the duck to the tub, then dumped her clothes onto the queen-size bed. She made a makeshift habitat out of an empty suitcase, a few towels, and a table lamp to keep the ducks warm.

After scouring the tub, she took a long, hot shower and dressed in pajama pants and a T-shirt that said CAJUNS LIKE IT HOT from her favorite New Orleans restaurant. Then she organized her closet and dresser.

When she went to pull up a new playlist, she flipped her phone ringer back on, and it instantly blared to life with "Jambalaya (On the Bayou)." Her mother's number glared at her like an accusation. Lily's head dropped back, and then she sent the call to voice mail.

Soon. She'd deal with her mother soon. She tapped in a quick text, assuring her mother she'd arrived safely and would call as soon as she was settled. She scrolled through the long list of recent calls and messages, all from her mom until a strange number popped up.

Her brows scrunched together. She fired off a text, praying the press hadn't found her already.

Who is this?

Her heart pounded a wild thwackity, thwack, thwack against her rib cage. She had a death grip on the phone and plopped onto the edge of the bed, waiting for a response. Time stopped until the dots finally began to skip and jump.

I'm the pilot from the airport.

The Voice. Better than the press. She let out the breath she hadn't realized she was holding and fell back on the bed, only to sit bolt upright again.

Why is your number in my phone?

You let me use it. Remember?

Lily thought for a second, then shook her head. Still didn't make sense. Why would he have borrowed a phone to call himself?

> Are you stalking me???? I own a gun.

She so did not. But the first chance she got, she intended to buy pepper spray. And maybe a Taser.

Whoa, I'm not a stalker.

> THEN WHY DID YOU CALL YOUR-SELF FROM MY PHONE?????

Another decade passed before he answered.

So, funny story . . .

She narrowed her eyes and typed.

> You have 10 seconds before I have the FBI trace your phone. My dad's well connected.

That sounded tough. The Voice didn't need to know that her father's connection to the FBI was from their investigation that had landed him in prison.

Calm down, Brienne of Tarth. YOU texted ME, not the other way around.

True. Plus, he was obviously a *Game of Thrones* fan, which put points on the board for him. Still . . .

> 5 seconds . . . And I'm MANLY????
> Cuz Brienne of Tarth is manly.

> Meant you're obviously badass with the threats. Truth . . . siblings dared me to get a pretty girl's number. Kinda juvenile. Sorry.

Honesty. She wasn't sure how to deal with that one. Except to be impressed. Lily's false identity, albeit well intentioned, made her feel like the bird droppings she'd just scrubbed out of the bottom of her tub. This guy sounded legit, though. For some reason she believed him, especially since he'd apologized.

> Why me?

> Obvious—you were the prettiest. More Daenerys with brown hair.

Lily smiled, even though she shouldn't let this continue. He was a stranger, and she planned to stay emotionally unavailable until she got her life on track.

> How would you know? Don't think you saw my face.

She had to admit, flirting with the Voice was fun. Without getting creepy, he'd already shown more interest in her in five minutes of texting than Andrew had during their entire engagement.

Saw enough. Is SWAT about
to break down my door?

> No, but don't get comfortable.
> That the only reason you picked
> me?

This time she added a smiley face.

Don't ask a question unless
you can handle an honest
answer.

> Go for it.

Wouldn't have contacted
you since I got your # w/o
permission, but if you want
truth, I owe you. As long as
my house isn't swarming
with cops soon.

She laughed out loud. Did she really want to hear his answer? She wasn't sure, so she hung more clothes in the closet while she thought about it. Finally, her phone dinged with another text.

Still there?

Here, just taking care of something. Kind of have a life going
here.

Not really, but she was trying.

Want to know or not? Your
choice.

Shoot.

She hurried to send another text, since she'd threatened to sic law
enforcement on him.

Not literally. I mean continue.

His response came swiftly.

You caught my attention
with your sexy moan.
That gorgeous body and
the moaning made it
impossible NOT to talk to
you. Imagination went wild.

Heat flooded her cheeks.
Good Lord.
Was this sexting? *With a stranger!* She wasn't entirely sure, but she
wanted to hear more. His response was so real. So raw. So refreshing. It
made a tingle rush through her veins, and lady land sighed. She'd never
had a sensual text conversation with anyone, but after the day she'd
had . . . after the *year* she'd had, she needed to feel alive. Needed to feel

sexy. Needed to feel anything besides Andrew's rejection and the humiliation that had nearly drained every last ounce of self-esteem she possessed.

Sexting with a guy she'd never see again couldn't hurt, and it was all she had for the foreseeable future.

◆ ◆ ◆

The night had taken an interesting turn.

Trace stared at his phone, waiting for Sexy Airport Girl to respond. He'd never texted with strange women before, but he had to admit, it was a nice diversion from the stress caused by talking to his ex-wife. Not to mention his finding Ben in Lily's cottage, getting chummy with her and her ducks.

"Ben, I ran your bath. Go jump in." Trace found a bag of cough drops in the medicine cabinet and popped one in his mouth. He pulled up the "For Sale" listing for a new cargo plane on his laptop and set it on the coffee table while he waited for his phone to ding again.

Ben sat on the floor in front of the coffee table with Legos scattered around him. He rocked back and forth on his knees as he separated yellow blocks from the rest. Two duck-shaped figures were complete, and he was almost finished building a third.

Oh boy.

"Go on, buddy. It's getting late, and you've got school tomorrow." Trace retrieved a mechanical pencil and a legal pad with his scribbled notes and numbers. "How about tomorrow we build dinosaurs instead? You like dinosaurs." Dinosaurs were a safe bet. No way Ben could get attached to a live one.

Ben shrugged and padded toward the bathroom. "I like ducks better."

Trace sighed and focused on the cargo plane listing on his laptop. A fair price for a plane in good condition.

The only delivery service still operating on Cape Celeste was unreliable at best and one of the primary reasons the resort and the island in general weren't flourishing. Trace saw no reason to rely on a delivery service based on the mainland. Why not start one right there in Angel Fire Falls? Unfortunately, his plane was equipped for passengers and didn't have enough tail room for major cargo. The financial projections Elliott had put together made it clear the Remington couldn't afford both a new hospitality director and a new cargo plane, though.

His only option was to take out a loan, using his existing plane as collateral. That was a risk he wasn't sure he could take. If he lost it, the Remington might go under completely with only the ferry to transport guests.

Trace slouched on the sofa. He'd rather text with Sexy Airport Girl than deal with all the problems that had surfaced today. There were so damn many.

He stared at his silent phone.

Call him crazy, but her attempt at intimidation had been fun. A challenge. Until he'd gone and screwed it up by mentioning her sexy moan and his filthy imagination.

The dots still didn't budge.

Ben came out of the bathroom, smelling of Superman bubble bath and toothpaste. He scrambled onto the sofa with a book in one hand and a Lego duckling in the other. Trace slung an arm on the back of the sofa and deposited his phone onto the side table to read with his son. It was their nightly ritual.

"Lily's nice." Ben opened the book.

A little too nice, in Trace's opinion. Inviting Ben into her cottage and then letting him name the ducks was an overstep. One that would leave his kid crushed when the birds were gone. And Trace would be left to help his son cope with the loss.

No thank you. He had to do enough of that every time Megan let Ben down.

So Trace would push Lily Barns to find a new home for the ducks, ASAP, before Ben fell hopelessly in love with them.

The phone dinged. Trace flipped the screen facedown, as though that would make the temptation to text disappear so he could devote one hundred percent of his attention to his son. "What are we reading tonight?"

Ben's smile reached from one ear to the other. *"Quackers the Duck Goes to School,"* he said.

Hell.

Ben got stuck on a few words, and Trace had him sound them out. Fifteen minutes later, Ben was tucked under his blue sheets and comforter decorated all over with airplanes and clouds. "Night, buddy." Trace kissed his forehead. "Sleep tight." He switched off the airplane-shaped lamp.

"Don't let the duckies bite." Ben yawned on the last word.

Trace grabbed a beer from the fridge, dimmed the lights, and pulled up his DVR recordings to catch up on *Game of Thrones*, hoping to satisfy his sudden hankering for fiery women. The cargo plane was a lost cause, at least for the time being, so he closed the laptop and pushed it aside. With his feet propped on the coffee table, he flipped through the recordings. When his phone dinged again, he settled on a random channel and read the last text.

Was the moaning that bad?

Trace put his beer down and texted back.

I'm a guy. Wouldn't call it "bad."

More like sensual. In a late-night-premium-channel kind of way.

What would you call it?

Answer comes with a
warning label. Doubt we
should go there.

Seriously want to know.

Trace considered her request.

Curiosity killed the cat, but
it's your funeral, beautiful. It
was a porn-flick moan only
classier. Won't forget it in this
lifetime. Was dying to kiss you
to see if you'd moan louder.

His pulse revved just thinking about it.

How did you imagine kissing me?

He took a long pull from his beer bottle before responding. No way
could he follow through with any of this, but damned if he didn't want to.
Every cell ached to touch that gorgeous girl until she moaned just for him.

Which was stupid, since she obviously didn't live in the area. Then
again, maybe that was safest. She'd been the first woman to catch his eye
and his interest in longer than he could remember, and a relationship
of the moaning variety was off the table because of Ben.

We'd watch the sunset from
the cliffs over the ocean.
Bottle of wine and a blanket.

And?

Trace hadn't thrown caution to the wind since the day Megan told him she was pregnant. Maybe he was overdue. His fingers flew over the keys, typing in a message he'd erase just as soon as he got it out of his system.

> I'd lay you back and kiss you deep. Hard. Slide my tongue over every inch of you until I found the spots that made you moan. I'd lift your skirt and move your thong to one side, because hell yes, you'd be wearing a thong, and I'd put my mouth on your—

A familiar voice tore his attention from the long monologue-text, and he glanced up at the television, doing a double take so fast it nearly gave him whiplash. There was his ex-wife. With a motherly look of love and concern on her face, Megan talked about the challenges and the joys of parenting an autistic child. She implored viewers to call the number on the screen with their generous donations to a nationally recognized charity for autism that helped children just like hers.

A picture of Megan and Ben flashed on the screen. Trace had taken it himself the last time she'd visited. She'd shown up wearing an outfit better suited for a conservative country-club brunch instead of a day trip to a vacation island. The second she'd stepped out of Trace's plane, Ben had grabbed her hand and dragged her off the dock and into the grass to show her a frog. Her expensive stilettos had sunk into the mud, and one heel had snapped off.

Her forty-five-minute visit with Ben was mostly spent fidgeting with her broken shoe while she mumbled under her breath. She'd insisted Trace take a few pictures with her phone, and then she asked him to fly her back to the Cape so she could take the next flight to LA.

Now Trace understood Megan's sudden interest in spending more time with their son. Ben would be a set prop.

Searing anger pounded through his veins, and his grip tightened around the phone. A swoosh sounded, and he looked down. Openmouthed, he stared at his cell.

No. *No, no, no!*

The word *Delivered* appeared in light gray under his racy text, and he wanted to reach through cyberspace and snatch it back.

His head fell back on the sofa. So much for throwing caution to the wind. Apparently, he sucked at it.

Chapter Six

Lily spent two days with Lawrence while he brought her up to speed on resort business and they set up her office space. She spent those two nights tossing and turning over the Voice's last text. On her third full day, she wasn't exactly bright-eyed and bushy-tailed as she put her makeup on in the bathroom of her cozy cottage. Her eyes were bleary, and her tail was dragging.

It didn't help that the ducks chirped a chorus starting at sunrise. They frolicked in the tub, and one of them squeaked. Lily turned to find they'd already eaten all the bread crumbs and dry oatmeal she'd tossed in for their breakfast, and one of them made its unhappiness apparent.

"I know how you feel." Lily dug through her makeup bag. "I promise I'll look for a better habitat today." Not only did they need more room, but she'd really like her tub back.

She found a tube of mascara and leaned into the mirror to brush it over her lashes. So far, mostly what she'd done at the resort was listen to Lawrence. Today, she planned to start developing a plan of action.

She finished one eye and stepped back to look at herself. The drowned-rat appearance she'd sported when she arrived hadn't been a good look for her. Unfortunately, the I've-been-up-for-two-nights-fantasizing look wasn't much better.

And those fantasies had her insides wound so tight, she might unravel with the least little nudge. His words had been as sensual as the velvety tone of his masculine voice, and Lily wasn't sure she could resist it if they ever did meet face-to-face again.

Which they wouldn't because now, on top of the new no-men-allowed policy she'd adopted, she could never look the Voice in the eye. Not after his last text, which had spun her mind into the gutter. It had been dreamy and daring and dangerous. And so far out of Lily's depth that she'd gasped when it popped onto her screen.

He'd left the last part—the part about where he would put his mouth after he moved her thong out of the way—open-ended. She'd wanted to text back and ask him *where? WHERE?* Even though it'd been pretty obvious, she'd still wanted him to explain. In vivid detail. Instead, she'd stayed quiet and didn't respond at all.

And he hadn't texted since.

She stabbed the mascara wand into the tube and gave it three rapid-fire pumps, then went to work on the other eye. When she finished getting dressed, she grabbed her iPad and a map Lawrence had given her. She opened it as she headed for the door to find a colorful diagram of the island on one side and the resort on the other. One hand on the doorknob, she stopped and drew in a weighty breath. Then she went back for her phone, checked to make sure the ringer was on, and shoved it into her pocket. She'd have to work up the courage to call her mother today.

Lily stepped outside to a gloomy gray sky. She drew the thick moist air into her lungs. The worst of the storm had finally passed, but a heavy dampness still hung in the air.

Using the map, she started with the campfire area on the west end of the resort. Aging Adirondack chairs surrounded a stone fire pit. A fresh coat of paint on the chairs and a few log benches and stools made of tree stumps for kids would transform it into a perfect family gathering place for roasting marshmallows, singing songs, or telling stories. From there, she followed a paved walkway to the front of the resort where a tattered net hung across a sand volleyball court . . . which was missing a fair amount of the sand.

The basketball court that stood adjacent wasn't any better. Useable, but deteriorating.

She pecked at the screen of her iPad, making a bullet list.

She crossed the property along the front entrance to an open-air but covered structure with a concrete floor. Perfect for group activities.

A lush green lawn swept around the east end of the resort, where hiking trails meandered off into the hilly landscape. Lily studied the map. When she was interviewing with Lawrence over the phone, she hadn't realized how big the grounds were. At the time, she'd scoured their outdated website, but it hadn't offered many details.

She tapped another bullet onto her list—*update website*.

Seeing the resort in person while looking at the map, it was clear the Remington encompassed acres upon acres of the island. The hiking trails butted up against the rocky cliffs and looped back around the rear of the resort. She'd explore those later. Today, she wanted the abbreviated tour.

Picnic tables, outdoor grills, and lawn swings dotted the expansive back lawn. She could see a large playground on the opposite end, so Lily headed that way. As far as she could tell, the playground equipment was new, and it was the only part of the property that had been kept well manicured.

For such a beautiful family-owned place, it hadn't been shown much TLC. She walked along the back of the resort toward the playground. According to the map, if she followed the path that skirted the playground and disappeared around a dense hedgerow of trees, vines, and flowery bushes, there should be a fishing pier beyond and an inlet.

Sounded lovely, and Lily couldn't wait to see it. She veered to the right and headed down the trail. Only to stop just as she cleared the hedgerow.

All three Remington brothers were down by the dock, which led to a pier. From a distance, their interaction seemed smooth and natural as they repaired a section that looked to have been damaged by the storm.

Lily's gaze landed on Trace. Even though the temperatures were moderate, the air was muggy, and he'd already worked up a sweat. One of his brothers tore out the damaged planks. The other Remington brother retrieved a new piece of lumber from what looked like a boathouse to the left, then made sure it was level. Trace hammered in nails to secure it in place.

Lily couldn't help it. She ducked behind the hedgerow and stared. Just *stared*. Even from her hiding spot, she could see the glistening sweat that coated his tanned arms. Ropey muscles where his neck met his shoulders flexed and released with each swing of the hammer. The hammer he wielded with his left hand.

She swallowed hard. She hadn't noticed he was left-handed when he picked her up on the road.

When he was done, he straightened and used the bottom of his shirt to swipe the perspiration from his face.

And holy hotness. She could do laundry on his abs. A gasp whispered through Lily's parted lips, moistness gathering in intimate places she'd rather ignore.

The twinlike Remingtons stopped to drink long and hard from water bottles, and Trace pulled out his phone, tapping on the screen as all three disappeared into the boathouse.

Lily's phone dinged, and she chuckled at the timing.

My last text was out of line.
I apologize for being an ass.

Did it make her a texting slut because she'd enjoyed it?

"You there," a scratchy voice said from behind her.

She whirled to find an elderly man shaking a bony finger in her direction.

"Yes, you, hiding in the bushes!" The man shuffled toward her, his sparse comb-over falling to the wrong side.

She stepped back onto the path, turning her phone screen-down so she could focus on the guest and not on the Voice. "Sir, I'm not hiding." She so was. "I'm . . ." She glanced over her shoulder and was relieved to find Trace still inside the boathouse. "I'm working. What can I help you with?"

"That racket has to stop." His pointing finger shifted over Lily's shoulder to the dock. "We paid good money to come here for peace and quiet, and my wife is a light sleeper. That hammering has had her up complaining since the crack of dawn." He shuffled right up to Lily and moved his baby-blue cardigan aside so he could plant both hands on his hips. "Good thing my hearing aids have an off switch."

And *that* would seem to be the problem. The resort didn't have any *life*. Even during the off-season, the grounds should be humming with energy. Bustling with fun activities to accommodate all stamina levels, each designed to help the vacationers relax so they could return home refreshed. This old fella was one of the few guests Lily had seen, and he was busy trying to stop the only sign of life at the resort.

"I'm so sorry you were disturbed." Lily's smooth professionalism kicked in to do what she did best—defuse volatile situations before they blew up and appeared on a popular vacation review site with a one-star rating. "The storm caused damage that needs to be repaired, so I'm afraid some noise is unavoidable, but I'd be happy to move you to a room as far from the dock as possible."

He harrumphed—half-satisfied, half-irritated. "Well, the storm didn't cause that awful breakfast this morning. The eggs were cold, and the bacon was rubber," he grumbled. "If it wasn't for the doughnuts and coffee, we'd have to go eat somewhere else."

Lily offered him a genuine smile while making a mental note to tour the kitchen and sample the food herself. So far, she'd eaten at her cottage. "Again, I'm so sorry, Mr. . . . ?"

"Walters." He pursed his lips. "Name's Walter Walters."

Wow. His parents really liked the name to give it to the poor guy twice.

"Mr. Walters." Lily placed a reassuring hand on his arm. "I'll personally guarantee you get a warm, tasty meal for lunch." Even if she had to cook it herself. Like most Cajuns, she knew her way around a kitchen and could make a gourmet meal out of nothing more than rice and a bottle of Tabasco. The motto in the French Quarter wasn't *Life's short, so make it hot and spicy* for no reason.

Involuntarily, she glanced toward the boathouse. Still no sign of the hot and spicy Trace Remington going back to his hammering. Or his sweating.

"I want to speak to the owner."

She refocused on Walter Walters. "I understand, Mr. Walters." Using someone's name tended to create a personal connection and settle feelings of anger.

Like naming baby ducks.

Guilt flooded through her at the trouble she'd caused Ben and the irritation she'd caused Ben's dad. But one problem at a time.

Walter Walters's bushy eyebrows stopped bunching between his eyes so much, and his lips unpinched.

She hooked her arm in his and led him toward a bench on the playground. "How about you wait here while I ask for the keys to one of the resort Jeeps so I can take you and your wife on a private island drive? Maybe the views will relax your wife and make up for the sleep she lost." And Lily could get acquainted with the island at the same time. Two birds, one stone.

No offense to her new feathered friends.

Mr. Walters mumbled under his breath but clasped his free hand over Lily's, and she knew she'd scored her first victory as the Remington's hospitality manager. Unhappy guests mostly wanted someone to care. She did care, and that was the reason she was good at her job.

After depositing Mr. Walters on a bench, she headed toward the boathouse. She passed the hedgerow and rounded a copse of giant pampas grass so the dock and inlet were fully visible.

Then she skidded to a halt.

A Cessna floatplane sat at the far end, tethered to the dock.

A prickle of worry rushed up her spine. Lawrence never mentioned the resort had a plane. There had been no mention of it on the resort's website either. Then again, the website seemed to have been created before airplanes could actually fly. Or at least on the very day the internet went live, and the site didn't look to have been updated since.

Lily shook off a shiver of worry. Premature assumptions were never a good idea. No reason to assume the plane belonged to the resort—other than the fact that growing up on the Gulf Coast had taught her a few things about boats and planes and docks. And the far end of the dock was *definitely* outfitted to moor a plane.

And where there was a plane, there was usually a pilot nearby.

"So about calling the lady I met at the airport," Trace said to his brothers after Sexy Airport Girl didn't respond. His voice was back to normal, and he could finally eat something besides soup. He set the cell aside and picked up a dusty nail gun from the workbench that ran along one wall inside the boathouse. "I'm calling uncle on this one." He'd already crossed enough lines with a woman he didn't know. It was time to let it go and admit defeat.

"She shot you down?" Elliott teased as he and Spence sorted through the extra lumber they kept stacked in one corner for repairs.

All four boat slips had been empty for years. Since that fateful day when his mother took a rowboat out and never came back. His dad had built a makeshift floor across the length of the boathouse and converted it into a tool and supply shed.

Trace didn't answer because of the nine kinds of hell his brothers would rain down on him. When the nail gun didn't work, Trace jiggled the cord to make sure the connection wasn't loose. He finally gave up and tossed it in the trash can. "We need new tools."

Spence threw two pieces of lumber onto the stack. "This place needs new everything. Try the drill and get screws from the toolbox." He pointed to the red metal cabinet against the wall. As a master builder, he slid easily into the role of foreman.

Trace went to the toolbox and found a drill, drill bits, and several different screws. He held them out for Spence to examine.

"You didn't answer the question." Spence pointed to a particular bit and screw, indicating the right size and strength for the dock repairs.

Trace went back to the toolbox to dig out more. "Long story."

Elliott settled a plank across two sawhorses. "Time is something we've got lots of now that we're back on the island."

No sense hiding it. He'd screwed up royally and probably needed to get it off his chest just to clear his conscience. Maybe it would help him feel less like an ass. He recited every detail, starting with the airport massage station all the way through accidentally sending the last inappropriate message because he'd been shocked by Megan's appearance on television.

His brothers went from scowling over Megan's absurd maneuvering to doubling over with laughter at his accidental erotic text to Sexy Airport Girl.

"Knew you had no game with women," Spence snorted out between wheezes of laughter. "Who the hell tries to compliment a woman by comparing her to a character in *Game of Thrones?*"

"What?" Trace held his hand palm up. "Daenerys is smokin' hot."

"She has fire-breathing dragons burn her enemies alive, dumbass," Spence said.

Confiding in his brothers didn't make Trace feel less like an ass. It made him feel like a complete moron. So he was a little rusty when it came to dating. He was a good dad, and that counted a lot more than his ability to smooth-talk women.

"What was the most memorable thing about her?" Elliott asked.

Trace rubbed his chin. "Besides the way she moaned?"

Elliott stilled. "Maybe I should visit the airport to find a date."

"Her ringtone," Trace said. "She had this funky ringtone about strange Cajun food."

Spence rolled his eyes. "You focused on her ringtone?"

"It was loud." Trace let a thread of defensiveness seep into his voice. "She was facedown in a massage chair, so I didn't get a good look at her face. Her hair was nice, though."

Elliott shook his head. "So you couldn't compliment her hair?"

The fact that he'd had a very similar conversation with Ben about complimenting his teacher instead of unintentionally insulting her wasn't lost on Trace. "Whatever." He waved them off. "It's over. You win."

Elliott feigned shock. "You're giving in? To *us*?"

Thing One and Thing Two gave each other high fives.

"If you're going to rub it in, maybe I should go ahead and call her." Trace grabbed his phone. Worst-case scenario—she'd hang up on him or not answer at all. Wait. No, that wasn't the worst that could happen. The FBI swarming his cottage and hauling him off in cuffs with Ben watching would be the worst.

Spence gave him a cocky grin. "I was kind of rooting for you." Spence pulled safety goggles into place. "If you're gonna call her, make it quick before I fire up the electric saw."

"You realize this makes me the winner?" Trace pulled up her number. "The dare was for me to call her with you two in the room. You

never said she had to accept, which means you'll both owe me. Big."
He hit "Call."

Just as Lily Barns appeared in the doorway. "Good morning."
Elliott and Spence got a friendly nod from the new hospitality manager,
but Trace got nothing more than a fleeting glance. "I was wondering if
I could borrow a Jeep to take Mr. and Mrs. Walters for a drive?"

And then her phone sprang to life.

With a familiar ringtone.

About having fun on the bayou and all kinds of Cajun food.

Which was all kinds of fucked up because . . .

Everyone stilled. And then one by one, all heads turned toward
Lily, including Trace's.

His gut twisted into a thousand knots as she flipped her phone over
and stared at it. The obnoxious tune wailed on about crawfish pie and
filé gumbo and a son-of-a-gun, who was obviously Trace because, *damn.*

His eyes slid shut for a beat. He'd had *sext* with Lily Barns.

Spence hid an *Oh shit* behind a cough.

Elliott busied himself with shuffling more planks of wood for no
apparent reason.

Trace raked a hand down his face, then gave his phone a gentle
waggle. "I'm sorry." *So very, very sorry.*

Lily's head shot up to lock her wide-eyed gaze onto Trace's. "No." It
slipped through her lips in a hushed whisper. "It can't be."

"You have no idea how much I wish it wasn't." He ended the unanswered call. Made an exaggerated gesture to hit "Redial," and her phone
bawled out the same song.

She took a step back and tossed a frantic look over her shoulder
toward the dock. "*You're* the pilot?" She said the word *pilot* like she was
delivering the highest of insults.

"And you're the moaner," he mumbled before he could stop himself.

Her face went up in flames.

Elliott looked at Spence and pulled at his left earlobe, the Remington brothers' code for *Let's get out of here*. Since they were leaving him to deal with a mess they'd helped create with their stupid dare, Trace was going to make sure the consequences of losing would be well worth his while. When Thing One and Thing Two least expected it.

"Lily, we'll take care of Mr. and Mrs. Walters," Elliott said.

Her expression—the one that said she wanted to punch someone in the throat—didn't waver. "Mr. Walters is waiting on a bench just up the path. He and his wife need VIP treatment and a decent meal if we expect them to return to the Remington." She held up a finger before they reached the door. "And could you please move them to a room on the other side of the resort so they can't hear the hammering?"

"We'll see to it," Spence said as he and Elliott left.

Trace's eye twitched. "So this is awkward."

"Awkward." The tone of her voice was as flat as Kansas. "I'm the new employee, and you're my boss. This is so far beyond awkward, I can't even put a name to it." The sound of her tapping foot echoed off the hollow wooden floor.

"Look, I really am sorry."

She ignored his apology. "Out of all the women you could've picked from the crowd, it had to be me?"

He shrugged. "You *were* the only woman moaning."

Tap, tap, tap, tap, tap, tap.

He cringed under the heat of her scalding glare.

"I suppose you'll want to let me go now, since you didn't want your dad to hire me in the first place." Her foot tapping went to machine-gun speed.

"No." He might've acted like a jerk over text, but he wasn't unethical. "This is my fault. I started it by asking to use your phone. We're both adults." Said the guy who had set the whole mess in motion by giving in to his siblings' taunts.

The tapping came to an abrupt halt. "Good." She lifted her chin. "From now on, it's strictly professional between us."

"Absolutely." He sliced a hand through the air. "Professional."

"Then I better get back to work." She spun on her heel and left him staring at an empty doorway.

So the FBI swarming Trace's cottage wasn't the worst thing that could've happened. *This* was by far the most awful result. A woman whose moan had played hell with his imagination would be living and working at the resort. Where *he* lived and worked.

And Trace couldn't help but wonder how the sexy girl at the airport—with her strappy shoes and big-city clothes—had transformed into the girl he'd found just a few hours later on a tricycle wearing practical jeans and hiking boots.

Chapter Seven

Lily sat in the small office Lawrence had given her and delivered punishing strokes to the keyboard. It had taken three days of around-the-clock work, but the new online booking system she'd set up with automated billing and a downloadable smartphone app would make communication between guests and the Remington much smoother.

She glanced at her closed office door. Privacy was how she'd accomplished so much in such a short span of time. Keeping the door closed ever since the embarrassing revelation of the Voice's identity a few days ago wasn't to avoid Trace Remington.

It wasn't.

They'd agreed to keep things professional. *"Pffst,"* she mumbled. She planned to keep it so professional that *Merriam-Webster's Dictionary* would add her picture under the word instead of a definition. She'd prove her worth as an employee and outperform the Remington family's expectations. She'd done it before to prove she deserved the job she'd landed through her father. She'd do it again or die trying.

Which she just might if her heart pounded any faster.

Wasn't it just her luck that the most exciting relationship she'd had in two years was through text? Unfortunately, it also confirmed that swearing off men indefinitely was in her best interest since her judgment in that department was flawed.

She'd exchanged flirtatious texts with her *boss!*

Her incredibly attractive boss. With his silky and seductive voice. Who managed to have an unfair amount of sex appeal after he'd worked up a sweat repairing the dock.

Her keystrokes quickened right along with her breath.

The upside of working so hard and keeping things so *professional* was that she'd made considerable progress on the action plan Lawrence had approved for the resort's facelift. The Remington now showed up on every major travel and review site, and she'd toured every square inch of the property, inside and out. As far as Lily could tell, the inside had been kept in relatively good condition. The challenge would be bringing the exterior grounds up to snuff and creating enough buzz for vacationers to actually book the rooms.

She logged out of the booking program and pulled up the resort's new social media account to add a gallery of pictures she'd taken of the grounds. By the time she finished posting, it was lunchtime.

She stared at the closed door and drummed her fingers against the desk. A hospitality manager actually had to be hospitable. Which meant she couldn't stay holed up in her office forever, no matter how much work she checked off her to-do list.

She squared her shoulders and went to the door. Being a professional meant she could get past the awkwardness between Trace and her.

She could.

She tugged the door open and peeked out, first one way, then the next.

Relief feathered through her when she didn't encounter any of the Remington brothers, especially the oldest. She hurried to the kitchen, walking through the great room where a few guests sat in oversize chairs and read. Or snoozed, since the median age of the clientele seemed to be somewhere between retirement and the pearly gates.

She detoured to greet one of the guests who had their eyes open. "Ma'am, can I help make you more comfortable?"

A blue-haired lady looked up at her through thick glasses. "I've got everything I need." She pursed her lips. "Including antacid tablets after the breakfast we had." She lifted a hand and gave her wrist a flick. "The pastries were to die for, though."

Lily put on a smile. "I'll see what the problem is with the cook."

She walked through the empty dining hall and pushed through the swinging metal doors into the kitchen.

Charley was bent over a tray of exquisite looking doughnuts. "Hey there." She sprinkled pink sugar crystals over the tray. "How's it going?"

"Fantastic." Lily used her most enthusiastic hospitality manager's tone. She glanced around the kitchen. No cooking, no food preparation at all besides Charley's ninja baking skills.

"Getting settled in?" Charley switched to blue sprinkles and dusted another tray.

Yes, except the ducks were getting noisier every day, and she'd been so busy with work she hadn't had time to find them a bigger habitat. At least Ben had come by every evening to help with them, assuring her he'd cleared his visits with Trace. "Absolutely." Lily leaned against the counter and drummed it lightly. "Can I ask you a question?"

"Sure." Charley kept working.

"I've gathered you're in charge of desserts and coffee but not the cooking?"

Charley winced. "You must've heard complaints about the food."

Lily gave her a weak smile and nodded. "Afraid so."

"At the risk of throwing our cook under the bus, I can't take credit for anything other than coffee and dessert," Charley said.

Whew. Lily didn't want to start on the wrong foot with another Remington family member. At the rate she was going, she'd need to grow a dozen more feet. "Care to shed some light on the situation? It's my job to bring in new business, and food is paramount to guest retention and bookings."

"Mrs. Ferguson comes in before dawn, cooks, and sets up the buffet." Charley looked up from her creations. "Then she leaves. Breakfast doesn't start until seven, so you can imagine how dry the food is by the time the guests arrive." She went back to decorating. "I clean up the buffet in between when I'm baking."

"What about lunch and dinner?" Lily asked.

"Not served anymore." Charley shook her head. "Breakfast is the only meal. It's included with the room."

"I assume the guests go into town to eat?"

Charley nodded.

"But why does Lawrence run the kitchen like that?" Lily couldn't hide her exasperation.

Charley reached for a small pot on the burner to brush warm chocolate onto another tray. "Uncle Lawrence's wife used to prepare the food. Aunt Camilla was an incredible cook. They ran a tight ship back in the day."

Charley glanced around like she wanted to make sure no one was listening in. "Mrs. Ferguson took over after Aunt Camilla died."

"Oh," Lily whispered. Trace had lost a parent.

Charley shrugged. "Mrs. Ferguson was here all the time, either cooking or looking out for the boys. Uncle Lawrence can't bring himself to let her go now that she's gotten too old to manage the kitchen."

Loyalty. Lily had to give Lawrence credit for that, but a hotel needed to serve edible food. "This is a problem." A problem that was going to make Lily's job impossible unless they hired a cook. She stared longingly at the doughnuts. "Those look positively sinful. I'll trade a kidney for one."

Charley grabbed a spatula from a drawer to scoop two chocolaty masterpieces onto a plate. "This batch goes to a friend of mine in town who has a cute little food cart and mobile catering business. I provide her with doughnuts and pastries, which attracts more customers. She gives me the profits from the bakery items. I can spare a few for you, though." She slid the plate to Lily, then poured a mug of coffee. "Just got this new beauty." Charley returned the pot to the burner and ran a hand lovingly down the side of the industrial coffee machine. "I had to wring the money out of Elliott and his new budget, but this baby is mine now." She pretended to give it a hug. "It was love at first sight."

Lily chuckled and fixed her coffee before taking a long sip. The flavor exploded in her mouth. "My taste buds have died and gone to heaven."

Charley let out a knowing chuckle. "I come from a long line of gourmet coffee roasters in Seattle. I have the beans shipped in weekly."

Lily let the mug hover at her lips, thinking. The scent was every bit as enjoyable as the flavor, and it filled her with a sense of home and hearth. Exactly the type of feeling the guests should have when staying at the resort. That theme, that branding should be carried through to every aspect of the resort. "Your uncle is very lucky to have you. Seems like your desserts and coffee are the only sustenance the guests have to look forward to at the resort."

"Thanks, but I'm the lucky one." Charley wiped her hands and stacked dishes into the sink. "I needed to get away from Seattle. There were toxic people in my life."

Lily offered a sympathetic smile because she was there for the same reason.

"I better get back to work." Lily swiped her plate off the counter. "Nose to the grindstone and all that. Thanks." She gave her plate a boost. "I'm starving and didn't want to stop working long enough to go back to my place and make lunch."

She hurried back to her office as fast as she could manage without spilling her coffee. With a foot, she tried to kick the door closed. The door swung as she took a seat behind her desk, but it didn't close completely. According to the time on her computer screen, she had ten minutes to eat before meeting Lawrence to go over the new booking program.

She had to choose between the door and the doughnut.

Privacy could piss off for a minute or two.

She took a big bite of chocolaty doughnut. The chair creaked as she leaned back and let the rich, sweet flavor saturate her palate. She closed her eyes. *"Ooooh God."* Her moan of sheer pleasure came out louder than it should've. Just as a gentle knock sounded at her door.

"Uh." The Voice cleared his throat.

She stilled but kept her eyes closed. She did not want to open them and deal with the problem she knew was standing there. And Trace Remington was definitely a problem.

"Lily?"

His deep, velvety voice slid through her like the warm chocolaty flavor of the doughnut. And the owner of that voice had just heard her moan. Again.

Lily chewed and swallowed, the delicious dessert turning to chalk in her mouth. She forced her eyes open.

One side of Trace's mouth lifted into a half smile just smartass enough to set her on edge. "Am I interrupting?"

She didn't appreciate the glint in his eyes, so she returned his smart-assery. "Yes. I'm on a hot date with one of Charley's doughnuts."

His eyes dilated.

Professional. Keep it professional. Lily leveled an all-work-no-play stare at him. "What can I do for you, Mr. Remington?"

His subtle smile faded at her formality. "Got a minute?" He leaned farther into her office, the front of one shoulder propped against the doorframe.

"One or two." She sat straighter in her chair, wishing she'd not only shut her door all the way but locked it too. She was not going to eat moan-worthy sweets in front of Trace.

He took the only chair in front of her desk. "Look. You don't have to avoid me."

She sputtered, "I'm not avoiding you." She *so* was. "I'm working."

"Okay." He drew out the word. "Have you found a home for the ducks?"

"I haven't looked because I've been *working*." She turned to her computer and searched for bird refuges in the area. "The nearest place is a hundred and seventy miles down the coast."

"I'll fly them there myself tomorrow."

His parenting skills were none of Lily's business, but what kind of person didn't want their kid to have a pet? "Ben has come over to my place after school to take care of them the past few days. He insisted you were okay with it."

Trace's chafed look said he was anything but okay with it.

"He's very good with them. He's even been doing research at school on how to care for them. He brought me some printouts," Lily said. "He's a good kid. You should be proud of the job you've done."

His hardened expression softened a little. "Thanks, but even so, the ducks need to go. The longer they stay, the more crushed he'll be when they get big enough to fly away."

Lily wondered if Trace was really talking about himself and his son. Their bond was obvious, and she admired it. Envied it, even. But protecting Ben from the heartbreak of losing a pet was also depriving him of the joy a pet brought to a kid's life. And she had news for Trace. Ben was already crazy in love with the birds and was going to be crushed no matter what.

Still, it wasn't her business, so she nodded in agreement.

"Look, when I apologized the other day, I meant it. I never intended to send that inappropriate text. I shouldn't have typed it to begin with. I'm not usually a jerk."

"So that's a new development since I've been in town?" She threaded her fingers.

He gave his temple an absent scratch as if to say *You've got me there.* "Really, I'm an okay guy. Just ask my brothers." He faltered. "On second thought, don't ask them. I'd be screwed if you did." He let a lazy smile form on his lips.

It was adorable.

Lily's gaze was drawn to that beautiful smiling mouth. A mouth that, according to the text message in question, could do wicked things to her while she wore a thong.

Her pulse revved. Quite unprofessionally.

It took an incredible amount of effort, but Lily didn't let her no-nonsense expression waver. She tapped her two index fingers together and waited for him to leave.

Trace sobered. "Can I make it up to you somehow?"

Besides fulfilling his promise to move her imaginary thong to one side so he could put that delicious-looking mouth to work making her moan again?

No thank you. She'd damn well stick to doughnuts for that.

"Yes." She lifted her chin. "The other night at my place, you were worried about change. Give me the benefit of the doubt, and let me do my job. I'm actually good at it. The Remington will be a better place."

Something flashed in his eyes. Maybe it was worry. Maybe it was skepticism. Maybe it was attraction.

Lily fought off a shiver and picked a piece of imaginary lint from the sleeve of her chambray shirt. "And let Ben and me keep the ducks."

"That's not fair," Trace shot back. "And I don't appreciate interference when it comes to my son."

"Look, Mr. Remington—"

His eyes dimmed.

She ignored it. "I don't mean to interfere, and I really did think he had your permission to come to my place. It's just that he's been doing a great job helping take care of them when I'm busy, and he's already attached," Lily said. "So whatever hurt you're trying to spare him . . ." She sighed. "It's probably too late."

Trace tapped a finger against the space between his nose and mouth and kept his eyes planted firmly on her. If there'd been a clock on the wall, Lily was sure she could've heard it ticking. Clearly, he was annoyed. But the fact that he was even considering her request showed it might have some merit.

Finally, he drew in a breath. "Fine. I'll *try* to give you the benefit of the doubt when it comes to the resort. You can keep the ducks, but I'll need you to back me up when I have to prepare my son to accept that they won't be around forever. Under two conditions—we forget all about the texting."

"Consider it forgotten." She doubted she'd forget Trace's erotic text in this lifetime. Neither would her uterus, the mutinous little hussy. Every time Lily thought of that text she ovulated.

Whatever. She had a job to do, and that was that. "And the second condition?"

"Stop calling me Mr. Remington."

Her foot bounced under the desk. "It's professional."

"It's absurd," he countered.

"As absurd as, say, a grown man asking to borrow a woman's phone so he can get her number without permission?" She gave him an innocent smile.

He didn't return it. "Those are my conditions. Take it or leave it."

They stared at each other across the desk so long it was like a showdown without dueling pistols. "Fine," she mimicked his earlier one-word answer. "I'll *try* to remember to call you Trace. If that's all, I have an appointment with your father." She glanced at her wrist to make a point. Only to realize she wasn't wearing a watch. So she shuffled papers around on her desk. Seemed like a professional thing to do.

Trace didn't budge. Why wasn't he budging? Instead, he stayed put like he didn't want the conversation to end. "He's in the family's private den," he finally said.

"Thank you." She grabbed her iPad and strolled right out of her office. Cool as the spring breeze rolling in off the ocean.

Except for her quivering thighs. She should add another item to her bullet list of things to do around the resort—*more working, less quivering.*

She found Lawrence sitting at a small wicker table in the corner of the den reserved for family. It was modestly decorated with an island motif. He was writing checks to go with the stack of bills in front of him. Lily knocked on the open door, and he peered at her over reading glasses. "Come in, Lily."

"Thanks for seeing me." Lily took a seat across from Lawrence, ready to give him an update on her progress. Unfortunately, she also had a list of concerns that needed to be addressed, namely Mrs. Ferguson's lack of culinary skills.

"Sure thing." He pushed back from the table.

She cut right to it. "Since our summer kickoff is just five weeks away, I've set up several discounted packages that will be available for a limited time." She decided to start with a list of her accomplishments before bringing up the food. "I'm advertising those package deals on social media and travel sites to get the word out. The point is to fill up the rooms as early in the season as possible so reviews start showing up online."

He nodded. "Impressive work."

"Lawrence." She chose her words carefully. "I don't think we can keep the Remington's rooms filled without offering better food choices."

He frowned. "I don't think we can afford to hire more kitchen staff for lunch and dinner. We only have enough room in the budget for part-time help with maintenance and cleaning."

"What if I found a solution that wouldn't cost the Remington anything?" She crossed her legs and waited. Thanks to something Charley had said, Lily had an idea that just might work if she found the right person.

He scrubbed a hand over his jaw. "I can't let Mrs. Ferguson go."

Lily dipped her head once in a nod. "I haven't met her yet, but if I can find a way for the resort to keep Mrs. Ferguson while bringing in food from another source, would you be willing to try it?" She gave him the deets but asked him to keep it under wraps for the time being.

"If you can work that miracle, then I'm on board," he said.

"Excellent." She smiled, and the tension in her shoulders released. She pulled up the booking program. "The new system is up and running. I'll need to update our website, but it can be fully integrated with the booking program." She pointed to the top corner of the screen. "You log in and the system updates the calendar as the bookings are made online. Employees and guests can download this app—"

Lily froze when she glanced at Lawrence. The blank stare he gave the screen told her he'd zoned out.

Her pride deflated. "This will be a tremendous help in bringing in new clients. Everything is done online now."

"I understand," he said. "But it's hard to teach an old dog new tricks. I used to handle reservations, but I think it's time to pass the torch." He scratched his jaw.

Yes! She should be in charge of reservations until the resort could staff the front desk. She let out a breath. Lawrence was so much easier to be around than his son. Thank goodness she reported to Lawrence and didn't have to work closely with Trace.

"Sorry I'm late." Trace breezed in.

Speak of the hot and handsome devil. Every cell in Lily's body tensed.

"It took some finesse, but I talked Charley out of a doughnut." Trace faced them at the table, leaning against the back of the seashell-print sofa, and ate his prize over a napkin.

Lily narrowed her eyes. Because who made eating a doughnut look so seductive? Plus, her doughnuts were still mostly uneaten and sitting on her desk, thanks to him. No one got between her and a gourmet doughnut and lived to tell the tale.

"I asked Trace to be here because he's the best person to work with you on the changes you're bringing to the Remington."

Her head snapped around to gape at Lawrence.

No. Just no.

"Lawrence"—Lily couldn't hide the surprise in her voice, or the desperation—"I assure you, I won't let you down. No need to impose on Trace."

Trace, on the other hand, didn't seem the least bit surprised or desperate as he chomped on his damned doughnut. Obviously, he'd known this was coming. So much for giving her the benefit of the doubt. He'd have to approve every change. And reporting directly to Trace would make avoiding him a little difficult.

"I have complete confidence in you, Lily." Lawrence tapped his finger against the table thoughtfully. "But I can barely work my new-fangled television remote."

"I'm looking forward to taking the lead on this. It's about time Dad turned more responsibility over to me." Trace took another bite.

She'd wanted to immerse herself in work. Earn her place at the Remington. Maybe she should've sacrificed one of her coveted dough-nuts to the work gods or some such, because the last thing she intended was to be stuck working side by side with a man who'd sexted her. A man whose ridiculous good looks could cause her to make another mistake that would ruin her chances at a new life.

Obviously, *Be careful what you ask for* wasn't just a cliché.

The silence was painful, and Lily laced her fingers to keep them still.

Lawrence looked from one to the other. "Is there something I should know?"

"Nope," Trace said too quickly.

"Not a thing," Lily blurted at the same time.

"I'm flying to the Cape to pick up guests, and I've got an aerial tour this evening." Trace brushed off his fingers on his jeans. "Tomorrow's kind of busy too. How about you show me the new reservation system later this week?"

She nodded and gathered her iPad. "I'll get started on updating our website. Also, I need to drive into town soon," she said to Lawrence. "Can I check out a Jeep?"

He nodded. "Leave me a copy of your driver's license. You typed in the number on your employment forms, but if you're going to drive a company vehicle, we need a hard copy on file for insurance purposes."

A rush of anxiety hit Lily square in the chest. Her license listed her real name. Which was why she hadn't given the resort actual copies of her identification. Since they didn't insist on a background check, typing in the information without submitting photocopies had allowed her to remain incognito. "I just remembered, my license is expired. I'll take the shuttle."

Lawrence pointed at Trace. "He can drive you into Angel Fire Falls and fly you to the Cape whenever you need."

Trace thumbed his chest. "Pilot, remember?"

Lily couldn't quite force a smile. Of course she remembered. How could she possibly forget?

Chapter Eight

If life is easy, then you're not having fun.

Lily sat behind her desk, trying to integrate the new booking system with the Remington's outdated website, which she'd dubbed Webasaurus Rex.

Focusing on work was an impossible feat ever since she'd told Lawrence her driver's license had expired so he wouldn't discover her real name. Her conscience was proving to be a handicap. Apparently, she hadn't inherited her father's ability to lie without losing a wink of sleep. It was already wearing on her, and she'd only been in Angel Fire Falls a week and a half.

Lily rubbed her eyes and let her head fall back in defeat. The website was so outdated, it would be easier to start from scratch. Website design wasn't her thing, but with the shoestring budget she had to work with, she'd have to do it herself. Luckily, she'd found a user-friendly website-building-for-dummies program.

In need of a break after hours in front of her computer, she pushed out of her chair and walked to her cottage. Her ringtone blared from the back pocket of her black hiking pants. Lily made sure no one was in sight, then drew in a fortifying breath. "Hi, Mom." Why did she find talking to her mother so exhausting?

"Scarlett! You haven't called. I've been worried sick."

"I called a day and a half ago." Having to check in with her mother so often drained Lily's energy. Probably why she found her mother's conversations exhausting.

"How's Vermont? Maybe I should join you at the retreat." Her mother's tone told Lily she was in the middle of a full-blown pity party.

"*No.*" Lily choked down her rising panic. "Mom, you need to stay close to home so you can visit Dad."

"I can only visit him twice a month." She sighed like it was a relief. "And there's not much to do here." Her voice shook. "I'm not going back to the country club. The service has gone downhill."

They'd probably canceled the Devereaux family membership for nonpayment of dues.

"Mom, have you thought about getting a job? You used to work before you met Dad." Lily tried to sound encouraging. "At least it would get you out of the house." And off the sauce.

"I worked as a bank teller," her mom snapped. "What bank is going to hire me after what your father did?"

"I don't know, Mom. You could find a job that doesn't require handling money." Lily stepped off the path and onto the road that led to the cottages. "Or you could volunteer. Helping others might make you feel better."

Her mom let out an exaggerated sigh. "I'm not a strong woman like you, honey. You get that from your father."

Dear God, no. No, no, no.

Lily's heart squeezed because there was more truth in her mother's words than she knew. Yes, Lily was a hard worker and never took a penny she didn't earn. But she was also posing under an alias. Maybe for good reasons—one being survival—but it was still dishonest.

"Tell me about the retreat," her mother said.

"Well . . ." Lily's conscience already prickling, she settled on a thread of truth. "I've got my own cottage. It's adorable." She glanced up the road toward her house, and her heart warmed.

"Oh, sounds lovely. What else, sweetie?"

A bird flew overhead, and Lily thought of her ducks. "There's lots of wildlife on the grounds and a really great pastry chef." She leaned her head back to gaze up at the cloudy sky. "Rains a lot. At least there are no hurricanes, though."

The mention of the Gulf Coast's horrible weather provoked a lengthy complaint about heat and humidity from her mom.

Lily listened patiently as she reached the front steps of her cottage. Sitting on the front porch was a gigantic plastic container that hadn't been there when she'd left for work that morning. Her phone dinged. She held it out to read the new reservation notification on her booking app, and a sense of accomplishment welled inside her. The fruits of her hard work were already paying off. "Mom, can I let you go?"

Her mother groaned her disappointment.

"I'm in the middle of something," Lily said. "Promise I'll call next week."

"Make it a few days, and I'll let you off the phone," her mother whined.

Lily rolled her eyes. "All right, Mom. Love you."

She hung up and texted the guest's arrival information to Trace, since he still hadn't made time for her to train him on the new system. Then she walked onto her front porch to look inside the container. Puppy training pads lined the bottom, and a fleece hunting hat sat in one corner. Next to it was a reusable grocery bag that contained an assortment of fresh veggies, cornmeal, and more training pads.

Hammering echoed from the backyard, and Lily cocked her head to listen.

Bang, bang, bang.

Lily frowned.

Bang, bang, bang.

She walked around to the back of the cottage. Ben was hard at work hammering stakes into the ground to form a large circle.

"Hey, bud." Lily stuffed her phone back in her pocket. "Whatcha doing?"

"I'm building a pen so the ducks can play outside." His tongue slipped through his lips on one side of his mouth as he concentrated on hammering in another stake.

Lily nodded. "Is that your box on the front porch?"

"It's the ducks' new inside house." He kept hammering. "They can snuggle inside the fuzzy hat to keep warm."

Pretty resourceful for a kid his age. "Ben, where did you get the supplies?" She really hoped he wasn't asking his dad for money. She didn't want to push any more of Trace's buttons when it came to Ben and the ducks.

"Mostly from the boathouse." Ben finished hammering in the last stake, then unwound the roll of chicken wire. He tore open a package of colorful pipe cleaners. "My teacher gave me these because she had extra." He used them to secure the chicken wire to the stakes.

"Where did the stuff on the front porch come from?" Lily asked.

"Charley took me to the store." He moved to the next stake. "Hey, Lily!" he blurted. "You know how the ducks think you're their mom?" He didn't wait for her to answer. "That's called imprinting. It's *science*. My teacher said the ducks can be my science project! Can we take pictures of the ducks every day?" It all tumbled out at once. "My teacher helped me find more stuff online about raising them." He hammered some more. "And Miss Etheridge stopped being mad at me for saying her hair is ugly."

Um. Wow. Telling any female her hair was ugly couldn't have produced a positive result. "I have a few pictures of them, but we can take more each day." Lily shoved her hands in her pockets. "Have you cleared this with your dad? For real this time?"

Ben didn't look at her. "He says I have to do my own project. The other kids at school have their dads do all the work."

Lily smiled. She'd chosen a few science projects specifically because they required building something; having a dad who was a builder had been convenient.

Her chest squeezed. It had been a long time since she'd remembered anything good about her father. Working on those projects with him had been fun.

But Ben still hadn't answered her question.

"Ben"—Lily dropped the tenor of her voice—"is your dad okay with this?"

He still wouldn't meet her eye. "It's a surprise."

Sounded like a smooth way of not clearing it with his dad. "You need to tell him. There's a difference between a surprise and a lie."

She nearly choked on her own words.

Lily swallowed back the bitterness of guilt that welled up in her throat.

That was quite the moral platitude from someone whose mother thought she was at an exclusive retreat in Vermont instead of working hard on a tiny island in the Pacific Northwest. She'd tell her mother the truth eventually. For now, she couldn't deal with the threats and the verbal abuse from the public if her true identity got out, and her mother wasn't exactly discreet after too much scotch on the rocks.

Lily refocused on Ben. "I'll leave my front door unlocked so you can check on the ducks after school. But only if you promise to tell your dad about the science project."

His nod was reluctant.

"Want to feed the duckies?"

She didn't have to ask twice. Ben dropped the pipe cleaners and ran to her. She tousled his hair. "What are we going to do with the veggies and cornmeal?"

He skipped along. "Grind everything up and feed it to them."

95

They rounded the corner and climbed the front steps. She took out her key and opened the door. "Thanks for shopping for them. I'm almost out of oatmeal and bread, and I don't have a way to get to the store." She made a face. "They eat a lot for being such little things."

"And poop a lot too." Ben giggled.

They carried everything in, and the ducks tuned up. She pulled up the camera on her phone and handed it to him. "Take a few pictures, and make sure they have fresh water. I'll start their food."

Ben ran to the bathroom.

She searched the cabinets and found a mini chopper. "Here we go."

Ben emerged from the bathroom, rubbing one hand against his thigh rhythmically. "Megan looks sick." He slid Lily's phone onto the counter next to her purse.

Lily hurried to the bathroom. Nine of the ducks cheeped their lungs out, but one sat off to the side, quiet and still. She adjusted the shade of the table lamp she'd moved to the bathroom for warmth to direct more heat downward. Still, the little lone duck didn't seem right.

She glanced at Ben, who rubbed his thighs faster.

"Maybe she'll feel better after she eats." A tremor of regret flowed through her at Ben's worried expression. The last thing she wanted was to cause him heartache.

She had him follow her back to the kitchen and pulled a chair to the counter. He clambered onto it, and she gave him a mixing bowl and a spoon. "You read up on how to do this?"

He nodded and worked with painstaking diligence. When he was done, he scooped the smooth mixture into a shallow container and carried it to the bathroom.

The cheeping stopped the second Ben set the food bowl into the tub. The other ducks edged Megan out.

"Be right back." Lily filled another container with food and brought it back to the bathroom to feed the weak duckling separately from the others.

"They're getting bigger, aren't they?" Lily said. In fact, they'd doubled in size.

"Miss Etheridge helped me find a library book with pictures. They'll start getting real feathers soon." Ben sat by the tub. "Megan is the only one that hasn't gotten much bigger."

Lily studied the ducks. Ben was right; she was smaller than the others.

Ben pointed to one of the ducks. "Sir Walter Raleigh is the biggest." He named off each duck in order of size.

Her gaze ping-ponged between the ducklings and Ben, amazed at how observant he was. "So, Ben, what do you think about changing Megan's name to Molly?"

His little body rocked. "But her name is Megan."

"Hmm." Lily sat on the floor and pulled her knees to her chest. "I like the name Molly, though, don't you?" Megan was actually fine with her, but Trace had insisted on renaming it for some reason.

Ben shook his head and rocked.

"Is there another name besides Molly and Megan you like?"

"*No,*" he said and rocked harder. "Megan is her name. It wouldn't be right to change it."

Lily wanted to rock back and forth too. Or maybe draw into a fetal position and suck her thumb. Because she knew firsthand how strange it was to change her name. "We can talk about it later. Want to take them out of the tub for exercise?"

The rocking stopped, and Ben shot to his feet. In ten seconds flat, the ducks were following Ben around the den in a game of chase. He laughed and giggled as he slowed enough for them to catch up, then took off again. The only duckling that didn't play along was Megan. She stayed by her food in the bathroom, sitting idly like she had no energy. Lily's volunteer work at the wildlife rescue had taught her enough to know that something was wrong. She scooped Megan up and fished a knit cap out of her dresser drawer. She sat Megan inside of it and cuddled the tiny bird against her chest.

While Ben and the ducklings circled the den, Lily used her phone to search for a vet on the island. Only one came up. Problem was, she had no way of traveling to town. She couldn't ask anyone at the resort for a ride because it would get back to Trace, and he'd likely be upset with her for the worry and disappointment the duckling's downward turn would cause Ben. More importantly, Lily didn't *want* Ben to be worried or disappointed any more than his father did. She wanted to save the duck for Ben's sake.

"Hey, Ben, let's put the ducks in their new home."

"Sure!" His voice was a squeal of joy as the ducklings waddled after him. He led them to the plastic container and gently scooped them up one at a time while Lily moved the lamp out of the bathroom.

"Can you do me a favor?" she asked. "Do you happen to have an extra bicycle I could use?" She'd gotten most of the way to the resort on a tricycle; she could make it two miles into town on a bike. She'd moved here for independence. She'd take care of the situation herself without help from anyone, especially her boss.

The man with a voice so sexy, her bra unhooked on its own every time she heard it.

Gah!

"There's a girl's bike in the boathouse," Ben said.

"Great. Could you get it for me?"

As soon as he walked out, Lily dialed the vet. "Hi, I have an emergency. Can I bring a duckling in right away?"

"We're about to close, ma'am," the receptionist clipped out.

Lily glanced at the clock on her stove. *Dang it.* She hadn't realized it was getting so late. "Please. I'm afraid it might not make it through the night. I have to try to save it."

The receptionist heaved out an annoyed sigh. "Hold a moment." The line went quiet for an eternity.

Ben threw open the door without knocking. "The bike's out front!"

Lily nodded and held her phone away from her mouth. "Thanks, Ben."

The line beeped as the receptionist picked up the call again. "Dr. Shaw will wait for you."

"Thank you. I'm on my way, um, but a bicycle is my only way to get to your office."

The receptionist drew in another exaggerated breath.

"Tell Dr. Shaw I'll pedal as fast as I can." Lily hung up, grabbed her purse, and eased it over her head so it hung across her body.

"Is Megan gonna be okay?" Ben rubbed his thighs. "Can I go with you?"

Lily forced a brave smile. "Do you go to the doctor when you have a cold or fever?"

Ben nodded.

"Well, I think Megan . . . or Molly—"

Ben scowled.

"Or Megan probably has a cold, so I'm taking her to the vet to make sure. You can finish their pen while I'm gone, okay?" She hustled them both out the front door. "That way they'll have a place to play outside when I get home instead of being cooped up indoors all the time. I bet staying inside gets boring, don't you?" She tried to make light of the situation.

Ben didn't look any more convinced that Megan wasn't seriously ill than Lily was.

She straddled the bicycle, thankful it wasn't a racing bike. It was more like a let's-take-a-leisurely-ride-along-the-boardwalk kind of bike, and it had a wicker basket attached to the handlebars. The bird, still ensconced in Lily's winter cap, fit perfectly.

She looked up at the churning gray sky. Would she ever catch a break?

Her dad used to say, "If life is easy, then you're not having fun." She should be having a freakin' party by now. The kind of wild party New Orleans had every Fat Tuesday where the more adventurous tourists woke up in a strange place wearing nothing but colorful beads and a matching Mardi Gras mask.

Then again, living by that philosophy had landed her father in a place where orange jumpsuits were mandatory.

She grabbed both handlebars and flicked up the kickstand. "Ben, try not to worry." She'd do enough worrying for both of them. All she could do was get Megan to the vet and hope for the best.

Ben looked a little more optimistic.

She pushed off and pedaled, trusting that this one time since she'd boarded the plane to move to Angel Fire Falls, the universe wouldn't be against her.

Chapter Nine

LILY'S LIFE LESSON #9
Sometimes it's the little things in life.

Trace had spent the past few days making runs to and from the mainland because the Cape's only delivery company had decided not to deliver. Again. After the last run, he blew off steam at the vintage PAC-MAN machine in the back corner of the game room and waited for Ben. Meeting up after school for a game of pool was their father-son thing, and it wasn't like Ben to miss it.

Megan had called while Trace was in flight. A good excuse to let it go to voice mail. The insistent message she'd left about Ben staying the summer in Los Angeles had Trace's blood pressure spiked to stroke level, especially since their son's welfare wasn't her real concern.

Spence gave a victory shout from the other side of the room when he hit the bull's-eye to beat Elliott at a game of darts. They came over and flanked Trace, each leaning against a machine.

"So how awkward is it with Lily?" Spence asked.

"Pretty darned." Trace shifted and ran from a blue ghost. "Dad's having her report to me. I've been busy making delivery runs, but I've got to make time to look at the new system she insists is good for the resort. Good thing is, I'll know what changes she wants to make and can put a stop to anything that might upset Ben. Bad thing is—" He quieted. There were so many, he wasn't sure which one took priority. He reversed the chomping yellow circle's course and escaped certain death.

"You like her," Spence finished Trace's sentence.

"Bite me," Trace said.

"Now see, that's your problem, big brother." Spence crossed his arms. "You're asking me to bite you, when it's Lily's teeth marks you really want.'"

"Change the subject, or I'll shave your head while you sleep like I did when we were kids." He wasn't going to take the chance of trusting the wrong person again and putting himself or Ben at risk. "And I never want to hear another one of your childish dares again."

The PAC-MAN chewed up dots as Trace used the joystick to maneuver through the maze. Left then right, he gobbled up a power pellet and turned to face down a pink enemy ghost.

He secretly named it Megan.

"So we were in town at the Fallen Angel last night watching the fight over a beer." Elliott hesitated. "We saw Megan's commercial."

Trace focused on the game, determined not to lose to the ghost that chased him. "Ridiculous, isn't it?" He shook his head at the absurdity of his ex working as the spokesperson for an autistic charity.

"Uh, not that commercial." Spence pulled at his Adam's apple. That was never a good sign. "Apparently, she's landed a network series."

Trace's head jerked around. "*What?*"

The spiraling sound of defeat caused him to turn a blank stare back on the game as the pink ghost chomped him to pieces.

Go figure.

Trace couldn't let go of the joystick. His hold on it was so tight, it should've disintegrated in his hand.

"Her acting must've improved," Elliott said. "I mean, it doesn't seem like my kind of show, but it's a big step up from the laxative commercial. At least Ben won't be teased over it."

Trace turned his back to the machine and leaned against it.

"I'll google it for you." Spence pulled out his phone and tapped on the screen. "Looks like Ben's helping her career quite a bit." He stared at the phone and both brows lifted.

"What?" Trace reached for the cell.

Spence held it out of reach. "I don't think you want to see this."

"I don't think you want your ass kicked." Trace held out his hand.

Spence leveled a serious look at him. "Fine, but I warned you." He handed over the phone.

The list of Megan's interviews and articles on entertainment sites was so long, Trace had to thumb through them. He tapped on an interview given by her agent and read the first paragraph. *Lead actress of next season's most anticipated new series, Megan Remington was discovered through her goodwill efforts to draw awareness to the same disability her son suffers from . . .*

Steam billowed from his eye sockets.

He handed the cell back to Spence and pulled out his own phone. Without a word, he punched in Megan's number.

"Hellooooow," she answered with a new Garbo-esque accent.

Trace ground his teeth into dust. "Megan, how dare you use our son—"

"Dad!" Ben crashed through the door, barreling straight for Trace.

The desperate look on Ben's face set off Trace's instinctive parental alert. For his son's sake, he curbed the lecture he was about to deliver Megan. "I'll call you back," he said into the phone.

"Trace—"

He hung up without letting her finish. He'd spent years playing the peacemaker so that the pain of her rejection wouldn't completely destroy their son. Trace was done being the nice guy who covered for her lack of interest.

"What is it, buddy?" Trace shoved his phone in his pocket and held Ben's shoulders. "What's wrong?"

The way his chest heaved, he'd been running at full speed. "It's Megan," he panted.

Why did that not surprise him? Trace stiffened. "What about your mother?"

"No!" The panic in Ben's voice rose. "Megan the duckie!" He hollered like Trace was dense for not knowing the difference. "She's sick, and I was building a pen for them, but she wouldn't eat and she hasn't grown like the other duckies and Lily wanted to call her Molly, but Megan is her name . . . and . . ." His bottom lip puckered. "And . . ." A tear slid down his cheek.

Trace pulled his son into a hug. When Ben buried his face in Trace's midsection, he gave his two brothers a concerned look. "Shhhh." Trace swayed gently to match Ben's rocking. "It's okay." Trace's gut had told him not to keep the ducks, but he hadn't listened.

Precisely why both the ducks and the women in his life should be kept at arm's length.

"Duck?" Elliott mouthed.

"Named Megan?" Spence mouthed too.

Trace nodded and made the signal for *Tell you later.*

"I'll go find Lily and check on the duck." Trace stroked his son's arms to help soothe his soaring anxiety.

Ben shook his head and sniffed. "Lily's taking Megan to the doctor. I gave her the bicycle in the boathouse."

What the hell? The only vet on the island was on the far side of Angel Fire Falls. "Lily is using a bicycle to take the duck to the vet?"

Ben swiped the back of his hand under his nose and sniffled. "Yeah. She said she'd pedal fast."

Spence let out a snort of laughter but tried to hide it behind a cough.

Trace's eyes flitted between Ben and the pool table, and his brothers got the message.

Spence ruffled Ben's hair. "I just beat Uncle Elliott at darts. How about we make it a trouncing defeat and you wipe the floor with him at pool?"

Ben swiped another tear away, but his countenance brightened, and he ran to the table. "I'll break."

Trace dropped his voice and said to Spence, "I have an evening tour scheduled. Can you find the guests and reschedule for me?"

"On it," Spence said.

Trace nodded a thank-you to his brothers and left Ben in good hands. He headed straight for the garage. Since he'd already been around the block with Lily Barns and her apparent obsession with traveling across the island using pedal-powered transportation, he searched the garage for a few bungee cords to strap the bicycle to the roof. He fired up a Jeep and kicked up dust as he backed out.

It didn't take long until she came into view. He slowed as he came up behind her. Her slender torso was bent over the handlebars, and she pedaled with the same determination as that first day when she'd arrived on the island. He'd allowed this woman to get under his thick skin and into his overactive imagination from the very first moment he'd heard her moan.

He passed her and pulled off the road, trying hard to compose his emotions. She didn't have kids. She didn't understand what it was like to be disappointed and abandoned by a parent the way Megan had abandoned Ben. Trace had warned Lily about the ducks, but she likely didn't have experience with Asperger's and couldn't have known how much damage they could cause.

He pinched the bridge of his nose. He'd made similar excuses for Megan since Ben was born.

He opened his eyes and looked into the rearview mirror as Lily slowed, her silky brown hair blowing every which way in the breeze. He got out of the Jeep, went around the back, and crossed his arms as she pulled to a stop in front of him.

Her big brown eyes rounded, and the bike wobbled. She steadied it by putting her feet on the ground, and then she leaned forward to look in the basket.

Trace squinted up at the thunderclouds. "Really?"

"I, um . . . yeah." She tucked a lock of hair behind one ear, the tremor of her hand barely visible.

"You couldn't just ask for a ride like a normal person?" He peered into the basket at the little bird nesting in a knit cap.

"I knew you'd be pissed and worried about Ben, so I decided to handle it myself. I don't want Ben to be hurt either."

She cared that much about his feelings? His kid's feelings? No woman on the planet had shown that much concern over him or Ben. Certainly not his ex. Not even Trace's mom, who'd been careless enough to go out for a boat ride without a life vest, even knowing she couldn't swim very well. Knowing she had three young boys who needed her.

Leaving Trace to feel responsible for his younger brothers.

"And you thought the best solution was to carry a sick bird all the way into town on this old bicycle?" His mom's old bike. "It's so ancient, it could've throw a chain or gotten a flat." Trace picked the bird up in its cap with a slow, steady hand.

"I'm sorry," she said. "I just wanted to get to the vet because he's staying open just to see Meg—"

Trace couldn't stop a scowl, which made Lily go quiet. He couldn't blame her for the name. That was Ben's doing, but it scratched at his ears like sandpaper anyway.

"The vet's waiting," Lily said.

"Get in." He handed her the duck and grabbed the handlebars. "I've got the bike." He had it strapped to the roof before she could get in the passenger seat. They were moving as soon as her door closed. "Do me a favor?"

"Okay." Her voice was small.

"If you like leisurely bike rides, go for it. But when it's really important, ask someone at the resort to drive you. We don't mind."

"Thanks. Sorry. I just like taking care of myself."

Understandable. And admirable. "Then I'll fly you to the Cape soon so you can get your license renewed."

She coughed and put a hand to her chest. "It's not a priority. I'll be sure to ask for a ride until I can make a trip to the mainland."

Something in her tone, her posture, her expression changed.

Call it instinct, but for the second time that day Trace's blood pressure spiked.

Lily explained the whole story to the vet, starting with how she'd found the orphaned ducks on the road. Dr. Shaw was old, but he had a kind demeanor and a gentle touch with the duckling. He examined the tiny bird on a metal table in a private exam room.

"Will Megan live?" Lily used the duck's name since Trace was in the waiting room calling the resort to let Ben know they'd made it to the vet.

"It seems you have a lame duck on your hands." Dr. Shaw smiled. "It'll be fine with a little extra care."

Lily sagged against the exam table. Ben wouldn't be heartsick, and her boss wouldn't hate her for causing his son grief. She jumped when the door to the exam room opened, and Trace stepped inside.

"Ah, there's the proud father," Dr. Shaw said. "Good to have both parents present when we discuss their baby."

A deafening silence filled the room.

Trace stuffed his phone in the front pocket of his denim jacket. "We're not together."

Lily cleared her throat. "I work at the Remington. Trace gave me a ride."

Dr. Shaw eyed them. "I see." He retrieved a small bottle from the cabinet in the corner and handed it to Lily. "Ducks have fragile legs. Occasionally, they can strain a muscle, which makes it hard for them to move around." He bundled Megan into the cap again. "You said there's ten ducks in the brood?"

Lily nodded.

"The weakened leg is preventing it from fighting its way to the food trough," the vet explained. "It's likely getting pushed out by the stronger ducks. Keep feeding it separately." He nodded to the small bottle in Lily's hand. "Don't feed them bread. Add the niacin to their drinking water. It'll strengthen the muscles and help the strain heal quicker. A therapeutic swim in shallow water for exercise will do wonders. Toddler swimming pools work well if you have one." He scooped up the duck in the cap and handed her over to Lily. "A bigger problem is the wing." He pointed to one side of the duck. "It's a little smaller than the other, which means it may never fly. Only time will tell."

"Thank you for seeing her after hours." Lily cradled Megan.

"You're welcome." Dr. Shaw took off his latex gloves with a snap. "The visit's on the house. Least I can do for you trying to save them. And one more thing."

Both Lily and Trace waited for him to finish.

Dr. Shaw nodded to the duckling. "Megan is a he."

Trace stared at the duck, then lifted his gaze to Lily. A slow smile formed on his lips, and creases of happiness appeared around his eyes. His hearty laugh echoed through the empty clinic and filled Lily's chest with satisfaction. It was the first time she'd heard Trace laugh. Really laugh, like the seriousness that came from carrying the weight of the world on his shoulders had lifted and he could finally let himself experience real joy . . . and from such a simple thing.

His laugh was contagious, and she belted out a chuckle too.

The moment was comfortable. Easy. And Lily's smile was no longer forced. Trace's laughter made her feel at home for the first time since she stepped off the ferry.

Sometimes it was the little things in life that made the biggest impact.

Lily glanced at Dr. Shaw and did a double take, her laughter coming to a sputtering halt.

The vet's questioning sure-you're-not-a-couple look reminded Lily that the warm, hearty laughter that had her feeling like maybe she belonged in Angel Fire Falls came from the one person who could bring her new job, her new home, and her new life crashing down around her if she wasn't careful.

Trace's laughter died out too. They said their goodbyes to Dr. Shaw. Outside, a hint of purple lingered on the horizon. Trace opened the Jeep door for her, and Lily climbed into the passenger seat. He didn't close it. Instead, he kept one hand on the doorframe and glanced off into the distance.

Lily cradled the duckling at her chest. "Thank you."

His head swiveled back to her. "For what?"

"For the ride." Lily shrugged. "If it'd been serious, I might not have gotten here fast enough."

He studied her, finally stepping in close. "No. Thank *you*." His voice went low and throaty.

Her lips parted as his scent ebbed and flowed around her like an invisible mist. "For what?" She echoed his words, her voice soft and whispery.

"For thinking of my son." Trace's dark eyes smoothed over her face like he was taking in every detail. "Ben has high-functioning autism."

Ah. That explained a lot. Ben's mannerisms made sense. So did the serious way Trace seemed to take on the world. Raising a special-needs child would likely do that to a person.

"Not many people have the consideration or the patience with him that you've had." He drew in a breath so heavy with emotion, it was clear he'd spent many heart-wrenching years worrying over his son. "That's why his mother, Megan, isn't around much."

Megan. That explained even more. "I'm sorry," Lily said. "For you. For Ben." She put a hand on Trace's arm. "And for Ben's mom . . . because she's missing out on a great kid."

The breeze kicked up and blew a rogue lock of hair across her parted lips. She reached up to flick it away, but he stopped her hand, pushed it aside, and used his fingers to tuck the silky strands behind her ear. His fingers lingered, brushing against her ear.

She shivered, looking up at him with uncertainty. His quick, shallow breaths washed over her face, warming her from the inside out.

His hand dropped to her cheek and cupped it, his thumb caressing her chin. Like he was torn and contemplating his next move. That beautifully chiseled jaw tensed and released. The pad of his thumb found her bottom lip and brushed across it.

She couldn't help it. She drew in a sharp breath as a tremble started somewhere deep inside her and spiraled in every direction.

This was *so* not a good idea.

He leaned into the Jeep, his eyes hungry. Moving a hand to the back of her head, he gently drew her toward him.

"Cheep," Megan the duck protested before Trace could cover Lily's mouth with his.

He stopped, his nose almost brushing hers. He lingered there, their breaths mingling. "We should probably go."

Only he didn't look like he wanted to go anywhere. He looked like he wanted to stay right where he was, with his fingers stroking her cheek and his lips hovering a fraction of an inch from hers.

"Cheep, cheep. Cheep, cheep."

"Yes." Lily swallowed. "Definitely. We should go." She pulled away from his touch and adjusted herself in the seat to stare straight ahead.

He hesitated, then closed the door.

Leaving her to wonder if his kiss really could've made her moan louder than her masseuse had. Leaving her disappointed that she would never know for sure.

Chapter Ten

The next morning, Lily made sure to get up early enough to meet the elusive Mrs. Ferguson in the kitchen. It wasn't hard for Lily to pull herself out of bed at the ass-crack of dawn because she'd lost another night's sleep thinking about Trace and that almost-kiss in the parking lot of the vet's office.

Bundled up in an oversize wool sweater, leggings, and lined rubber boots, Lily used a flashlight she'd found in her kitchen drawer to follow the path to the back entrance of the resort. The smell of grease and burned toast nearly bowled her over the second she opened the door. With the back of one hand against her mouth, she waited until her stomach settled, then put on a brave face and entered the kitchen.

It could've been declared a national disaster area. Lily looked around at the piles of dirty pots and pans, and her admiration for Charley grew exponentially. The National Guard probably couldn't get a mess that size cleaned up in the amount of time Charley managed to do it every morning.

An old woman—with a hitch in her walk from what looked like a bad hip—limped into the kitchen from the pantry. She didn't notice

Lily, probably because her eyesight had gone long ago if the thickness of her glasses was any indication. She stirred a pan of scrambled eggs.

Lily didn't want to startle Mrs. Ferguson, so she coughed.

Did no good. Mrs. Ferguson picked up a clean frying pan and put it on a burner.

Lily guessed the cook's hearing was as long gone as her eyesight, so she inched forward, hoping Mrs. Ferguson would catch the movement in her peripheral vision.

No such luck.

Lily eased up to the counter. "Mrs. Ferguson?"

The cook whirled around and raised the empty frying pan high above her head in attack mode.

Lily stumbled back against the wall.

"Who are you?" Mrs. Ferguson fiddled with her hearing aid.

"I'm Lily Barns!" She stayed beyond swinging distance. "I work here," she hollered.

Mrs. Ferguson had obviously turned up her hearing aid at the same time Lily shouted because the old woman covered her ear with one hand. "No need to shout." She lowered the pan. "You almost got yourself clobbered. That'll teach you not to sneak up on folks."

Um. Lily couldn't have announced her presence any louder if she'd had a bullhorn. But she needed to win over Mrs. Ferguson for the good of the resort. And for the good of the guests' gastrointestinal systems. Lily glanced at the overcooked food, still sizzling over burners set too high.

"I'm the new hospitality manager." Lily peeled herself off the wall now that Mrs. Ferguson had discarded her cast-iron weapon. "I came to see if I could help with breakfast."

Mrs. Ferguson gave her a territorial look.

Lily veered toward the sink. "How about I get started on the dishes?"

Mrs. Ferguson nodded. "Suit yourself."

Lily stepped up to the industrial sink and filled it with soapy water. Thirty minutes later, she'd barely made a dent in the mountain of pots and pans. How someone could dirty so many dishes cooking eggs, bacon, and toast was beyond reason. Still, she whistled a tune her grandmother used to love, and she worked, keeping one eye on Mrs. Ferguson.

By the time she had the buffet set up and ready in the dining hall, Mrs. Ferguson was whistling the same tune.

Lily smiled. She took a break from dishwashing and dried her hands. "Mrs. Ferguson, would you be interested in helping Lawrence out with something really important?" Lily waved a hand across the kitchen. "I mean, cooking breakfast is important too." She tilted her head to one side. "Everyone agrees that no one makes breakfast quite like you." She plowed on. "But the resort is suffering in some areas, and something tells me you're the only employee here who can fix one particular problem."

"What problem?" Mrs. Ferguson retrieved her purse from a cabinet and hooked it in the notch of her elbow.

"Well, Lawrence wants to bring in a younger crowd of people. You know, couples with kids, families. But he doesn't want the empty nesters to feel left out." Lily propped a hip against the counter. "The guests would miss your . . . unique brand of breakfast, but I think you could help Lawrence fill a serious void at the resort in a different way."

"Who would cook breakfast? Lawrence depends on me." Mrs. Ferguson's concerned expression made Lily fall in love with her just like she loved her own grandmother.

"I promise I'll find someone to take over the cooking. No one could fill your shoes, of course, but I'll make sure the guests are happy." Lily kept her tone reassuring.

Mrs. Ferguson gave her a skeptical look. "What would I be doing?"

"Well, you'd be in charge of leading activities here at the resort for people your age. Bingo—" When Mrs. Ferguson's hand fluttered to her throat, Lily knew she'd scored a victory for the resort. "Maybe a basket-weaving class."

Mrs. Ferguson's other hand covered the first. "I adore bingo and basket weaving."

"Perfect!" Lily gave her a dazzling smile. "So you'll do it?"

"If it'll help the resort, then of course I'll do it." Her expression turned crestfallen. "But I feel like I'm abandoning Lawrence if I stop cooking. He's been like a son to me, you know."

Lily walked over and put an arm around Mrs. Ferguson's shoulders. "It'll be difficult, but we'll make do. Every time you start worrying, remember how important your new responsibilities are to the resort. And you have free rein to implement any activities you think the guests over fifty will enjoy. Lawrence is going to be so excited."

She saw Mrs. Ferguson out and tackled the rest of the dishes. Leaving them for Charley would be just plain heartless. As she finished up, Charley walked in with Sophie in tow, a tiara perched on her cute little head.

"*Heeeeey.*" Charley looked around the kitchen. "You're good. I take it you met Mrs. Ferguson."

"Yep." Lily dried her hands and waved at Sophie. "Hello, Your Highness."

Sophie scrunched her shoulders and climbed onto a stool at the opposite side of the counter.

Charley pulled a frying pan from the cabinet, spooned in butter, and turned on the burner. "I'm making breakfast here before I take the kids to school. My stove isn't working." She disappeared inside the walk-in fridge, then reappeared with a carton of eggs and several other ingredients. "Want an omelet?"

Lily's stomach rumbled, her appetite finally returning now that the smell of Mrs. Ferguson's burned food had receded. "Sure. You don't mind?"

"I owe you my paycheck for cleaning up after Mrs. Ferguson." Charley cracked eggs into the skillet and sliced mushrooms. "Obviously, you didn't eat her food since you aren't on your way to the dentist with a broken tooth." She raised both brows. "No joke, one guest really did break a tooth. On scrambled eggs."

Lily chuckled. "That's scary."

Charley tossed in the rest of the ingredients. "Mrs. Ferguson is a good person, but she has no business in the kitchen anymore."

Lily slid onto the stool next to Sophie. "Well, that won't be a problem. She won't be cooking anymore."

Charley's jaw fell open. "No way."

"Yes way," Lily said.

"How'd you manage it?" Charley's voice was all awe and hero worship.

Lily winked. "I have my ways." Really, she was just good at her job. Hospitality managers were problem solvers.

"Guest complaints just went down." Charley flipped the omelet and slid it onto a plate for Sophie. "So did the resort's liability insurance. How do you want your omelet cooked, Lily? The sky's the limit." Charley spooned more butter into the pan.

Lily tapped her chin. "Spicy." Sure, she was southern, but more specifically, she was Cajun, and she had to be true to those roots. "I like it *really* hot and spicy—"

Trace blew in at that exact moment, stopped cold, and gave her a cloudy stare.

"I like jalapeños and cayenne pepper," Lily hurried to explain.

Charley's assessing gaze lingered on Lily, then on Trace, who, in turn, hadn't taken his eyes off Lily.

"*Okaaaay*. Coming right up." Charley disappeared into the pantry.

Maybe it was his alpha-male swagger. Maybe it was his self-confidence. Maybe it was his devotion to his son. Or maybe it was the whole package, along with a face as good-looking as his body and a square jaw that sported a hint of stubble. Whatever the reason, just his presence made everyone else seem invisible.

From what Lily could tell, he was firm all over except for the softness that lingered in his chocolaty eyes as he looked at her.

That softness made Lily's heart do a flippity-flop.

"Morning," he finally said.

"Sleep well?" It was the first thing to pop into Lily's stuttering brain.

"Hell no." He didn't try to cover his bluntness. And the look in his eyes said he'd lain awake for the same reason Lily had—that almost-kiss. "You?"

"Like a baby," she said.

"Liar," he deadpanned.

Truer words.

Heat crept up her neck, slid down her torso, and settled in parts unknown. At least unknown to him. She, on the other hand, was well aware which parts heated every time she heard his voice. She shifted on her stool but didn't argue his point. No sense trying to deny the effect he had on her, especially after last night, when her uterus cried out *Give it to me, baby.* Probably loud enough for Trace to hear. It was one of the things she could be honest about without jeopardizing her safety.

It would, however, jeopardize her job. So even if her attraction was obvious, she couldn't let it go beyond a really good fantasy.

"Here we go." Charley emerged from the pantry with a jar of jalapeños. "Want an omelet, Trace?"

"No, thanks. I made breakfast at my place." He finally tore his gaze from Lily and focused on his cousin. "Ben's on his way. He's looking for his belt in that black hole he calls a room." Trace rubbed the back of his neck. "Listen, today was my day to pick the kids up from school, but would you mind getting them? I have to make several trips to the Cape for supplies again and then pick up a new guest." He shook his head in disgust. "The delivery company decided not to deliver this week's supplies until next week."

"Again?" Charley sounded as disgusted as Trace.

"Can't we use a different company?" Lily had dealt with similar issues at her previous job, and the delivery companies in NOLA had lined up with competitive bids to win the business.

Trace's gaze flitted to Lily again, and his brow knitted. "It's the only delivery company on the Cape with a cargo floatplane. Every other company I've found is a fair distance away and wants to gouge us simply because they can."

Ah. Those companies had the island by the cajones, and they knew it.

"We need a delivery company based here on the island. A reliable company that will actually deliver on time." Charley raised both brows at Trace. They'd obviously had the same discussion before today. "Know anyone who can fly a delivery plane from the mainland?" She waved a spatula around. "Anybody?"

Trace shook his head. "Not gonna happen anytime soon." He glanced at Lily, then looked at the ground. "The resort can't afford a cargo plane right now."

Her stomach quivered. Instinct told her the resort not being able to afford a new plane had something to do with her. Lawrence had said the budget was tight, and paying a new full-time employee had to chew up a lot of the resort's funds.

"Don't worry about picking up the kids. I've got it handled." Charley flipped Lily's omelet.

"Thanks." He shoved his hands in his pockets.

"Trace, we need to go over the new booking system so you can start using it," Lily said.

"Right. Sorry we haven't gotten to it. It's been . . . yesterday was . . . crazy." His expression turned brooding, and Lily knew right where his thoughts had gone. Both of them had definitely stared at their ceilings most of the night. "Unexpectedly crazy," he added. As if the one-two punch to emphasize that almost-kiss was necessary.

It wasn't.

Ben crashed through the door in his usual full-throttle manner. "Lily, can I go to your house and see Megan before we leave for school?"

"No." Trace gave his shoulder a squeeze. "Let her . . . *it* rest. You can feed them after school." His brooding expression vanished. "Son, the doctor said Megan is really a boy."

Ben's shoulders drooped.

Trace nudged him playfully. "Come on, it'll be fun thinking up a new name. Remember how much fun you had helping Lily name all the ducklings?"

Charley blinked twice, obviously not yet clued in on the ducks or the fact that one had been named after Trace's ex-wife. She shook her head, dishing up Lily's omelet. "I swear this place is like *The Twilight Zone*."

"I'd explain, but I've got to go." Trace glanced at his watch. "I'm already late." He looked at Lily. "We'll get to the new system soon."

"Sorry, boss. *Soon* isn't good enough." Lily dug into the scrumptious mix, but before she forked a generous helping into her mouth, she said, "This week, okay?"

He angled his body half-in and half-out of the back door, and the brooding was back.

And darned if he couldn't win a sexiest brooder alive contest. Really, *People* magazine should put his picture on the cover. Every year. Because Lily had yet to meet anyone who pulled it off quite as well as Trace.

Finally he nodded, said goodbye to his son, and let the door close in his wake.

As soon as they were alone, Charley said to the kids, "Go load up in the Jeep. I'm right behind you."

With backpacks strapped to their shoulders, both kids hurried out in a frenzy of excitement to start a new school day.

Charley crooked all four fingers at once in a give-it-up gesture. "What's going on?"

"Nothing," Lily said around a mouthful of omelet. She swallowed. "Nothing at all is going on with me and Trace. We're just friends." Her own words took her by surprise. "I mean we're not really friends. He's my boss, and I'm his employee, and it's strictly professional between us."

Charley folded her arms. "I meant what's going on with the duck."

"Oh." Lily's foot bounced against the barstool. "I found a bunch of orphaned ducks on the road when I was riding a tricycle from the ferry."

Charley's mouth fell open.

Once Lily started, she couldn't stop. "Trace was good enough to keep it a secret at first because I must've looked ridiculous, but then Ben named one Megan." She gobbled up more omelet. "Trace caught me trying to take Megan to the vet on a bicycle, and she turned out to be a male, so that sort of made up for the name, and then . . ." Lily bit off the part about her and Trace almost kissing. "So can I have a ride into town?"

It took Charley a minute to absorb everything. Finally, she recovered. "Do you have any idea how much I need a friend like you?" She pulled a large tray of pastries from a storage cabinet and set it on the counter. "You've managed more adventure in your life in less than two weeks at the Remington than I've had in the last year."

Lily could use a little less adventure at the moment.

Charley went back for a second tray of pastries. "Come on. We'll drop the kids off at school, I'll take you wherever you need to go, and then we can deliver these to my friend."

"Thanks." Lily picked up one of the trays. She very much wanted to meet Charley's friend. Lily had her fingers crossed that Charley and her friend could solve the food service problem at the resort. If it worked out, all she'd have to do was get Trace's stamp of approval.

Work. Work was her lifeline. She and Trace had already swerved way too far into the personal zone, so from now on, they would focus on work and nothing more.

She'd just keep telling herself that because she was her mother's daughter. Denial would help her cope with the growing chemistry between Trace and her that had become impossible to ignore.

◆ ◆ ◆

Angel Fire Falls Elementary School was bustling as they waited in line to drop off Ben and Sophie.

"It's bigger than I thought it would be," Lily said.

"This is a great place to raise kids." Charley inched the Jeep forward. "That draws people to the island. Keeping them here is another thing." She shrugged. "Small-town life isn't for everyone. Jobs are mostly based on tourism, so it's not always easy to make a living here."

That fact had become painfully clear to Lily already. Experience in the hotel industry told her the resort would eventually sink unless she turned things around. Part of the Remington's success would be finding a solution to its food-service problem. Fingers crossed, Charley and her friend who owned the food cart would consider the proposal Lily planned to pitch to them when they dropped off the pastries.

Two kids tumbled out of the car in front of them, so Charley inched forward.

"There's my teacher!" Ben shouted from the back seat.

A midtwenties woman with blue-tipped hair greeted the kids in the unloading zone.

Seemed like the perfect kind of person to help with the children's summer activities calendar Lily wanted to develop. She made a mental note to contact the school soon.

When it was their turn, Ben shouted a goodbye and scrambled out of the Jeep.

Sophie leaned through the front seats and gave her mom a kiss. Charley hugged her. "Have a good day, sweetie." She leaned back to peek through the open door as Sophie climbed out. "Hi, Miss Etheridge!"

The young teacher waved as Sophie shut the door.

Charley pulled away from the school. "My friend won't get to her food cart for another forty-five minutes. Any place you need to go first?"

"I need a few groceries," Lily said. "My fridge and cupboards are pretty bare."

Charley drove to the grocery store, where they wandered through the small market. It was mostly filled with healthy organic choices, and Lily loaded her cart.

"So you and Trace . . ." Charley walked beside the cart. She left the statement open-ended.

"There is no *me and Trace*."

"Uh-huh," Charley said, unconvinced.

They walked down the hygiene aisle, and Lily grabbed shampoo, conditioner, and body wash.

Charley stepped in front of the cart, bringing it to a halt. She grabbed a box of SECOND SKIN condoms and read the package. "Warms to the touch." She tossed it in the basket.

"Hey!" Lily snatched them up. "I do not need—"

A woman in her fifties wearing a T-shirt that said GOT MORALS? pushed her cart past and sniffed.

Lily waited for her to turn onto the next aisle. "I do not need condoms," she whispered.

"I've known Trace all his life. Trust me when I say he's never looked at any woman the way he looks at you." Charley snatched them out of Lily's hand. "Not even his ex-wife." She tossed the purple box back into the cart like it was a basketball free throw. *"Score."* She waggled both eyebrows.

Heat singed the tips of Lily's ears. "Seriously. I can't get involved with my boss again—"

Dammit.

Charley's expression went from sly to sympathetic. "For the record, Trace is a really good guy, but I don't blame you for not wanting things to get personal at work."

That sounded like the voice of experience.

"Still, there's *something* between you two, even if there isn't," Charley said. "Know what I mean?"

Did Lily ever. She couldn't stop her body from going up in flames every time she and Trace stepped into a room together.

Charley nodded to the box of condoms in the cart. "Never hurts to plan ahead. Just in case."

"Let's get outta here." Lily pushed the cart to the register and looked away when the male clerk rang them up with a quick, knowing look in her direction.

They loaded the bags into the back of the Jeep and got in.

"Need to go anywhere else?" Charley asked.

"Actually, if you're ready to deliver the pastries, I want to meet your friend. I'd like to run an idea by both of you."

"Sounds intriguing." Charley turned right onto Marina Boulevard, which ran straight through town.

Lily took in Angel Fire Falls for the first time in daylight. It had been almost dark when Trace had driven her to and from the vet, and her full attention had stayed on the duck. And what Trace would've tasted like if they'd actually kissed. Sightseeing had been the last thing on her mind.

The small tourist town was every bit as picturesque as the pictures she'd found online before she'd moved. It was nestled on the far eastern coast of the island where the landscape dipped into a valley between the soaring cliffs to the south and the rolling hills to the north.

If the landscape and harbor were gorgeous, the town itself was just as charming with its colorful clapboard buildings lining both sides of the main street. The flower boxes and hanging planters weren't in bloom yet, but it had to be breathtaking in its full summer glory.

This early in the morning, not many people were out and about on the main strip, home of numerous shops mostly geared to tourists. They parallel parked along the curb close to an old pink-and-white VW van that had been converted into a food cart. BRILEY'S BURGERS & BREWS was painted on the side.

"Best burgers on the West Coast," Charley said. "Briley will be inside setting up."

They carried both pastry trays to the back door of the van. Charley tapped out the knock-knock jingle, and the door slid open.

A woman about Lily's age—with black hair and an A-line haircut framing her beautiful face—greeted them. "Morning!"

"Briley, this is Lily. She's working at the Remington."

"Nice to meet you. Come on in." She disappeared inside the van.

They followed her, but Charley stood in the open door because there wasn't enough room for all three of them. Lily was impressed with Briley's ingenuity. On the outside, the van had wheels with a metal skirt all the way around to secure it to the street. On the inside, everything remotely related to an automobile had been gutted, including the floor so there was enough headroom to stand up and move around. It was a small space but so efficiently laid out that it worked as a full-service kitchen.

"This is remarkable." Lily took in the setup.

"Thanks." Briley shrugged. "It's not fancy, but it's mine. Between Charley's pastries and my burgers, we do pretty well." Briley poured three coffees from a commercial-grade travel container.

"I'm certain you do." Lily took one of the coffees. "I've had Charley's doughnuts." She sipped from the cup.

Lily ran a fingertip along the rim of the cup. "You two are pretty resourceful. How would you feel about teaming up with the Remington?"

A look passed between Briley and Charley.

"I assume this has something to do with you finally getting Mrs. Ferguson to retire?" Charley asked.

"Oh, I didn't get her to retire." Lily smiled. "I reassigned her to a different department that I think will be a better fit."

One of Charley's brows arched.

"Which leaves the Remington's kitchen and dining hall available for an independent restaurateur to rent the space." Lily took another sip, then let the cup hover at her lips. "At a very affordable price." She let the two ladies digest the idea, then added, "You'd need to be open for business by the Remington's summer kickoff weekend. Until then, you'd have to continue providing morning coffee and doughnuts for the guests. It's the only source of food left at the resort now that Mrs. Ferguson has other responsibilities." She sipped and swallowed. "Can you manage that?"

Charley and Briley shot each other another look that said this might be the opportunity they'd been waiting for.

Charley lifted her coffee cup in a toast. "I like the way you think, Lily Barns."

Briley joined her. "You're exactly what this island needs."

Lily took another drink and stared at their cups for a beat before lifting hers.

The sip of coffee didn't go down as smoothly this time. Charley was becoming a friend, and it didn't feel right to hold back the truth from people she was starting to care about.

And she was definitely starting to care about the entire Remington family.

Chapter Eleven

LILY'S LIFE LESSON #11
Everything that comes before the "but" is total bullshit.

Two weeks on the job and Lily was slaying her to-do list.

Lawrence was thrilled. Trace, on the other hand, was avoiding her, and they still hadn't gone over the new system because he'd come up with a new excuse each day.

Change was hard. Maybe he was as afraid of change as much for himself as he was for Ben.

So their conversations had taken place mostly over text or phone. Considering the circus-animal flips her insides did when he was around, avoiding him wasn't a bad thing, except communicating by phone and text slowed her progress.

The owners still weren't utilizing the booking program, and Lawrence was bringing on new employees every day to accommodate the approaching tourist season. Training the entire staff had to be a top priority.

Starting with Trace, no matter how busy Mr. Resistant-to-Change might be.

Lily posted FULL-SERVICE RESTAURANT COMING SOON! and CHECK OUT OUR SUMMER KIDS' CAMP ACTIVITIES CALENDAR! to social media and the new website. When she was done, she pulled out her cell and sent Trace a text.

> Need to meet about the booking
> system.

His response was swift.

Maybe tomorrow.

> You're avoiding me.

Funny how their roles had reversed.

No, I'm not. Been busy
hauling supplies.

Another problem she could help him solve if he'd meet with her.

> New system isn't hard. Promise.

He didn't respond as quickly that time. Finally the dots started to jump.

It'll have to wait. Landing in
a few with guest.

She smiled to herself, clutched her phone, and pushed back from her desk. A photo of a new guest stepping off the resort's plane would be great for social media.

She slid on a pair of retro Ray-Bans as she left through the front doors. The sun had finally come out, and the blue sky, the chirping birds, and the scent of the spring flowers she'd asked the groundskeepers to plant were divine. She rounded the corner and waved to Spence.

From his ladder, he nodded a greeting, then went back to rolling a new coat of paint onto the building's wood trim.

She made her way to the dock and took in the beauty of the property. The smooth water reflected the sky like a mirror. She slowly spun in a full circle and drew in a satisfying breath at the transformation. The Remington's appearance was fresher, more inviting, and she was proud of her work.

If she could accomplish that much in such a short time, then surely she could convince her boss to learn the new booking system.

And ducks could fly without feathers.

She snorted considering the ducklings were still covered in fuzz, but Ben had put different-colored Velcro bands around their legs, claiming it would prevent them from flying away. Lily knew it was so she could tell them apart. At school, he'd conveniently made a chart that listed each duck's name along with the color of its band.

The kid had color-coded a bunch of ducks. Pretty clever, especially for an eight-year-old.

A buzzing noise sounded in the distance, and Lily shielded her eyes as she stared into the sky to find Trace's plane. A speck appeared, the bright sun glaring off the metal when it got closer.

She pulled up the new booking app on her phone and thumbed through it to find the guest's name. Ronald Parker was staying through the weekend. Alone. She pulled up the vacant rooms and assigned one to him.

Then she recorded Trace's plane coming in for a landing. It skipped across the water and slowed to a stop. As he guided it toward the dock, he came into view through the front windshield.

The plane coasted right up to where she stood, and Lily's breath caught. Trace's aviators, his headset . . . not to mention the shadow of stubble on his face . . . were simply gorgeous.

"Hey, Lily." Elliott came from behind and secured the plane to the dock.

From the pilot's seat, Trace took off his headset. She couldn't see his eyes from behind the sunglasses, but Lily could feel his gaze licking over her skin like fire. He climbed out of the plane and opened the door for the passenger.

She lowered the phone and stopped recording.

A man, who looked to be in his late thirties, stepped out.

"I'll get the bags," Elliott said to Trace, who went to retrieve his things from the cockpit.

Lily stepped over to greet the guest. "Mr. Parker?" He was dressed in a trendy suit that was too slick for an island vacation.

"That's correct." His tone was smooth.

A chill slithered up her spine, and she disliked him instantly. She plastered on a smile. "I'm Lily, the hospitality manager. Welcome."

Mr. Parker's attention stayed more on Trace, even when he spoke to Lily. "Thanks." Stopping Elliott, Parker took charge of his carry-on.

Trace got his things from the cockpit and turned to walk toward her. His black polo stretched taut across his broad shoulders and muscular pecs. Each step he took made her thighs quiver a little more.

Professional, professional, professional.

"Is Mr. Parker's room ready?" Trace came to a stop in front of her.

His soapy scent and ridiculous good looks scrambled her thoughts. "Um." There went her amazing command of the English language. She gave herself a mental slap and held up her phone. "It is. I just assigned him a room through the new system's app." She gave Trace a dazzling smile. "Standing right here on the dock. That's how easy it is."

His jaw ticked.

She looked around Trace and spoke to Elliott. "Please deliver Mr. Parker's luggage to room 213."

She turned her attention to the new guest. "Would you mind if I got a picture for our social media?" He fit the new age demographic Lily was trying to bring into the resort.

He fidgeted. "Yes, I would mind." His words were terse, but then his demeanor shifted, and he gave her a friendly smile. "I'm not fond of cameras." He gave Trace an unreadable look. "But you two would look great together on camera." He held his hand out toward Lily's phone. "Why don't I take your picture for your page?"

Lily took a step back. "No, but thanks." She could not let her picture show up on social media.

A wrinkle appeared across Trace's forehead. Maybe he thought she didn't want her picture taken with him, or maybe she looked as guilty as she felt. Didn't matter. If her picture went public in connection with the Remington, it would only be a matter of time before the press showed up. And maybe even the unsavory characters who'd made it their life's work to threaten the Devereaux family, even the members who hadn't stolen a dime from FEMA or anyone else.

"Mr. Parker, let's get you a room key." Lily led the guest and Trace up the path.

Once they reached the front desk, she slid her glasses to the top of her head and programmed a card key.

He cocked his head to one side. "Have we met? You look familiar."

"No!" she said too quickly. "No." She smoothed a hand over a hip. Maybe the press had already found her. "I'm sure I would remember."

He gave her a suspicious stare.

She wanted to return it in spades. Because there was no doubt in Lily's mind that Ronald Parker wasn't who he said he was. No question he had a good reason not to let his picture show up on the internet.

Took one to know one.

She handed over the card key. "Enjoy your stay."

"I'll show you the way," Trace said.

She managed to keep smiling until Trace and Ronald Parker disappeared around a corner. Then she hurried to her office and shut the door to pace in private.

When her eyes locked on her computer, she came to an abrupt stop. Frantic, she sat behind the computer and googled Ronald Parker. A few hundred names came up on various background check sites, but there was no way to tell which one was him.

She brought up Facebook and typed in the name. Several popped up, and she quickly scrolled through them, none with his picture.

When someone knocked, she jumped and stood up. "Come in."

Trace's head appeared. "Mr. Parker's all settled. He scheduled an aerial tour for this weekend." He gave her the same curious look he had when she'd refused to take a picture with him at the dock. "Everything okay?"

"Yes!" *Ack!* The adrenaline rush had her volume dialed up. "Yes." She took a calming breath and walked around to the front of her desk. "I'm antsy to show you the new system and train the staff." She reached behind her back with one hand and steadied herself against the desk.

His mocha eyes swept over her. Finally, he sighed as if surrendering and pushed the door all the way open. "All right. If it's got you this excited, then let's do it." A lopsided smile formed on his lips.

This is about work. There was no innuendo in his words. There wasn't.

She slid one butt cheek onto the desk and kicked a leg to work off nervous energy. "When?" She pulled up her calendar and waited.

"Seven o'clock? I've got more supply runs. My plane isn't outfitted for cargo, so I have to make several trips." He hooked a thumb in his belt loop.

She typed it onto her calendar. "Great. I'll get the rest of the staff trained this week. I'll let you know when in case you want to be there."

"I'm starting to feel like you're *my* boss," he said.

"Speaking of supply runs and cargo, there's something else we need to talk about." When his look turned skeptical, she hurried to explain. "I think you'll like it." Plus, talking about work might calm her racing heart. Mr. Parker had really spooked her.

Trace pushed off the doorframe and eased past her to sit in the chair in front of the desk. "Okay, hit me with it."

She leaned in, unable to contain her enthusiasm. "Of course, the financial decisions are above my pay grade, but maybe we could consider using the money from the restaurant lease for a cargo plane."

He made a face that said he did indeed like what she had to say. He slouched down in his chair, getting comfortable, and his muscular thigh brushed against her swinging leg. She stilled but didn't break the contact. Neither did he. Instead, he shifted, the friction of that powerful thigh massaging against hers.

A current of electricity didn't just shimmy up her spine. It scorched through her entire body.

"I've spoken to Elliott about the budget." The roughness of Trace's voice caused Lily's stomach to do a flip. "With all the changes we're making, he doesn't think we'll be able to afford a plane right now. Not even with the lease money from the restaurant space." Another small shift of his thigh, and that wonderful current shot through her again. "Maybe"—his voice turned to gravel, and he cleared his throat— "maybe if we have a successful summer we can reconsider."

She leaned back and shuffled through the papers on her desk, which pressed her leg harder into his. Heat steamrolled through her. She ignored it, found what she was looking for, and handed it to him. "If you knew how to use the booking system, you'd already know that our summer season is filling up." She pointed to a number. "That's how much our bookings have increased."

He studied the page.

"Besides a few B&Bs, we're the only major resort on the island, right?" She fiddled with a lock of hair.

He nodded without looking up.

"If more people stay on the island instead of the mainland, business will increase for everyone in Angel Fire Falls. The restaurants, the souvenir shops—they won't be able to keep up with the new demand unless they've prepared in advance."

His eyes sparkled up at her. With a finger, he flicked the page. "I can use this to convince the island's business owners to sign up for my delivery service, and open for business with a full client list."

Bubbling with enthusiasm, Lily kicked her foot again. The friction of their legs made her brain stutter. "It's just a thought." She stilled her foot. It was the only way she could think straight.

He angled his head to one side. "At this rate, you'll have a solution for global warming soon."

"Is that approval I hear? From the man who didn't want to hire me?" She stood and tried not to stare at his mouth. That damned unholy mouth that had so much promise.

He eased out of the chair, his eyes never leaving her. They stood toe to toe, him looking down at her from under shuttered lashes. His heat reached for her. Blanketed her.

"See you at seven." His tone went husky.

So did her breathing. "Yes. Seven. I'll be ready for you."

Dear Lord.

"I'll be ready to work," she said in a small voice.

He let his gaze drop to her lips before finally stepping away. At the door, he turned back. "I'll bring dinner to your place."

Before she could protest that dinner at her place would be too much like a date, he was gone.

She stared at the empty doorway. Waiting for seven o'clock would seem like an eternity. And Lily cursed herself for feeling like it couldn't come soon enough.

Lily got off work later than expected and hurried home to freshen up before Trace landed on her doorstep with dinner.

Then again, maybe she should make herself look worse. Mat her hair or smudge her makeup. Unless she'd misread the situation in her office earlier, his husky tone and sparkling eyes held a promise. A promise that was far too tempting.

Noise drew her around to the rear of her cottage. Ben had the ducks in their outside pen. "Lily!" he blurted the second he saw her. "Megan was strong enough to eat with the rest of the ducks today!"

Right. They still hadn't renamed the duckling formerly known as Megan.

"Awesome sauce." She walked over to the pen and handed Ben her phone. It had become their evening ritual; he took daily pictures for his science project and documented their growth. "It'll be dark soon. Want to bring them inside for the night?"

One at a time, Ben scooped the ducks into a box so they could carry them back into the cottage.

A Jeep rumbled down the lane. By the sound of it pulling to a stop in front of her cottage, Lily knew it must be seven o'clock.

A tingle started low in her belly and seeped into her arms, her legs, her nipples, her . . .

She shot to her feet. "I'll carry the box."

They rounded the corner just as Trace propped a plastic toddler swimming pool on her front porch.

"What's that, Dad?" Ben lumbered up the steps.

Trace spoke to Ben but looked at Lily. "Dr. Shaw suggested it. I figured Lily's tired of sharing her tub . . . with ducks." Something glinted in Trace's mocha eyes. Something sultry and seductive. Something that said maybe she should consider sharing it with him instead.

The thought of water sluicing off him in the shower made Lily want to lick her lips.

Having to live with that mental picture was so unfair. And uncalled for.

Trace went back to the Jeep and pulled two bags out of the back seat that had VINCENZO'S RISTORANTE written across the front. "Anybody hungry?"

"Yeah!" Ben hollered and threw open her front door.

Lily climbed the steps with the birds. "Starved." She went inside and set the box next to the duck habitat. "Ben, can you put the birds back in their house? I'll help your dad with dinner."

Lily washed up at the kitchen sink. "Thanks," she said to Trace as he pulled to-go boxes out of the bags. "It'll be nice to soak in a hot bath."

Trace froze with a Styrofoam container in his hand. His expression clouded . . . like maybe he was picturing her in nothing but bubble bath suds.

"I mean without having to scrub it out every time." Her pulse kicked up a notch. She dried her hands on a dish towel and folded it. And refolded it. Twice. "I'll get utensils."

Trace finished setting out the boxes. "You should've seen me trying to get that thing into the plane. I thought I might have to strap it to the top. I drove the Jeep down to the dock so I wouldn't have to drag the damn thing all the way here."

She laughed. "Now *that* would've made great pictures for our social media advertising." She arranged forks and knives on the table.

"No way." He put both hands on the back of a chair. "I draw the line at embarrassing social media pictures."

Lily had to draw the line at *any* social media pictures. "Same goes for me. I promise not to post any pictures of you if you'll agree to the same." She held out her little finger. "Pinkie swear."

He looked at her hand, his gaze traveling up her arm, across her neck, then raking over her face. Slowly, he hooked his little finger in hers, and all the air seemed to leave the room. He stepped closer. "I hope you know I've never pinkie sworn." That husky voice was back, and it caressed her cheeks. "Ever. It's not what guys do." He didn't untwine their fingers, holding on longer than the customary it's-sworn-in-pinkies-if-not-in-blood length of time.

When Lily's phone rang, they broke apart. She checked her cell, and a tremor of guilt raced through her when her mother's number popped onto the screen. Lily sent it to voice mail and flicked off the ringer.

"Need to take that?" Trace extracted a can of soda and a bottle of wine from a bag.

"Nope." She squirmed.

He held up the wine. "Got a corkscrew?" His eyes dilated on the last word.

A shiver raced over her. Without a word, she hurried to the kitchen to search the drawers. "Here we go." She held it up like a prize.

"Ben, go wash up." Trace's gaze didn't leave her.

Lily got two wine glasses out of the cupboard and brought them to the table without making eye contact. She should declare a no-fly zone because her girl parts were waving him onto the tarmac with orange batons.

Once Ben was ready, they sat down and opened their meals.

Trace opened the wine and popped the soda for Ben, who dug in like he hadn't eaten in a month.

"Ben, slow down." Trace gave Lily an apologetic look. "I don't want him to eat like a caveman. It's one of the symptoms of growing up with only guys in the house."

Lily's heart squeezed because Trace hadn't had a mom around and neither did Ben.

"I distinctly remember getting stabbed with a fork by one of my brothers when I reached for the last pork chop."

Lily laughed. "Stabbing aside, I think what your family has is pretty special. I'm an only child, so I didn't have that." She twirled her wine glass in a circle.

Trace's brow knitted. "Are your parents gone?"

Her head snapped up. "What?" Loneliness sliced bone-deep because her parents *weren't* gone. At least not in the way he meant, but both her parents had been absent emotionally since she was a teenager. So she'd left them behind and hadn't spoken to her father since the day he was convicted. "Why?"

"You used past tense. I just thought—"

"What if the other ducks aren't named right?" Ben blurted.

Lily polished off her wine, trying to steady her shaking hand.

Ben rocked gently and moved food around his plate with a fork. "What if Sir Walter Raleigh is a girl? And Belle is a boy?"

Trace refilled Lily's glass. "Why don't we focus on renaming . . . Megan . . ." It seemed painful for him to speak the name. "And soon we can take the rest of the ducks to Dr. Shaw, if you want. He can tell us their genders."

"It might be fun to figure it out on your own," Lily said to Ben. "And you'd be learning something in the process that you could include in your science project."

Trace's brow wrinkled again. "The ducks are your science project?"

Ben rocked harder.

Lily knew a guilty face when she saw one. How could she not, when one stared back at her every time she looked in a mirror? And didn't that just suck, because the Remingtons had already become the kind of people she didn't want to keep secrets from. Especially the two sitting at her table.

She lowered her voice. "He was supposed to tell you."

Trace dragged a hand over his face. "I'm sorry, buddy. I've been so busy with work, I forgot all about your project. We never talked about it, did we?"

Ben shrugged. "It's okay. Lily helped me."

Trace turned a heart-stopping look on her. "Thank you. I'll have to find a way to show my gratitude."

Her throat closed. "Let's think up a name," she said to Ben with an unnatural amount of cheer. "How about Captain Quackers?"

Ben belly-laughed.

Trace joined the fun. "Or Count Quackula?"

The rocking stopped as Ben laughed harder.

"I've got one." Lily held up a finger. "Firequacker."

All three of them burst out laughing.

Trace slid a hand over until his little finger brushed hers. The thrill of his touch rushed up her arm, and her breath hitched.

Their eyes locked, and time seemed to stop.

"What else?" Ben obviously didn't want the game to end.

Lily moved her hand away, using her fork to pick at the rest of her lasagna. "Since you and I named all the ducks, I think it's only fair to let your dad name this one."

Ben nodded.

Trace rubbed his chin like it was a life-changing decision. "I think Waddles fits because of his injured leg. He still limps a little, so what do you think?"

Ben giggled and cheered.

"Perfect." Lily gave him a warm smile.

"Hey, Ben, why don't you spend time with them while I help Lily clean the kitchen?" Trace's chair scraped along the wood floor as he got up and took his dish to the sink.

Lily stood and gathered up the silverware. "You brought dinner. I'll clean up." She forgot to breathe when he came up behind her, his chest brushing against her back. Heat arrowed through her, striking at her core.

He reached around her and took her dish. "I don't mind. It's the least I can do after you've been so kind to my son."

When they were done cleaning the kitchen, Ben was curled in a ball, watching the ducks through the plastic wall of the habitat. She grabbed a throw pillow from a chair and put it under his head. Then she got a blanket and tucked it around him.

Trace took a seat on the sofa and watched.

She got out her iPad and phone and sat next to him. "Ready to learn the system?" His scent wrapped around her, and his firm thigh pressing into hers played tricks on her concentration.

"I was worried about Ben handling the changes you'd make at the resort." He adjusted his position, the leather under his large frame squeaking as he moved closer to look at the screen of her iPad. "It seems I'm the one having trouble adapting. We've never taken reservations online before."

She brought up the program. "Once you learn, you'll see how much easier your life will be." She held out her hand. "Give me your phone, and I'll download the app."

His sigh was heavy as he pulled it from his pocket and handed it over.

A few minutes later they huddled shoulder to shoulder as she led him through the new system. "I've added the family members as admins, and I've put in phone numbers for the entire staff." She gave him a tutorial, reminding herself this was work. His presence, his scent, his body touching hers as they sat was not personal. Not exciting. Not in the least. "Everyone will know when a new guest is checking in and scheduled to leave." She tapped on the calendar to show him the bookings. Several weeks were already blacked out, which meant there were no vacancies. "You've seen the stats, but here's the daily calendar. It's very useful."

With that, he turned a smoky gaze on her, and it dropped to her mouth. "I was wrong."

Not what she expected. "Um, about what?" Wrong to trust her? Wrong to bring over dinner? Wrong not to kiss her? *Wrong about what? WHAT?*

"The changes you're making are really good for the resort." His look shifted to Ben, whose eyelids had grown heavy with sleep. "And you've been good for my son. Thank you."

"I don't deserve credit." She nodded in Ben's direction. "He does." Ben's eyes slid shut as he dozed.

Trace let out a hollow chuckle. "Trust me when I say, not everyone has parental instincts. You've been great with him."

She could not take credit for being great with his kid. Not while she was hiding the truth from both of them. "I want to show you something." She got up and found the color-coded list Ben had made for her about the ducks. "He did this for me because I can't tell them apart. But he can. Without the bands. Without a chart. Without any help from anyone." She glanced in Ben's direction. "He's extremely intelligent. Observant in a way that blows my mind."

Trace's eyes glistened at her when he looked up from the chart. "Not everyone sees that."

She lifted a shoulder. "Maybe it's easier for me to see because I've been lucky enough to find something in common with him." She squeezed Trace's hand. "Come with me." She quietly retrieved a flashlight from the closet and led Trace outside. When they were behind the cottage, she shined the light on the pen. "Did you know your son built that? All by himself . . . with supplies he found in the boathouse."

"No, I didn't." Trace's shoulders sagged. "I feel like I've failed him."

She put a hand on his upper arm, and a thick muscle flexed. "Failed him?"

"I've ignored him lately because of work. His science project slipped my mind, and that makes me just like his mother."

"I don't know what the deal is with Ben's mom, but it's your turn to trust what I'm saying." Lily closed the space between them. "Not everyone devotes as much time and attention to their child as you. He's an incredible kid. I'm no expert, but I doubt that happens by accident."

Her heart punched against her chest.

Her father was in prison. Her mother drank to avoid reality. Together they'd produced a person willing to keep the truth from everyone.

Trace reached out and put a hand on her hip.

Heat rushed from his fingertips, up through her center, and hardened her nipples. God, but she wanted him to kiss her. She absolutely couldn't lie about that any longer.

He hesitated like he was torn, then pulled her into his arms.

"Trace—"

His finger covered her lips. "Shh." He caressed her lip with his calloused finger, sending a shock wave of desire rioting through her. "Don't say anything, or I'll change my mind." His hand slid around to the back of her head and pulled her mouth to his. He grazed his lips gently across hers, then went in for more. His other hand settled on the small of her back just firmly enough to hold her in place.

She should step away. End the insanity before she made a terrible mistake. For the second time in her life.

Her feet didn't move. Instead, her lips parted, and his tongue found hers. Soft yet unyielding, it coaxed a moan from her.

His grip tightened, and he pulled her flush against him. And oh, the hardness pressing into her belly was impressive and frightening at the same time because this was a man she shouldn't want.

His strong arms closed around her, and she melted into him with a soft sigh of pleasure. Her hand coasted up his back. His firm, muscular back. Her arms encircled him, pulling him into a red-hot openmouthed kiss that rocked her world. It must've knocked his world off balance too, because he did a little moaning of his own.

A branch snapped somewhere near them, and all six-feet-plus of him went rigid. He broke the kiss, and they stilled. Except for the pounding of their hearts. Their quickened breaths swirled a thin mist of fog around them as Trace stared over her head into the darkness.

She leaned her cheek against his chest and listened. Finally, Trace's fingertips moved against the back of her head to gently caress her hair.

"Probably a raccoon," he said.

She looked up at him, and he let his nose skim hers. Let his mouth linger just a hair above her lips.

His fingers moved to her throat, and he caressed the sensitive skin with small circles.

Another tremor of need slid through her.

"My situation with Ben is complicated."

She understood *complicated* far better than Trace could imagine.

"But I had to do that just once." His voice was full of disappointment.

"Just once," she repeated.

He nodded. "I haven't gotten a good night's sleep since you got here because I lie awake every night wondering what you taste like." He ran the back of one finger down her cheek.

The roughness of his fingertip against her skin made her quiver, and her nipples shouted for her to demand that he do her against the tree. Her common sense told her he was spot-on, and one kiss would have to be enough. "Now maybe we can both sleep better," she said. "Because I think about you too."

"You're an amazing woman, Lily. It's so damn hard to be around you and not kiss you. Not touch you." The pad of his thumb brushed across her bottom lip. "But . . ."

He drew that one word out in a way that arrowed straight to her pounding heart, making it flatline.

"This isn't fair to you. Ben needs all my time and attention," Trace breathed out.

He was right, and the rejection shouldn't hurt. But it did.

His thumb swept over her mouth again. Her lips parted to tell him it was okay. She understood. She agreed. But the words didn't come.

She had to hand it to her father. He'd always told her everything that came before the *but* was total bullshit.

And he'd been right.

141

Chapter Twelve

Saturday evening, Trace stood under the shower, bracing his weight against the tiled wall with both hands. The hot water washed over him, and the tension in his tired muscles relaxed. He'd already lined up half the island's business owners as clients, all of whom were just as frustrated as he was with the inconsistency of their current deliveries. The solution had been right in front of him, but it took Lily's creative business mind for him to see it.

Same way it took Lily's involvement with Ben's science project for Trace to realize what a crummy father he'd been lately. Something he couldn't allow to continue.

He hadn't been completely honest with her. Work wasn't the only thing distracting him. He wanted her. Badly. And if he'd thought one kiss would be enough to get her out of his head, he'd been terribly wrong. She'd tasted like the ocean breeze that blew in the tide on a warm summer evening.

Ocean breeze? Tide? Dudes didn't use words like that to describe a woman.

He'd damn sure pump iron—or something just as manly—as soon as he got out of the shower. Elliott had a weight bench set up at his place. Trace would pay him a visit and bench-press a few thousand pounds to get his manhood back.

He stood under the water so long, it ran cold. Trace didn't move. First time in his life he'd hoped for shrinkage. Did absolutely no good.

That kiss had only stoked his flames of desire, making his nights more restless while he thought of how soft and sexy she'd felt molded against him . . . of how much he wanted her against him again with his mouth exploring every crevice.

A thump sounded from the den, and Trace leaned back out of the stream of water. A swipe of a palm over his face wiped the drops away, and he listened.

Another thump sounded.

Trace slowly reached for the knobs and shut off the water. His father had taken Ben and Sophie to the mainland for the night, leaving Trace alone in the house. Either the raccoon that'd interrupted his kiss with Lily was back and making himself at home in the den, or the Remington had a prowler on the grounds.

He draped a towel around his waist and snuck down the hall to peek around the corner into the den.

Thing One and Thing Two had their feet propped on the coffee table and were helping themselves to beer. Far worse than a raccoon.

Trace relaxed. "Sure. Make yourselves comfortable." He walked through the den to the kitchen to get a beer for himself.

"Hey, asshat," Elliott said.

Spence took a swig. "We're going to the Fallen Angel for a beer. Get dressed. You're going with us."

Trace sank into the chair and popped the cap off the bottle. "Too tired. I'm gonna catch up on sleep." It had been in short supply lately. "Get your feet off my table."

"Wuss." Elliott uncrossed his ankles and put his leather all-weather boots on the floor. "Ben's gone, and you want to sleep?"

Maybe he'd be a better father if he were well rested by the time Ben got home. "Yup."

Thing One and Thing Two gave each other eye rolls.

"I've been working long hours, which you two slackers wouldn't understand." Trace took a long pull from his beer.

Spence snorted. "While you've been flying the friendly skies, Lily's been working our tails off." He still had his feet on the table. "I've done more painting and repairs the past two weeks than I did all the years I was in the building industry."

"It shows." Trace stopped razzing his brothers. "The place hasn't looked this good since . . ." *Since Mom was alive.* He didn't finish because of the pain that sliced through his brothers every time her name came up. "What do you guys think of Lily so far?" He studied the label on his bottle.

"I think she's fucking smart," Elliott answered without hesitation. "A few days ago, she asked to sit down with me to discuss the budget. I thought she'd ask for more money because of the list of repairs and upgrades she wants to make." He shook his head. "I wasn't even close. She'd already figured out a way to acquire the materials we need to complete her entire list without spending an extra dime."

Trace frowned. "How?" He'd approved Lily's list but told her to prioritize, tackle the most important items first, then ask Elliott when the resort could afford the rest.

"She went to Howard's Hardware and convinced them to barter supplies." He took a drink. "In exchange, she's organizing a community improvement month after the summer season is over to bring in extra business for them. Howard's will give a discount to any business on the island that starts a renovation or building project during that month."

Howard's was one of the businesses already signed up for Trace's delivery service. If their demand increased, they'd need more supplies delivered. It was a win-win for everyone involved. Trace nodded, impressed but not surprised by Lily's skill.

"And that's not the best part." Spence chuckled. "She asked me to pick up the materials because she couldn't haul them on her bicycle." He punctuated that with a moment of silence. "Talk about self-sufficient."

Lily had agreed to ask one of them when she needed a ride, but she was keeping everyone so busy she'd managed on her own. Again. The woman had crazy stamina at work and a real knack for winning people over. Trace had slipped in to observe the training session when she'd introduced the new booking system to the staff. By the time she was done, the employees were so enamored, Trace was surprised they hadn't carried her around the grounds on their shoulders.

"Have you heard any more from Megan?" Elliott changed the subject.

The question pulled Trace back to the present, and he shook his head. "No. My guess is she's already lost interest in having Ben stay with her over the summer." One less thing he had to worry about. "But I've been screwing up with Ben the same way she does."

His brothers both gave him a look that said, "Really?" So Trace rattled off the whole story about the ducks and the forgotten science project and kissing Lily because of how amazing she was with his son who'd never had a real mother.

"You forgot a science project. Ben'll get over it," Elliott said.

"He's had to get over way too much already." Trace stabbed his fingers through his tangled wet hair. "He didn't pick Megan to be his mother. I did. I can't help but wonder if he'll hold it against me someday."

"He's a kid," Spence said. "Not a Mafia foot soldier bent on revenge."

"You're nothing like your ex-wife," Spence said, "which is why we're dragging your ass into town tonight for a beer. You deserve to unwind while Ben's gone." He snapped his fingers in a hurry-up gesture. "Get dressed, or we'll be forced to do the public a disservice and carry you out of here in that towel."

Trace pushed Spence's feet off the table and stood. "I'd like to see you try." He strolled toward his room. "Give me ten."

Maybe his brothers were right. He could use a break. And he doubted unwinding over a beer at the Fallen Angel would cause him to screw up any worse than he already had.

The Fallen Angel was the most unusual bar Lily had ever seen. That was saying something, considering she'd worked in the French Quarter and spent a lot of time on Bourbon Street.

She followed Charley and Briley through a glass door on Marina Boulevard for her first official girls' night out in Angel Fire Falls. The door led to a set of dark wood stairs that descended into a basement. Basements weren't common where she was from, so the light streaming in from small horizontal windows close to the ceiling was interesting, especially since the only thing visible through the windows were people's feet as they walked past on the sidewalk.

Retro rock-and-roll music played in the background as they commandeered a small table with barstools around it.

"Thanks for inviting me out. I needed a break from work." Lily had even dressed up for the first time since she'd changed out of her flashy clothes in the airport restroom. The white-and-aqua paisley miniskirt was comfortable and fresh looking with a pair of platform flip-flops. She added a jean jacket since the nights were cool in the Pacific Northwest. "So how's the new restaurant coming?"

"I thought you were taking a break from work?" Charley asked.

"Habit, I guess." Lily shrugged.

"Well, you *are* kicking butt and taking names, so I guess you're entitled," Charley said.

Briley tried to flag a server. "The menu will be on your desk by Monday. We're starting fairly simple."

"Wise. We're promoting a family atmosphere, so simple works." Lily nodded. "I have another favor to ask," she said to Charley. "Can you hook me up with Ben's teacher? I need someone to help develop our children's activities calendar for the summer."

"Sure thing," Charley said. "Ride with me to pick up the kids from school next week."

"Great. Thanks." There was something gratifying about scratching items off her to-do list, and it grew shorter each day.

Finally, a blonde waitress stepped up to the table and offered to take their order. They all asked for a beer.

"Can I see IDs?" asked the server, who looked barely old enough to drink herself.

Fear pierced Lily's chest and nearly stopped her heart. "Um." She patted the front pocket of her jacket, then withdrew some of the cash she'd been rationing. She still hadn't cashed her first paycheck because the name on it didn't match her license. Would that be a crime? She wasn't sure. Working on the small island where employers seemed to be pretty lax about requiring identification had allowed her to keep her identity a secret so far. She wasn't about to start flashing her license around now. "I must've forgotten mine." She thumbed through the bills and smiled at the server. "I'll just have a Coke."

"Never mind." Charley hopped off the stool. "My cousins are friends with the owners, who happen to be tending bar tonight. Let me see if I can fix this." She tugged Lily over to the bar. "Hi, Mason. This is my friend. She's new to Angel Fire Falls."

His black hair tapered perfectly to his neckline. It took a minute for his smoky gray eyes to leave Charley and greet Lily. "Lily *Barns*." He drew out her last name with an exaggerated air of familiarity. "Nice to meet you."

Lily creased her brow. "You know my name?"

"Everybody knows your name. Your ideas could mean great things for the entire island." Mason tossed a towel over one shoulder. "The Fallen Angel signed up for Trace's new delivery service, which he credits to you."

Oh. No. She had no idea anyone outside the resort knew she existed, except for maybe Howard's Hardware. And that was because she'd visited them personally with a business proposition. She forced a smile. "Nice to meet you, Mason."

"Lily forgot her ID. Can you help us out?" Charley asked.

He gave Lily an appreciative look, then turned smoky eyes back on Charley. "Beers are on the house tonight."

"Thanks, Mason." Charley picked up two mugs.

Lily grabbed the third and followed Charley back to the table. As they talked, the bar filled up. Without them having to ask, Mason sent fresh mugs to their table as soon as the first round was empty.

"Charley's got an admirer," Briley teased, the beer already loosening them up. They had to dial up their volume as the chatter of the full room had grown loud.

Charley swallowed a mouthful of brew and shook her head. "Not interested. I've been burned. Fool me once and all that."

"Me too," Lily chimed in. "My ex was a jerk."

"That makes three of us." Mischief twinkled in Briley's eyes. "Hey, let's get our hoo-has tattooed as a show of solidarity."

The three of them threw their heads back and laughed.

"Charley and I know each other's stories," Briley said. "What's yours, Lily?"

Beer caught in Lily's throat. She coughed and covered her mouth.

Her two new BFFs waited expectantly for details.

Lily twirled her frosty mug in a circle, a sudden urge to pour out the painful memories of Andrew's betrayal welling up inside her. None of her old friends had been left to talk to by the time Andrew had sunk the knife in and twisted it.

"Andrew hired me right out of college." Because her father knew him from renovating the chain of upscale hotels Andrew managed. "He was nice looking." But not drop-dead gorgeous like a certain pilot she knew. "Very romantic at first and a gentleman." Both in and out of bed, which she wouldn't describe as satisfying. "We settled. Mostly, I think I wanted to make my parents happy." Not to mention her mother had pushed her into the engagement because Andrew's annual salary contained a lot of zeroes. "We both worked all the time, so I'd lost touch with a lot of my friends from high school and college. Since we worked *together*, it was a convenient choice for me. Eventually, his friends became my friends, and it was all very easy." At least that's what she'd told herself. She shrugged. "Unfortunately, he got the friends in the breakup."

"You said *we* settled. What was in it for him?" Charley drew on her mug.

Mainly her father's name and reputation. Once that started circling the bowl, Andrew pulled the plug and flushed both their relationship and her career. Lily took a long, slow drink of beer. "Corporate execs love the family-man look. I was good for his career."

Until she wasn't.

She lifted her mug with a smile. "I'm not dropping my panties anytime soon for anyone, not even a tattoo artist, so I'll settle for a toast. Here's to not making the same mistake twice."

They toasted and took a big gulp each.

She looked toward the entrance and saw Trace following his two brothers into the bar. As though he could sense her presence, his gaze found hers and locked on instantly.

She forced down another sip, hoping the cold beer would cool the heat building low in her belly.

The Remington brothers weaved through the crowded room toward the bar. If all the handshakes and backslaps were any indication, the Remingtons were well liked.

Charley cleared her throat to get Lily's attention. "You sure about not dropping your panties anytime soon?"

Lily angled her chair away from the bar so she wouldn't be tempted to stare at Trace. "Absolutely certain. My ex was also my boss. Hard work might be a habit I can't break, but hooking up with my employer isn't a mistake I plan to make again."

A flash went off at Lily's side, and her head swiveled to see Ronald Parker pointing a phone in her direction.

She held up a hand to block her face and looked away.

Oh God. Oh God, oh God, oh God.

She kept her face hidden.

"Oh. Sorry, Lily." Parker stepped up to the table. "I forgot you don't want your picture taken."

No more than he did. She had to bite her tongue to keep from snapping at him for taking her picture without permission. "Mr. Parker." She glanced at his phone, hoping he hadn't gotten a full-on shot of her face.

He waved it around. "Don't mind me. I'm just taking a few vacation photos before I go home tomorrow."

Thank the Baby Jesus the guy was leaving the island.

"I hope you've enjoyed your stay enough to visit us again." Not really, but she was paid to attract business and not chase it away because she got creeped out by a guest. "How was your aerial tour?"

"It was excellent." He looked thoughtful. "I couldn't find you on social media."

Her heart skipped a beat. Then another. "Why would you want to find me on social media?"

Briley and Charley stayed quiet, but their looks said they didn't like him any more than Lily did.

"Oh, I friend everyone I meet." He stepped closer until his arm brushed hers.

Her skin crawled, and she leaned away.

"It's a hobby." He put his hand on the back of her chair. Not only was it a possessive gesture, but it also invaded her personal space in a way that was far too familiar.

She sliced a hand across the span of her two friends. "Mr. Parker, we're having a private conversa—"

"Ladies." The rich timbre of that voice at her back skated over Lily. "Enjoying yourselves?" A warm, firm hand closed over her shoulder, and she knew it was Trace's without looking.

His scent. His touch. His sound. His very presence might as well be foreplay by the way her body reacted.

"Lily, I know it's after hours, but can you spare a few minutes to discuss business in the back office?" An easy smile played at his lips. "The bar is a new client, and I need your input. I figured since we're here, it would save us an extra trip."

She was supposed to be taking a night off from work. Just a few hours to let her hair down and relax. But Ronald Parker had become more than a nuisance, and this was her chance to escape. "Sure." She slid off the stool. "But I don't have my iPad with me to make notes."

Trace smiled. "You do seem to run the universe through that iPad, but we can get by without it tonight." He turned to Charley. "I'll return Lily shortly." The waver of his smile was so slight Lily almost missed it. "Mr. Parker." Trace steadied his friendly expression, but pure alpha testosterone fell off him in waves. "I see you're on the schedule to fly back to the Cape tomorrow." As he waited for an answer, he drew in a breath that seemed to increase his height several inches.

Parker shrank back a step. "I am." His questioning gaze slithered back and forth between Lily and Trace.

"I've bought you a drink to say thank you for staying with us." Trace pointed to the bar. "The bartender is waiting for your order."

With a hand on her elbow, Trace led her toward the back of the room. When they passed Elliott and Spence sitting at the bar, Trace said, "If that guy doesn't leave Charley and Briley alone, run interference."

Both of his brothers tensed, bowed out their chests, and leaned back on their stools to look in their cousin's direction.

Trace tried the handle on a door down the hall, and it opened. He flipped the light on and held the door open for her.

The room was lined with shelves filled with everything she'd expect to find in a bar. "So what input do you need?" She perused the cluttered shelves. "The owners might benefit more from Charley and Briley's input on inventory organization; it's a mess in here."

Trace closed the door and came to stand in front of her, one broad shoulder propped against a metal shelf. "What's with that Parker guy?"

Good question. Instinct told Lily the answer wouldn't be good. "No idea."

Trace crossed his arms, and Lily couldn't help but stare at his chest as it flexed and flowed under his stonewashed T-shirt. "He seems to think he knows you. Or is that just a come-on?"

As much as Parker creeped her out, it would be a relief if it was a come-on. Otherwise, the press might be closing in. "I've never seen the guy before." If she never saw him again, it would be too soon. "Why?"

Trace made a face. "My gut tells me he's not straight up. Maybe he was a guest from your previous job?" Trace's eyes roamed her face. When they swept her length and snagged on the bare skin below the hem of her miniskirt, her knees went weak.

"I don't think so." Trace's concern for her, his willingness to protect her, made her bite her lip to keep the truth from tumbling out. "So you really don't need my input for your new client?" she asked.

"Not at the moment." His eyes sparkled. "Unless I misread your body language, Mr. Parker's advances looked unwelcome. I figured I'd help you out."

She blew out a chuckle. "I thought I was being subtle."

"About as subtle as, oh, I don't know"—he scratched his ear— "pedaling a giant tricycle with ducks riding shotgun during a storm."

They laughed.

"Nice bodyguard detail you and your brothers provide," she joked. "You guys could hire out your services for a nice price."

"There's no charge. Looking out for women we care about is free."

She blinked at him. The Remingtons cared about her. *He* cared about her. Coming to her rescue in a crowded bar was proof of that, which was why she wanted to bare her soul right then and there.

His hungry look said he wanted her to bare everything else.

"I'm not used to having anyone look out for me." At that moment, Lily felt so alone. So abandoned by everyone in her life. Her father, her fiancé, her friends. No one was left from her old life. Her new life at the Remington offered her more than a job. It offered real relationships and security. And she couldn't fully embrace it because she wasn't being honest.

Trace took her in from the top of her ponytailed hair all the way to her dressy flip-flops. "You've got someone looking out for you now." He shifted like he was going to close the space between them but stopped.

So she took two steps, went up on the tips of her toes, and placed a gentle kiss on his cheek. "Thank you," she whispered.

When she tried to step away, he took the opening of her jean jacket between his fingers and tugged. "You look nice." His voice went throaty. "More like the girl I saw at the airport getting a massage." He eased a hand inside her jean jacket and stroked her hip.

"You mean the girl who was moaning?" She smiled as heat rushed up her neck to settle in her cheeks. And several other parts of her anatomy.

"One and the same." He covered her mouth with his and kissed her deeply.

It was wrong. Stupid, even. She knew where it might lead. How it could end.

Bad habits really did die hard because she sighed against Trace's lips, and his arms circled her. The hand at her waist smoothed up her back until it reached the sensitive skin at the base of her neck. The roughness of his fingertips made her skin pebble, and she moaned.

"I love that sexy moan of yours," he breathed against her mouth, then claimed it again to search out her tongue with his.

His kiss, his taste was everything she thought it would be and so much more.

She sighed against his lips, and as if it was the most natural thing in the world, her palms moved over his chest, up his neck, and sank into his hair. He tasted like fresh morning dew on a hot summer day, and Lily melted against him.

He eased her back against the shelves, feathering soft kisses across her neck.

"That's. So. Good," she panted out. *And so wrong,* she tried to remind herself.

"I promise it would be much better if we were skin to skin." He whispered the wicked promise against her neck. "If we weren't in a storage room, I'd prove it to you." He slid one hand up her rib cage and tugged her tank and bra down. When his hand cupped her aching breast, her head fell back and thudded against a shelf.

He kneaded her breast into a hard peak, while nibbling the flesh at the crook of her neck. Then he dipped his head and pulled a nipple into his mouth.

She couldn't stop a small cry of pleasure from escaping when his warm mouth closed around her throbbing peak. *"Oh God."*

He chuckled, and his hot breath made her insides heat to nuclear temperatures. Nice guy that he obviously was, he paid her other breast the same attention. His lovely tongue swiped across her nipple. Once, twice, three times. Then circled it and gently suckled.

She fisted his hair, which caused him to moan too.

"I'd give an arm to see you naked." He found her mouth with his again and kissed her. This time more urgently. He cupped her ass in his palms and lifted her off the ground.

She squeaked, but her legs closed around his waist.

"No, not an arm. I like what you're doing with both hands." She trailed kisses along his neck.

"Hands are more like an accessory," he said with a laugh. "They're not the body parts that are going to make you moan the loudest." He carried her to a bare wall around the corner and steadied her against it. "My tongue and"—he pressed his hips into her center—"*this* are all I need."

A shudder of pleasure raked through her. Her panties were already hot with moisture from the sheer pleasure of his rigid shaft grinding against her.

She couldn't stop. Couldn't get enough of him.

"Trace," she whispered against his lips. "This is wrong."

"So wrong." His mouth consumed hers as his fingers flexed into her butt cheeks.

She feathered kisses along his jaw to his ear. When she sank her teeth into his earlobe, he shuddered and rolled his hips into her. His granite shaft made her want to puddle at his feet. Made her want to scream for more skin and fewer clothes between them. He moved against her until she shimmied and shuddered and raced toward the edge.

A knock sounded at the door, and Trace stilled. His hot breaths washed over her ear, and she buried her face in his neck.

"What?" he barked out.

The door wasn't in view, but they heard it open.

"Trace?" Spence asked.

Trace leaned his forehead against hers and stared down at her, lust still clouding his eyes.

She eased one foot to the ground. "It's okay," she mouthed.

"Yeah, what is it?" Trace said, helping her find her balance before he let go.

"Someone's out here asking for you."

"Who?" Trace helped straighten her top.

She pushed against his chest so he'd step back far enough for her to smooth her skirt. The last thing she needed was to walk back into a crowded bar with her clothes twisted into an I-almost-had-closet-sex kind of way.

"I don't know." Spence sounded irritated. "One of your clients maybe?"

Trace let out a breath that was just as annoyed. "Be right there."

The door shut.

Gently, he brushed a stray strand of hair off her forehead.

He gave her another long, luxurious kiss before he took her hand and led her to the door.

She pulled it free as they stepped out into the hall. The din of the crowded bar came rushing at them. Trace gave her a reassuring look before they walked back into the fray.

The second they stepped into the crowded bar, a young hipster kid wearing skinny jeans and a knit cap moved into their path. "Trace Remington?"

Trace stopped short to keep from colliding with the guy, who was half Trace's size. "Yes?"

Lily eased up behind him, every instinct she had going on high alert.

The kid pushed an envelope into Trace's chest.

It all happened so fast, yet it was like it was in slow motion. Before she could tell him to back away and not accept what the kid was offering, Trace grabbed it.

"You've been served." The kid disappeared into the crowd.

Trace stared at the envelope with rounded eyes. He slowly opened it and skimmed the page. "My ex," he mumbled like he couldn't believe what he was seeing.

Lily placed a reassuring hand on his forearm. "What is it, Trace?"

"She's suing me for custody of Ben."

Chapter Thirteen

Trace crumpled the legal papers in his hands. The noise of the Fallen Angel's busy weekend crowd faded into the distance, even though patrons stood shoulder to shoulder in the bar.

A warm hand closed around his upper arm and squeezed. "Trace." A soft, comforting voice pierced the fog of silence that engulfed him.

He looked to his right, blinking Lily into focus. "I can't . . ." He rubbed the corners of his eyes with a thumb and forefinger. "I've got to go." He had to get out of there and talk to Megan. Ask her why she was doing this to their son because they both knew she didn't really want custody of Ben. "You've got a ride with Charley?"

She nodded. "Don't worry about me."

The concern creasing the soft skin between her brows made him want to take her in his arms. The kindness glinting in her eyes made him want to take her to his bed.

The way she'd melted into his arms in the storage room, the way her body quivered and heated everywhere he'd touched had only whetted his appetite.

But was it fair to pursue Lily with Megan throwing shade his way? Was it right for him to take one second of his attention off Ben while Megan was making threats?

Trace glanced down at the wadded paper in his hand. None of it was fair or right, but it had landed squarely in his hands nonetheless.

"Thanks. I'll—" He couldn't think. "We'll talk later."

He blazed a trail through the thick crowd and found his brothers sitting at the bar. "Let's go." His expression and his tone were enough for his brothers to know he was serious.

Elliott tossed a few bills on the counter, and Spence pulled jingling keys out of his pocket. They were in the Jeep in less than a minute. Spence fired up the engine, did a quick U-turn on Marina Boulevard, and headed home.

Trace told them everything.

"Man," Spence said. "If I'd known why the kid was looking for you, I would've tossed him out of the bar."

Trace propped an elbow on the passenger door and tapped a fist against his mouth. "He'd have found me someplace else."

"What happens now?" Elliott asked.

Trace wished he knew. He was tired. So damned tired that his bones ached. He let his head fall back on the headrest and stared straight ahead, only the Jeep's dual streams of light illuminating the way home. "First, I'm going to get Megan on the phone and ask her what the hell she's thinking. If she had custody of Ben, her interest would last about ten minutes." No way in hell would he allow her to take their son away only to dump him on a stranger. Trace didn't care if the special-ed-teacher-nanny Megan planned to hire had a wall full of credentials; no stranger was taking care of his son.

"This is fucked up." The dash lights weren't bright enough to show Spence's expression, but his tone said he was pissed.

"What about Lily?" Elliott asked.

Trace tensed. "What about her?" He'd been wondering the same thing ever since the hipster kid, who was dressed like he probably skateboarded all the way from Los Angeles, had shoved the papers into Trace's chest.

"You two weren't in the storage room looking for pretzels," Spence said.

"First time I've seen a woman turn your head since you became a single dad." Elliott reached through the seats and bumped the edge of his fist against Trace's shoulder. "It'd be a cryin'-ass shame to let Megan screw it up for you."

Trace blew out his cheeks. "I don't know." He said it more to himself. Before he could figure out his relationship with Lily, he had to deal with Megan.

Spence slowed and turned into the resort.

"I'll talk to you tomorrow." The Jeep had barely rolled to a stop in front of Trace's cottage when his feet hit the ground. As the Jeep rumbled away and he had privacy, Trace pulled out his phone and dialed Megan's number. He climbed the steps and got her voice mail without the phone ringing once.

He growled.

He unlocked the door and flicked on a light. Then he sent Megan a text telling her she might as well answer, or he would call her cell and her landline every ten minutes for the rest of the night. If that didn't work, he'd fly to LA and do the same with her doorbell.

He knew how much she hated losing precious sleep. He'd certainly spent plenty of nights getting up with Ben because she wouldn't.

He dialed up her number again, and she answered on the second ring.

"What, Trace?" she snapped.

"Are you seriously going to use Ben like a circus animal to help your career? Because that's low, even for you," he snapped back. He couldn't help it; this was about their *son*.

"You gave me no choice!" Megan insisted. "If you'd at least considered letting Ben come stay with me over the summer, I wouldn't have had to take such drastic measures. This one's on you. Not me."

"According to the articles I've read in the news about your busy career, you won't be available over the summer," he said through clenched teeth. "You'll be on set. So how will you spend time with Ben?"

She went quiet.

"That's the plan, isn't it?" He let out a bitter laugh. "You won't have any time to spend with him. That's the whole reason you actually want custody after all these years."

"I want my son with me," she argued.

"Because of what he can do for your career." He let his head hang forward as he paced. "Not because you care about him."

"Don't make this harder than it needs to be."

That was rich, coming from a woman who penciled in visits with her son twice each year and managed to miss most of them. "He's an eight-year-old boy. Don't put him through this. Drop the custody suit." No way in hell would he let her take their son only to dump him on someone else. A little reminder of how she didn't actually like to be around their son was long overdue. "Come to the island next week. If all goes well, I'll bring him to visit you a few times over the summer."

She stayed silent like she was considering his proposal.

"If it goes *really* well, I'll bring him to visit while you're working." He sweetened the offer, knowing his ex would focus on the on-set publicity opportunity instead of the needs of their child. He just needed to get Megan to the island, and she'd screw the rest up on her own.

She always did.

"Fine," she said. "I'll be there. But I'm not dropping the custody suit yet. Not unless we can come up with an arrangement that's acceptable for me."

Megan ending that last sentence with the word *me* was typical since it was her favorite subject.

Still, he could be polite if it meant ending her custody nonsense without a fight and saving Ben any unnecessary emotional damage. "What day should I expect you?"

"I don't know yet," she clipped out.

Her no-show rate was pretty high, which was why he never told Ben when she planned to visit.

"I'll be in touch," she said, and the line went dead.

Why did that not surprise Trace in the least?

Lily said goodnight when Charley dropped her off in front of her cottage. Her lips still burned from Trace's kiss. Her girl parts hadn't cooled off either, but she couldn't let Trace be the one to put out the flames.

Her job at the Remington was off and running. She couldn't risk the promising new start she had by getting involved with Trace.

With the porch light on, she dug her keys from her purse.

Maybe she should walk down to his cottage and knock on the door. Obviously, they needed to have a heart-to-heart about boundaries. Boundaries would save them both a lot of trouble. So yes, she should go talk to him. As soon as she figured out how *not* to catapult right over those boundaries and shrink-wrap around him.

She let herself in and flung her purse and keys onto the counter.

Trace's exquisite tongue, his clever hands, and the large-and-in-charge package he'd pressed between her legs in the Fallen Angel's storage room would be difficult to walk away from now that she'd gotten a small sample.

Good Lord, if he could get her that worked up fully clothed, it would likely be mind-altering if they were naked.

A shudder of lust quaked through her, and she tried to shake off the thrill of anticipation.

When her entire body broke out in a sweat, she opened the fridge, letting the cold air work its magic.

Did no good.

She slammed the fridge and went to the front door. It was late, but she had to talk to Trace and set things straight for both of them. Maybe ask him to be the strong one even if she couldn't be because fraternization between employers and employees wasn't good for either of them.

With a hand on the knob, she drew in a deep breath and opened the door before she lost her nerve.

The butterflies in her stomach turned to hornets when she caught a glimpse of the gorgeous man sitting on her front porch, his back against a post and one leg slung over the side.

"Trace." She stepped outside and closed the door.

"I heard Charley drive past my place, so I knew you were home."

Lily closed the front of her jacket and hugged herself against the night chill that hung in the air. "And you figured you'd sit on my porch instead of knocking?"

He chuckled. "Truth?"

She had to break eye contact on that one. "Sure." She took a seat next to him but left enough room so they didn't touch.

"I was trying to figure out a way *not* to have to say this." He went quiet.

"I'm a big girl," she said softy. "I can take it."

He drew a long breath into his lungs. "I told you my situation with Ben is complicated." Trace bent a knee and propped his arm over it. "He needs all my time and attention."

She crossed her ankles and swung her legs back and forth. "I remember."

"This is why." He pulled a folded batch of papers from his jacket. He'd obviously smoothed them out after wadding them up at the bar.

"Ben's always been high maintenance because of his condition, but if his mother gets custody, it'll crush him and any hope he has of a stable, productive life." His voice rasped with the grief. "I can't let that happen."

Lily's heart thudded.

"My ex-wife already has ammunition she can use against me." Trace stuffed the papers back in his pocket, a muscle in his jaw twitching.

Once upon a time, Lily's father had cared about her the way Trace cared about Ben. She missed it and could never fault Trace for loving his son enough to do whatever was necessary to protect him. Trace's devotion to his son was one of the things Lily admired about him most.

"You're an incredible father. I doubt you've done anything bad enough for you to lose custody."

Trace looked down and sighed heavily. Lily had to lace her fingers in her lap to keep from reaching out to comfort him.

"Before I moved back to the island, I flew private jets in Los Angeles. The job played hell with my schedule. I was always on call, never any rhyme or reason to my hours." He stared into the darkness. "I was called out one night when my regular sitter was out of town. I called Ben's mom." His tone went hard. "She refused to come stay with him because she had an audition the next morning, or so she said. So I called a nanny service."

Lily knew the story wasn't going to end well for Ben, and a seed of anger sprouted in her chest.

"I was so worried about Ben waking up with a strange person in the house that I misread the weather report and flew right into turbulence that nearly caused us to crash." His head thumped back against the post. "That's the first time I've ever had passengers scream in terror on a flight."

She couldn't help but let the pain and regret behind his words seep into her chest. "I'm so sorry."

He let out a sarcastic chuckle. "I wish that were the end of the story." He closed his eyes for a beat. "Ben *did* wake up, had a complete meltdown when he didn't know the nanny, and she . . ." The grinding of his teeth was audible. "To calm him down, she gave him a tranquilizer that was prescribed to her."

Lily's intake of air was sharp. She closed her hand over his. "That bitch."

A husky laugh escaped through his lips. "I quit my job the next day and moved back to the island."

Lily's heart tumbled end over end.

She squeezed his hand again. "Ben's such a good kid. He deserves the life you're building for him here." She tried to pull her hand from Trace's, but he didn't let go. "It's for the best we keep it professional . . . and friendly." She was so full of it. She wanted him now more than ever. "I made the mistake of getting involved with my boss once." She breathed deep. "It didn't end well for me. He used it against me. I worked my heart out for that company and threw it all away because I trusted a person who had power over my career. I would be foolish to go down that road again." She caressed her thumb across his calloused hand. "Even if you're nothing like him."

"Give me a name, and you can consider his ass kicked," Trace said.

She laughed. "Thank you, but it's not necessary."

"He was a fool." Trace reached out and gently molded his fingers to her neck. "You're everything I want in a woman." He let his gaze roam over her face, the moonlight glinting off his eyes. "You're wonderful with Ben." Trace let the calloused pad of his thumb sweep over her bottom lip, sending a delicious shiver racing through her. "I'm the problem, not you. I have to keep all my attention on my son, and that's not fair to you, Lily." His thumb traveled across her lips again. "You deserve better than playing second string." He took her hand and placed a sweet kiss on the inside of her wrist. "If circumstances were different . . ." The next kiss to her wrist was a nip.

Every cell in her body went up in flames.

"But they're not," she whispered. "And this can't be. No matter how much we might want it." Gently, she pulled her hand away.

He stared at her mouth for a long, long time. The regret, the sorrow, the turmoil in his expression said he alone was responsible for the wall that kept them apart.

Lily couldn't let him believe that . . . because it wasn't true. So she took a deep breath and went for honest. "I've made mistakes." Like trying to start over with a new name. "I'm not great girlfriend material." Even though she wanted to be. "You don't know me very well . . . but, um, you see, before I moved here . . . I . . ."

Her phone blared to life from inside the cottage, belting out the song that reminded her of her Cajun roots and the painful mess in her past that had brought her to the island in the first place. She swallowed, blinking back to the present.

"You should get that." He stood. "It might be important if someone's calling you this late." He backed away, his eyes never leaving hers. "Goodbye, Lily."

Those words stopped time. Lily couldn't move as she watched him turn and recede into the darkness.

She went inside and answered the phone. For once, her mother's slurred self-pity rant seemed like a blessing. It was the only thing keeping Lily from marching over to Trace's cottage and kissing him silly. Then telling him everything.

Chapter Fourteen

LILY'S LIFE LESSON #14
Spandex should come with a warning label: *Can cause blindness
if not used with caution.*

In the hotel business, there wasn't much difference between the work-week and the weekend. Except weekends were usually much busier. Despite the lack of sleep after the previous night's near miss in the Fallen Angel's storage room, Lily got an early start to take care of her responsibilities.

She made the rounds, following up with the guests who were leaving. Everyone but Ronald Parker. Him she'd rather avoid, so she texted Elliott and Spence to see if one of them could check on the guest who'd become a thorn in her side. With her phone app, she scheduled departure times for everyone else so Trace would know when they needed to fly to the Cape to catch their connecting flights. Then she popped into the kitchen to find Charley.

"Good morning." Lily put her phone and iPad on the counter. She helped herself to a cup of Charley's famous coffee.

Charley bustled around the kitchen. "Morning."

Lily leaned against the stainless-steel island and sipped her brew. "If I ride with you to school tomorrow, will you make introductions to Ben's teacher? I need to get the children's summer activities calendar firmed up."

"Sure thing." Charley stopped to wipe her hands and really looked at Lily for the first time. "You look as fresh as a spring flower."

Lily looked down at her choice of clothing. She'd pulled on a pair of black capris, a breezy off-the-shoulder top, and a pair of stylish sandals. The ensemble was more like what she would've worn on her day off in New Orleans. Not at all like the microfiber hiking pants and all-weather boots she'd been sporting since she moved to Angel Fire Falls.

Her subconscious probably had something to do with her outfit; deep down, Lily knew there was meaning behind it. The truth about her roots, her identity, her life had to come out eventually. She might as well start preparing for it. Might as well give the Remingtons a glimpse of who she really was. When the time was right, she wanted the Remington family to hear the truth from her. They deserved as much after the way they'd welcomed her. Trusted her.

Until then, she'd work her tail off, for them as much as for herself, to make this the Remington Resort's most successful tourist season on record.

She lifted a bare shoulder. "The weather's nice, and it's getting warmer. I'm enjoying it."

Charley pulled a tray of pastries from the oven and put in another. "Well, you look nice." Her eyes twinkled with mischief. "I'm sure Trace agrees." She leaned to the right to look around Lily. "Don't you, Cuz?"

"I absolutely do." Trace's velvety voice came from behind her and slid right through her.

She tensed and tingled all over.

Slowly, she angled her body so she could speak to both of them, hoping her cheeks weren't as red as they felt. "Thank you." She transferred her weight from one sandal to the other. "Can we meet later about a few more ideas I have?" Lily shifted the conversation into a more professional gear.

He glanced at the watch on his right wrist. "I've got time now." He tapped the phone in his pocket. "Thanks to your handy-dandy app, I already know my first scheduled trip to the Cape isn't for a few hours." He scratched his temple. "First, can I ask what's going on in the great room?"

She had no idea.

"I think Lily's created a monster," Charley said.

"Um . . ." Lily lifted both brows in a question.

"Oh, you haven't seen it for yourself?" Charley laughed, drizzling the pastries with white chocolate.

Lily shook her head, the coffee mug hovering at her lips. "I came in through the back entrance."

"Oh, this is gonna be good." Charley chuckled and wiped her hands again. "I've got to see your reaction for myself."

Lily didn't wait for them to explain. She set her coffee mug down, picked up her phone, and went to the great room as fast as her sparkly sandals could carry her. When she rounded the corner of the great room, she came to an abrupt stop.

Charley and Trace caught up and flanked her.

The furniture had been pushed back against the walls, and folding chairs were scattered around the center of the room. Mrs. Ferguson sat facing the guests as gentle ocean music played. She wore bright-orange yoga pants, a neon-turquoise spandex shirt, and a sweatband around her head.

Oh dear. Lily had suggested Mrs. Ferguson start bingo and a basket-weaving class for their senior guests. This was . . .

Actually, Lily couldn't put *this* into words.

Mrs. Ferguson touched her forefingers to her thumbs so they formed a circle and rested them on her thighs. "Deep breath in," she said, and the participants complied with exaggerated enthusiasm. "Exhale." Her tone was soothing. She called out a pose that required the participants to bend forward in their chairs. An older gentleman's toupee fell forward.

"Oh my," Charley whispered.

Lily covered a gasp with one hand.

Mrs. Ferguson could barely cook without starting a five-alarm fire. Now she was teaching yoga?

She led the seniors through a series of yoga moves, their butts never leaving the seats of their chairs. When she got to the warrior pose, Lily's mouth fell open.

Charley stifled a laugh by clearing her throat.

Trace rubbed his jaw.

When the class finished, Charley squeezed Lily's arm and headed to the kitchen, still trying to hold back laughter.

Lily put a hand to her cheek. "I should ask Mrs. Ferguson what else she's got planned that we don't know about." Lily turned a reluctant look on Trace and drew in a breath. "I'm going in. Wish me luck."

"Oh, uh-uh," he said. "I'm coming with. Growing up, if we threw down with Mrs. F., we rarely won. So this I've got to see."

As Lily approached, Mrs. Ferguson wiped imaginary sweat from her neck with a gym towel. "I see you're hard at work for our senior guests," Lily said.

"It's given me a new lease on life." She panted, still not a bead of sweat visible. "Thank you so much, dear. I owe it all to you."

Lily slid a look at Trace, and he lifted an I-told-you-so brow.

No wonder Mrs. Ferguson won throw downs with the Remington brothers, who were big and built enough to scare most people away with their alpha swaggers. She played dirty with her cooing voice and comments that made her seem like a sweet little old lady—one who probably wore a skirt, orthopedic shoes, and her socks rolled down. Plus, she'd been savvy enough to credit Lily in the process.

"Tomorrow is bingo, Tuesday is flower pressing, and Wednesday is kite flying on the back lawn." Her expression brightened with excitement. "Next weekend will be our first Fifty-Plus Book Club for female guests only." She leaned in, batted her lashes, and gave Trace a bashful glance. "To christen the group, we're starting with *Fifty Shades*."

He wheezed out a cough.

"Um, Mrs. Ferguson . . ." Lily shot an SOS look at Trace.

He just shrugged as if to say *You're on your own.*

Lily had to stop an eye roll. She turned her hospitality charm right back on Mrs. Ferguson. "Since the Remington is trying to build a family-friendly reputation, I think *Lawrence* would prefer to keep the activities we offer more clean and wholesome, don't you?"

Mrs. Ferguson frowned with uncertainty when Lily mentioned Lawrence's name. "I didn't think of that. I suppose you're right."

"You're doing a fantastic job." Lily invoked her knack for persuasion. Mrs. Ferguson had no idea who she was dealing with.

And for a second Lily froze. Because that's exactly what her father had done to get people to trust him. He'd charmed them first, making them trust him, and then he'd charmed them out of their money. He'd started as an honest businessman but had gotten carried away and had abused his power of persuasion.

She nibbled at the corner of her lip, then forged on. "Put together a list of activities you plan to offer." Hopefully, the list would be rated G. "Trace and I will make sure Lawrence approves."

"I'll bring it tomorrow morning. Wonderful idea, dear." She stood, giving them a full-length view of her clinging orange yoga pants.

Trace shrank back a step. "I'll be in the kitchen getting another cup of strong coffee." He walked away with a shake of his head.

Lily needed another cup too. With the image of Mrs. Ferguson in spandex burning her retinas, Lily could use a shot of bourbon to go with it. Spandex should come with a warning label: *Can cause blindness if not used with caution.* "Thank you, Mrs. Ferguson. I'll look forward to adding it to our website. And let me know if I need to order any supplies or materials for flower pressing or any other activities."

Lily hurried through the lobby and made a quick stop in her office before tracking Trace down again so she could pitch a few more ideas to him.

"Lily!" Ben shouted as he, Sophie, and Lawrence came through the front door. "We took the ferry home!" He threw his arms around her waist and hugged her like he hadn't seen her in a week, even though it'd only been two days. "And we saw a movie and jumped on trampolines at this big place that had a whole bunch of them!"

It made Lily's heart sing, and she hugged him back.

"Hey, Lily. How'd it go while I was gone?" Lawrence asked.

"Everything went great." She stroked Ben's hair. He still hadn't let go of her waist.

"Where's Mommy?" Sophie asked in a small, cherubic voice. It was the first time Lily could remember having heard it.

"She's in the kitchen." Lily looked at Lawrence. "And there's fresh coffee too."

"Music to my ears." Lawrence sniffed the air and followed his nose, Sophie skipping along after him.

"Ms. Barns." Ronald Parker's voice came from the great room and crawled over her skin. "Lovely to see you."

She glanced over her shoulder and found him leaning against the doorframe, watching her and Ben. She didn't turn to face him. Rude, she knew, but the man made a habit of skulking.

He gave her a curious look. "You have an accent I can't quite place. You're not from around here, are you?"

A dull throb started behind Lily's eye.

"I missed the duckies!" Ben hollered, still holding on to her waist.

Something eerie skated over Lily, and she glanced over her shoulder again just in time to catch Ronald Parker pointing his phone in her direction. She ducked her head and blocked Ben's face with her hand just as Parker's flash went off.

"Mr. Parker," Lily hissed. Who *was* this guy? She had enough experience with the press to know he didn't fit the mold, but something about him made her bristle. "It's highly inappropriate to take pictures of a child without the parent's consent."

Trace strolled into the lobby just as she spoke. He came to a halt. Instead of Ben running to his father as he normally would, he stayed attached to Lily like glue.

"Pardon me." Parker seemed contrite, but Lily had her doubts. "You seem so fond of each other, I thought it would make a great vacation shot."

"The resort is beautiful." It wasn't easy, but she forced a cordial tone. "You're free to take as many photos of the grounds as you like."

"What's going on?" Trace's tone held an edge as he sized up the situation.

"I stopped in to schedule a lift back to the mainland," Parker said with a casual smile.

"Ben," Lily said, handing him her phone, "can you go take today's pictures of the ducks and feed them?" They'd already been fed, but the protective instinct gnawing at her gut told her Ben should leave.

He grabbed the phone, but before he could barrel toward the front door, Lily leaned down and whispered, "Go give your dad a hello hug."

Trace's eyes clouded with both relief and sadness when Ben ran over and threw his arms around his middle. "Meet you in the game room later for pool?"

Ben cheered, then flew outdoors.

"What time do you need to leave?" Trace's tone stayed stiff when he spoke to Parker.

Parker pushed off the wall. "Now would work for me if you're available."

Trace nodded.

Good riddance. "We'll send someone to your room in a few minutes to pick up your bags," Lily said.

When they were alone, Trace asked, "Is there a way to flag unwanted guests in the booking system?"

"Consider it done." Anxiety ebbed from Lily's tightened stomach. "We can wait to meet this afternoon after you fly the guests to the Cape." Getting rid of Parker was far more important than discussing more ideas for the resort with Trace.

"Thank you for looking out for Ben." Trace glanced toward the doors where Ben had just left. "I think he's starting to like you better than me."

Lily shook her head gently. "Not possible. He obviously worships you."

His expression filled with need, and he took a breath so deep, so filled with desire that Lily thought he might cross those few steps between them and pull her into a kiss. "He obviously worships you too."

They stared at each other, the heavy silence communicating so much more than words ever could.

"It's the ducks." She winked. "They're my ace in the hole." It was either break the moment with a joke or drag him into an empty room and redefine the word *worship*. By using her tongue.

Trace blew out a sad chuckle and stared down at his boots.

"Seriously, Ben was my first friend on the island. He's easy to love." Her voice went low. "It's going to be okay. You're not going to lose him."

Trace's head snapped up, and he gave her a hollow look. Then his gaze swept her face, and the hollowness disappeared. He shifted and brought them close enough that his scent wound around her, and his breath coasted over her skin.

She had to stop her traitorous body from swaying into him. "I'll check on Ben while you're gone." She forced herself to take a step back. "See you later."

Not one muscle in Trace's large frame moved except the one in his jaw. It twitched like he was exercising a good deal of willpower.

Lily didn't have much willpower left, so she turned and flew out the front doors just like Ben had.

After Lily checked on Ben at her place and retrieved her phone, she went to her office to lay the groundwork for the idea she planned to pitch to her *boss*—because it didn't hurt to keep reminding herself that Trace was her employer. It might help keep her thoughts off him and the way he'd looked at her for caring so much about his son.

And featherless ducklings could fly.

She sank into her office chair and covered her face. After a few minutes, she blew out a breath that sent the papers on her desk fluttering and turned to her computer screen.

Hammering at the keyboard, she posted COMING SOON—NEW ACTIVITIES CALENDAR FOR OUR FIFTY-PLUS CROWD! to the website and social media. She checked the new bookings, then placed two calls. One to Buzzbee Electronics & Gaming and another to Billiards & More, both located in Portland. It took some negotiating, but by late afternoon, Lily had everything in place to make a good case for the next changes she wanted to make.

Now all she had to do was convince her *boss*.

Lily propped her feet on her desk and rubbed her eyes. Then she dialed her mom.

She answered on the second ring. "Scarlett!" Her mother immediately groaned about her credit card getting declined and the bank calling about their overdue mortgage.

Lily stopped breathing every time her mom used the name *Scarlett*.

She'd never cared much for her name. How many *Gone with the Wind* jokes could one suffer in a lifetime without committing a violent crime?

She snorted out loud.

Her mom didn't seem to notice and kept rambling.

Lily had left that name and the life it represented behind just three weeks ago, yet it already seemed like another lifetime. With each passing day, the weight of her decision to disassociate from her past closed in on her a little more.

"Scarlett? Are you there?"

Lily snapped out of her trance. "Yes." She sighed. "I'm distracted. Sorry."

"How's the retreat?" her mom asked.

The dull throb behind her eyes, which had started when Ronald Parker tried to take a picture of her and Ben, turned into searing pain. Lily rubbed her temple. "Mom, does the name Ronald Parker ring a bell? Maybe a reporter or someone sniffing around for information on Dad?"

"Can we talk about something more pleasant?" Her mother sniffed.

For the first time, Lily mustered the courage to confront her mom instead of enabling her denial. "No, we can't. We've ignored our situation long enough, and now we're going to deal with it. Answer my question. It's important."

Her mother's sigh whistled through the phone. "No, the name doesn't sound familiar. Why?"

Lily slowly removed her feet from the desk one at a time. "There's a guy . . ." Her conscience wouldn't let her keep up the charade much longer, so she avoided some of the details. "He's visiting the resort where I'm staying. Something's not right about him."

"I told you to let me hire a bodyguard for you," her mother insisted. "Now I'm worried. Maybe you should come home. Or I should come to Vermont."

"We can't afford bodyguards, Mom." Lily put a palm to her forehead. "You can't pay your bills. It's time for you to face it and figure out a plan for your future." Lily still hadn't told her mother about the money she'd left behind. She wouldn't until her mother finally pulled herself together and faced reality. Otherwise, the modest savings she'd hidden away in her old room would be used for booze or a shopping spree to keep up appearances.

A sob echoed through the phone.

"I'm not trying to upset you, but we can't continue to ignore the turn our life has taken."

"Oh, honey," her mom sobbed. "The mortgage isn't just overdue. The Feds are seizing our home."

"I'm sorry, Mom." Lily kept a soothing tone. "But it's just a house. Considering everything Dad did to pay for it, I can't imagine staying there anyway."

"He did those things for me. He knew how much I'd wanted to get out of that tiny Podunk town on the bayou where I'd spent my entire childhood milking cows and slopping pigs when all the other girls were at cheerleading practice." She blew her nose. "I know that's no excuse, but he did it because his business was going under. One of his partners embezzled a lot of money before your father finally caught on. By then it was too late, and he was desperate to keep me from having to go back to the world I'd spent my life trying to escape."

Lily sat up straight. "Dad . . . Dad's business was going under?"

"Yes! Do you think he would've done the awful things he did for no reason?"

That's exactly what Lily thought.

"Mom, when did this happen?"

"You were just starting high school. You were so smart, and he wanted to send you to college the way he'd always promised."

Lily's eyes widened as a glimmer of understanding sprang to life. For the first time, she could see why her father must've buried himself in his work and paid attention to little else. To take care of his family, he'd sacrificed his own happiness, his integrity. His freedom.

It was still no excuse for his crimes, but his situation had obviously been desperate. And he was human.

"How come you and Dad never told me?"

"Your father was ashamed." She sniffed. "And so was I."

Lily sighed. "I had a right to know."

"Maybe so, but your father is a proud man. He wanted to provide for me and for his baby girl." She sniffled. "Your father didn't go to college. He grew up just as poor as I did and worked hard to build his business and a reputation in his industry. He wanted you to have the opportunities he and I never had. Working all the time was the only way he knew to prove himself. His actions may have been misguided, but his heart was in the right place."

"What are you going to do now?" Lily asked.

"I . . ." her mom stammered. "I've joined a twelve-step program."

Lily's eyes welled. "Oh, Mom."

"It was time." Her mother drew in a heavy breath. "There's something else you should know. When my mom left me the old farmhouse, your father and I put it in your name. The Feds can't touch it."

Lily stood. "I own Grandma's old house?"

"It was your father's idea. I actually wanted to sell it, but he knew how much you loved Grandma Barns." She chuckled and sniffed. "You never wanted to leave there when we'd visit, and you wanted us to call you by your middle name because *Lily* was her name too."

Lily rubbed a palm across her forehead. Was it hot? Because a fine sheen of perspiration had broken out over her entire body.

"If it's okay with you, I'll move back there." Her mother let out a bitter laugh. "Ironic that the one place I spent my life avoiding is the only place left for me to go."

"Of course it's okay with me if you live there. As far as I'm concerned, it's more your house than it is mine." Lily's heart thumped against her chest. "Mom, you'll need money to turn on the utilities and buy basic necessities."

"Once I move, I plan to look for a job." Her voice cracked. "I'm not qualified for much, but I'm going to try."

Lily smiled, a tear streaking down her cheek. "I'm proud of you. Until you find a job, I've got something tucked away for you." She told her mother where to find the stash of money that had been Lily's savings from her previous job.

"You know, your father would like to talk to you sometime." Her mother's voice was stoic. "He doesn't call because he's afraid you won't answer."

Lily hesitated, then finally said, "Tell him he can call me . . . but not yet. I need more time." A tremor of guilt slid through her. "And when I get hom—" She could not call New Orleans her home anymore. She felt more at home in Angel Fire Falls than she ever had in her life. They just might not want her to stay when she finally fessed up. "When I can, I'll go visit him."

"He'll love knowing you want to see him and talk to him."

"I love you, Mom." Lily squared her shoulders. "And tell Dad I love him too."

"Scarlett," her mother sniffed. "I'm sorry. I should've told you the truth sooner. You *did* have a right to know."

Lily drew in a sigh so weighty she felt it to her bones. "Better late than never."

They ended the call, and for the first time since the whole mess with her father began, Lily's heart opened to forgiveness. Her father had seemed cold and distant to a young woman who'd only wanted his approval. He'd worked hard for his family, allowing his pride to drive him to do dishonest things when work wasn't enough. And his shame had kept him from repairing the damage he'd done to the people he cared about most.

History didn't have to repeat itself. If Lily could forgive her father, in turn maybe she could find forgiveness.

Telling the Remingtons the truth was a given. Timing was the tricky part.

If she did it now and they asked her to leave, it would hurt the resort. She'd made promises to other businesses on the island in exchange for the materials and supplies the Remington needed. Promises she couldn't keep if she left. The best way to fulfill her obligation to Trace and his family was to finish what she'd started, see them through a successful summer season, make good on the bartering arrangements she'd made with other businesses, and then tell Trace and Lawrence the truth so they could decide her fate.

She just hoped her conscience held out long enough for her to accomplish the things she'd set in motion to ensure the Remington's success.

Chapter Fifteen

Work hard, but play harder.

Once the bustle of the Sunday guest exodus was over, Lily downloaded a measuring app that her dad had often used when visiting a new construction site. She brought her iPad along as she strolled to the game room to investigate her next renovation project. Remodeling the game room would be a huge hook for the younger family demographic they were trying to reach. Lily might not be around long enough to see all the fruits of her labor, but she was going to try like hell to make sure the Remington's makeover put the resort in the best possible position to keep its rooms filled.

She took the covered walkway that connected the game room to the main lodge and stepped up to the glass-paned door. When she peeked in, Trace was alone on the sofa, staring at the ceiling, brooding.

His head leaning back against the sofa, he rolled it to one side when she stepped in.

"Hi." She closed the door.

He didn't say anything. Just gave her a half-hearted smile.

His resigned mood had her worried, and she hurried over to sit next to him. "Did something bad happen?" Her stomach did a flip-flop. Maybe there were more threats from Ben's mom. "I mean, it's none of my business, but do you want to talk?"

He blew out a dull laugh. "It's everything. I don't even know where to begin."

She laid her iPad on the cushion and waited. If he didn't want to go into it with her, she wasn't going to push him.

"This mess with Meg . . . with Ben's mom made me realize he's growing up, and he *is* going to leave some day. How is he going to function on his own?"

Lily covered Trace's hand with hers. "That's the protective father in you talking." She caressed a thumb over the back of his hand. "It's an ugly world out there, and you don't want to see him hurt by it. He's much more capable than you think, and that's because of you."

When Trace gave their hands a blank stare, she pulled hers free.

"Sorry." Just last night, he'd told her they had zero future together, and she'd agreed. So she picked up her iPad and shifted into business mode. "I'm glad I found you here." Lily crossed her legs, one foot bobbing. "We're trying to attract families to the resort, right? Parents want both outdoor and indoor activities to keep their kids busy." Her foot bobbing sped. "I think renovations to this room are necessary."

"We don't have the budget for new equipment." Trace went back to staring at the ceiling like the conversation was over.

Not even close.

"I've got everything worked out so that it won't cost anything." She gave him a dazzling smile. "I've struck a bargain with an electronics store in Portland. They're willing to barter the equipment we need in exchange for free weekend packages at the resort. We also have to give the electronics store credit on our website along with their links."

He shook his head. "I don't know. Ben's extremely attached to this room."

Lily plowed on. "I also have a billiards store lined up to re-cover the pool table. Same bartering arrangement. We just have to get it to the mainland."

"Well, that's a definite *no*." His mood wasn't lightened one bit by her kick-ass business negotiations. "Ben can't go a day without pool. It's how he unwinds."

Lily let a self-assured smile form on her lips. "I arranged for them to give us a loaner while they're working on ours."

"You have a solution for every problem, don't you?" His tone grew flatter.

His foul mood had to go. "That's what you pay me for." She rubbed her nails against her shirt and blew on them.

Funny thing was, she wasn't playing the I-care-about-your-son card just to get Trace to agree to her plan. She truly did think the renovations would make Ben happy, and if the resort benefited from it, then even better.

She hopped off the arm of the sofa and went to the dartboard. "Okay, Mr. Grinch. It won't be Christmas for several more months. Why don't we settle it with a game of darts?" She plucked the darts off the board one by one. "If I win, we remodel the game room, and Ben can help pick out the new equipment if he wants." She held out a fistful of darts to Trace. "If you win, you make the call, and I won't mention it again." She shrugged playfully. "Even if you make the wrong decision."

Trace stared at her outstretched hand before slowly rising from the sofa. "You're on." He walked over, took the darts, then parked one butt cheek on the edge of the pool table. "Too bad for you, I'm pretty good at darts."

She took a dart in her left hand. She might work hard, but she played harder. "Best round wins?"

With an air of confidence that said he knew he'd win, he said, "Be my guest."

Lily closed one eye to aim and let the dart fly. It hit the outer ring of the board. She made a point to frown as hard as she could at her poor performance. When the next shot wasn't much better, she harrumphed. Loudly.

Trace just tapped the darts against his muscled thigh and smiled like he'd already won.

Her third dart hit a wire and bounced off. She gave Trace a pouty look. "Your turn."

He stepped up, aimed, and thwack, thwack, thwack, his three darts landed pretty close to the bull's-eye.

He gathered his darts and slid onto the edge of the pool table, bracing one hand against his thigh.

"Wow," Lily said, oh-so innocently. "You're good."

He smirked.

So she sashayed over, took aim, then frowned as she stared at the dart in her hand. Her *left* hand. She slid a sly smile in his direction. "Did I mention the game room my father added on to our house when I was a kid? It was a birthday present." A pretty extravagant gift, but it had been her haven as an only child. Kind of like Ben.

His smirk faded. "No, I don't recall your mentioning it."

"Oh, and I also forgot to mention . . ." She switched the dart from her left hand to her right. "I'm not left-handed. My bad."

Trace's eyes rounded.

Thwack, thwack, thwack. All three of her darts hit the red circle in the center of the board.

"You little"—as if he couldn't stop himself, he tossed his darts on the pool table and was on her before she could protest—"cheater." He pulled her flush against his rock-hard body.

She whispered out something inaudible, and good Lord, she hoped she hadn't just begged him to kiss her, because that's what both her mind and her body wanted. "I didn't cheat." Her voice was a throaty whisper. "I just didn't tell the whole truth."

And that statement made her gasp because half truths seemed to be her new modus operandi.

Before she could pull out of his embrace, his nose brushed hers. He anchored her against him with one hand at the small of her back, while his other fingers molded to her neck and his thumb caressed her cheek. "Is there anything else I need to know about you, Lily? Because I can't resist the pull you have on me. God help me, I've tried, but whatever this thing is between us"—he grazed his lips across hers, and they both drew in a lusty breath—"it's stronger than my willpower."

There were so many things she wanted him to know . . . but not yet. Not until she was done transforming the Remington so it could function without her should they cut her loose.

She tilted her face up to look him in the eye. What she saw there stole her breath. The unchecked emotion. The raw attraction. The pure honesty.

It split her heart in two, and she nodded. "There's lots you need to kn—"

He swallowed her words with a blazing-hot kiss.

It was crazy. Or stupid. Or both.

He wanted her. Wanted her so badly it hurt.

"Trace," Lily whispered, gliding her palms up his chest. "I work for you."

Her touch turned his insides to fire. Made him crazy with need.

"This isn't a good idea," she finished.

"I know." He backed her to the door and fumbled with the shade and lock. Then dipped a hand to her beautifully rounded ass and pulled her into his erection, which had his pants feeling two sizes too small. "But this says otherwise."

A gasp slipped from her lush lips as his hips pressed into her. Her fingernails curled into his shoulders. "God, I've wanted you to do that since we were at the Fallen Angel."

His fingers found the hem of her shirt, and he slipped one palm up her bare back. "Tell me to stop, and I will. But first I want you to trust me when I say I'm not your old boss. He was an idiot for letting you go and an ass for taking advantage of his position of power over you." When Trace outlined each of her ribs with a fingertip, her skin pebbled, and she shivered against him. With his other hand, he traced her jawline with a thumb. "Do you want me to stop, Lily? Just one word from you, and I'll walk away."

Her breaths grew heavy, and she shook her head. The need and want he saw in her eyes was his undoing.

Relief threaded through him when she didn't ask him to stop, because he couldn't go another minute without tasting her. Touching her. His face a breath from hers, their eyes hooked into each other's as he picked her up and carried her to the sofa with her legs firmly surrounding his waist.

She broke the kiss just long enough to ask, "What if someone tries to come in?" She devoured his mouth with another kiss, then leaned back to look at him with wide eyes. "What if Ben shows up?"

"He's in town with my brothers." Trace dipped his head to suckle the soft skin of her neck. "We've got the place to ourselves." He ran his tongue along her collarbone, dipping into the crevice just above it.

Her petite, lush body shuddered from top to bottom.

"You may be onto something with remodeling the game room." He suckled the soft skin behind her ear. "We're definitely gonna need a new sofa after we're done here today." He smiled against the curve of her neck.

"That's. Really. Naughty," she panted out.

"Not nearly as naughty as we're about to get." He set her on her feet, slid his hand around her neck, and threaded all five fingers into her hair to wind it around his hand. Gently, he pulled back just enough so her creamy neck was fully exposed, calling him, taunting him. Her soft black shirt, which showed off her toned shoulders, had driven him wild since the second he saw her in the kitchen that morning.

He devoured her long, slender neck with his mouth and tongue, blazing a fiery trail down her bare shoulder, which had been calling his name, begging him to peel the rest of her clothes off one stitch at a time. He sucked and licked and laved until she transformed into a whimpering puddle of need.

When she was limp in his arms, he took an earlobe between his teeth and nipped. Then he took her mouth in a scorching kiss that had her soft, luscious body squirming against his.

Her hands were curious to explore him. She fumbled with the bottom of his shirt until her palms connected with his skin. His abs tightened against her frantic touch, which left a heated trail as she traversed every dip, every contour, every muscle that grew more taut with each pass of her fingers.

"Take it off." Lily pulled at his shirt, her voice frustrated with desire. "I want to see you."

He reached behind his head and one-handed the collar of his polo. It sailed across the room.

Her eyes darkened with desire as they coasted over his torso, and Trace couldn't help but feel a twinge of pride well up at her look of hunger.

"Your turn," he said.

She didn't hesitate and grabbed at the hem of her shirt.

He pushed her hands aside. "Let me." He should take it slow. Savor the moment he'd fantasized about for weeks. But hell no. He wanted her right then, and her needy hands and wandering eyes said she wanted the same. He pulled her shirt up, revealing delicious, creamy skin. Then he tugged it over her head and sent it flying in the same direction as his.

He took two steps back to look at her. "Fuck me, but you're gorgeous," he said with a groan. His gaze cruised over her flat belly, the rise and fall of her panting chest, and snagged on her lacy strapless bra.

When he looked up, he caught her mischievous grin.

"You play dirty." His voice was hoarse with desire.

She shrugged. "Maybe, but something tells me you won't mind." Her fingers went to the button of the black capris that were molded to her slender thighs and perfect hips. With a flick of two fingers, the button came undone.

His mouth turned to gravel when she kicked off her sandals, hooked both thumbs in her waistband, and lowered them to the ground with a swoosh. She stepped out of the pants.

Lucky bastard that he was, the triangle of lace covering her front was the size of a Doritos chip—his new favorite snack.

With one long stride, he had her back in his arms, sliding both hands around to cup her bottom. And holy shit, his palms filled with soft bare flesh because the panties were a thong. A jolt of need shot through him, and he took her mouth in a ravenous kiss, gently lowering her onto the sofa until she was fully stretched along its length.

She folded her hands behind her head and smiled, like she wanted to enjoy the show. "I never thought I'd see you naked."

His prick strained against his jeans at the way her wandering gaze took him in. No shame. No reservations. She was a woman who knew what she wanted and went after it, and he loved that about her. It showed in the way she tackled every project at the resort.

And it definitely showed in the way her eyes flickered with passion and need when he unzipped his jeans and slid them off. The way the tip of her pink tongue darted out to trace her bottom lip when he tugged off his boxer briefs. The way she opened for him when he lowered himself to her and covered her beautiful body with his.

And that accidental erotic text he'd sent her when she first arrived on the island? He kissed his way down her flat stomach, moved her thong aside, and made good on his promise.

Chapter Sixteen

Lily's Life Lesson #16
Scratch lesson #5, because sexting *definitely* isn't better
than the real thing.

Lily could no more stop herself from wrapping around Trace any more than she could stop the sun from setting in the west. Yes, he was her boss. Yes, she'd played with fire in the past and gotten burned.

Yes, she was going to roll the dice again with Trace because he was a different kind of man, and she trusted him.

His smoldering kisses left a burning trail over her rib cage, then her stomach. Everywhere his lips touched, her muscles involuntarily tensed into balls of fire that singed every nerve ending she possessed, and she moaned.

"That's what I want to hear." He circled her belly button with the tip of his tongue.

She fisted his hair in one hand. "You do things to my body I didn't think possible."

He chuckled against her belly, his breath making her skin pebble. Then he slid both hands under her ass and flexed his fingers into her flesh.

Need crashed through her, and she pulled at his shoulder. "Trace." Her tone was practically begging him. "I want you. Now."

"Babe, this is one thing we're doing my way." His breathy whisper against the dark triangle where her thighs met caused a shudder to rush from the top of her head to the tips of her curling toes. "Promise I'll get the job done to your satisfaction." There was a smile in his words.

He settled between her thighs and placed a hot openmouthed kiss on the inside of one leg, then the other. And he did the same at her center.

She cried out as his heated breath and his wonderful tongue washed over the thin fabric of her panties, creating just enough friction to drive her insane. She writhed under him, her nails digging into his shoulders.

True to his naughty text, he moved the small strip of lace aside, and his mouth closed over her center.

Nothing prepared her for the electrifying shock of pure bliss that scorched across every cell in her body. *"Trace!"* she screamed.

He chuckled against her throbbing nub. "The walls aren't sound-proof, babe."

"I don't *care*." And at that moment she didn't. The only thing she cared about was his mouth and his tongue and his fingers fulfilling the long-overdue promise of his erotic text. She hooked her legs around his shoulders. "Don't stop."

He didn't speak. Didn't have to. Their bodies communicated in a way that didn't require words. The suckling movement of his mouth and the stroking of his tongue were rhythmic and controlled, coaxing her closer to the edge. But the punishing way his hands gripped her thighs said his self-restraint was hanging on by a thread. He was obviously gritting it out to satisfy her with the loveliest swipes of his tongue and the warmth of his mouth.

Lily clutched at the edge of the sofa cushion to hold on to her sanity as long as she could. She'd never been wanted like this. Never been worshipped like this. And it made her body come alive like never before.

The incredible sensation became almost painful, and just when she thought she couldn't stand it another minute, he eased two fingers inside, reaching the deepest, most intimate part of her.

She bit down on her lip to stop another shout of pure unchecked pleasure.

Until he curled those talented fingers and hit just the right spot.

She cried out something completely indiscernible as the most powerful climax she'd ever experienced barreled through her. She thrashed under him at the wonderful torment, and his hold on her hips tightened to keep her in place. He gave his fingers another twitch-and-curl combo, wringing every ounce of orgasm from her throbbing core.

He laid soft, sweet kisses across her abdomen as her breathing slowed. It was intimate and sexy and all for her. He rose to his knees and tugged off her panties. "Don't move." He wrapped a hand around her foot and pulled it to his mouth to place a tender kiss on the inside of her ankle.

"I'm not going anywhere." She watched the flex and flow of his toned body as he bent to find his pants, pulled a foil square out of his wallet, and covered himself. With slow, stealthy movements, he walked back to her, letting her enjoy the view. His impressive erection made the tide of sexual heat rush through her again, even before the first orgasm had completely receded.

Her body pulsed and hummed and cried for him as he covered her with more than six feet of pure male hardness. He delivered a punishing kiss, then hooked one arm behind her knee. He inched his steel shaft into her center, hesitating long enough to let her adjust to his thickness.

His gaze locked onto hers as he pressed farther in.

Her lips parted in a hushed plea for more, and she arched up to meet him.

He got her message loud and clear and sank into her to his root with one long, scorching thrust.

She moaned.

He groaned.

And he rested his forehead against hers, their breaths mingling and mixing from the excruciating pleasure where their bodies joined.

"Christ, you're so tight," he breathed out. "Our fit is so perfect."

Like they were made for each other. She nodded. "Better than I thought possible."

He dipped his head and pulled her bottom lip between his teeth to nibble. With a shift of his hips, he withdrew and plunged into her again. They found that perfect rhythm, and he reached deeper inside her with each stroke.

Every part of Lily's body tightened. Her nipples, her throat. When her muscles clenched and clamped around his shaft, his eyes closed, and he stopped breathing. "Jesus, that's so good."

"Pure perfection." She lifted her hips to match his movements.

With his arm still hooked behind her knee, he lifted her leg higher. Spread her wider. His strokes quickened, deepened, until Lily was on the edge and ready to jump into the abyss. He drove into her over and over, then without warning, he rotated his hips in the opposite direction, and—bingo.

She fell, a white-hot orgasm spiraling through her so powerfully that her world went hazy for a few seconds. When she opened her eyes, he stared down at her with a self-satisfied smile. Her muscles convulsed around his stiff cock, but he still hadn't come yet. Obviously, he enjoyed the fact that he'd just rocked her world. Her heart filled because she'd never had anyone care about her pleasure so much. So openly.

And she wanted to return it.

When she flattened her palms against his chest and pushed, his eyes widened.

"Sit up." She guided him into a sitting position. "Let me do the rest." She straddled him.

When he realized what she was doing, a wicked gleam showed in his eyes. "You're so bossy," he teased and sank his teeth into her earlobe.

She shivered. "You pretend not to like it, but you do."

He chuckled and feathered kisses across her jaw. "I just let you think you're in charge." He molded both hands around her waist and guided her onto his throbbing hard-on, filling her completely.

Her head fell back, and she moaned again.

"You're so damn beautiful like this, Lily." He rested his head on the back of the sofa. "I could watch you like this every day." His jaw twitched, and his eyes widened with realization. "Or every night in my bed."

A chill skated over her. She'd love to explore that possibility. See where their relationship might go. But when she told Trace the whole truth, any hope they had of a future together might be destroyed just as they were getting started.

She lifted to his tip and sank down on him again.

"Damn, woman," he said in a gritty voice.

The here and the now was her focus until Trace was just as sexually satisfied as she was. "Let's concentrate on the present." She lifted again, her strokes picking up speed. Their thrusts came faster, harder. She circled her hips and adjusted her angle. Another storm started to brew at her core, and she rode him hard . . . until she tightened and twitched around him, another orgasm overtaking her.

Her shout of approval pulled him over the edge with her, and his generous flesh pulsed inside her. She wrapped both arms around his head and buried her face in his neck. Their hearts beat in a steady cadence where their chests molded together.

With a finger and thumb, she toyed with his hair, enjoying the feel of his body against hers, both of them dewy and slick.

When she'd moved to the island, she'd been ready to give up on men altogether. Ready to settle for a little harmless flirtation via text, because in her experience, sexting had been better than the real thing.

Lucky for her, she was wrong.

The three orgasms Trace had just given her were incredible, and she doubted she'd ever experience anything so powerful again.

As she caressed his ear with the tip of her nose, he went hard inside of her again.

Yep, she hadn't just been wrong. She'd been *dead* wrong. Because he reached for his wallet again, and they made the most of the old felt on the pool table.

Since it was getting re-covered and all.

Heart thundering, she clamped her legs to his firm, fine ass. Every inch of him was hard, muscular male. Her body hummed with so much sexual energy that within minutes they were pulled into the vortex of another powerful orgasm.

She cried out, but he swallowed it with the most incredible mind-melting kiss.

As their breathing slowed, her palms slid up his back, the muscles dancing under her fingertips. She traced the contours, the hard angles and planes of his firm yet smooth skin.

He suckled her nipple, circling it, teasing it with his tongue, and she buried her hands in his hair. Dipping his head, he gently bit at the underside of her breast, then placed a tender kiss in the same spot. Then he did the same to the other breast. She arched, filling his mouth as much as she could with the trembling flesh of her breast. And he obliged with long, thorough flicks of his tongue until she moaned.

Lily's heart squeezed, and she pulled his mouth to hers. After a long, languid kiss, she said, "Hold me. Just hold me." It had been a long time since she'd felt so safe, so secure. She wanted to enjoy the moment, because it likely wouldn't last forever.

Chapter Seventeen

The weather was getting warmer and the ducks were getting louder, so Trace and Ben got dressed earlier than usual to stop at Lily's every morning and move the growing ducks to their outside pen. It was Trace's day to take the kids to school, so he dropped them off, then raced home, practically fishtailing into the resort so he could get to Lily's.

Since he and Lily had taken their relationship to the next level a little over a week ago, it had become their routine to steal whatever time alone they could. Going several rounds in the game room had been just the beginning, and they continued their inventive streak every morning after Ben was at school. Not surprisingly, she tackled sex with the same incredible creative mind as she did her job.

Fine by him.

The dining room table, the kitchen counter, against the wall, in the shower, or in bed, it was all good. The best, actually. She was the bright spot in his life, even with everything else turning to shit.

Trace turned onto the lane that led to the cottages.

Megan still hadn't shown up on the island, and if he couldn't get her to drop the custody suit, he'd have to hire an attorney. He'd spare no expense when it came to protecting his son, so a lawyer would cost a hell of a lot of money. Money he'd intended to use for a cargo plane.

He parked in front of Lily's cottage and cantered up the steps, whistling. He stopped with his fist raised to knock on the door.

The bounce in his step and the glee-club tune flowing through his puckered lips was proof that Lily made him happy. Even with so much to worry about, he felt as though he could face anything because of her.

He knocked.

Her voice was distant as she hollered "Come in" from somewhere deep inside the cottage.

He cracked the door. "Lily?"

"In here," she said from the bathroom.

Awesome. Maybe she was just getting out of the shower and he could towel off her sexy wet body.

As he headed to the bathroom, her phone dinged from the kitchen counter. He stopped and picked it up. Lily seemed to manage the entire resort from her phone and iPad, so it might be important. He glanced at the screen as he turned into the hallway, and it made him stumble.

With a hand, he reached out and steadied himself against the wall. And reread the text from Mom.

> I've been trying to reach you.
> Why aren't you returning my
> calls?

A tiny sliver of guilt pricked at his heart for invading Lily's privacy. A big bolt of worry caused his heart to stutter because the text made something prickle at the back of his skull. Lily never talked about her parents. He'd asked her about them once, thinking they weren't living because she'd used the past tense to refer to them.

"Trace?" she said from the bathroom.

He swallowed down the cotton in his mouth. "Yeah. Are you decent?" Stupid question, because he and Lily hadn't been *decent* when they were alone together for more than a week.

Lily's upper body appeared through a crack in the bathroom door. "You've seen me without a stich on." Her smile was mischievous. "Several times. Up close." She was wrapped in a towel, secured by a corner tucked between her mouthwatering breasts. Tastefully applied makeup accentuated the perfect bone structure of her beautiful face. Upswept hair drew his attention to her slender shoulders and neck.

He followed her into the bathroom, where she swiped on mascara. He placed a hand on her hip. "Yes, I've seen every inch of you, and I gotta say . . . you've got some prime real estate under that towel."

She laughed and kept working the brush across her lashes.

He traced a finger up her arm all the way to her neck, staring over her shoulder into the mirror. "Your phone dinged." He slid Lily's phone onto the counter. "I thought it might be important."

She stopped brushing the wand over her lashes. "Thanks," she said slowly. "I'll check it in a sec. I'm in a hurry." She pumped the tube of mascara and went to work on the other eye, stealing glances at him in the mirror.

He eased closer until his chest molded to her back. With a flattened palm against the side of her thigh, he smoothed it upward until his hand disappeared under the towel.

Her skin pebbled. "I've got work to do in my office before I ride into town with Charley."

"The only word I heard was *ride*." He made sure his breath was at her ear.

She shivered. "We're finalizing the menu and swinging by the school during the kids' lunch break. Ben's teacher agreed to brainstorm with me on our children's summer program."

He nuzzled the nape of her neck, and another shiver raced over her.

"I thought we could spend time together before going to work. Maybe talk." With the cuff of Lily's ear between his teeth, he glanced into the mirror to find one of her silky brows arched high.

"Talk?" She leaned back against him, and his hard-on pressed into her lush ass. She hissed in a breath.

"Yes, talk." His fingers moved around to her front, and he stroked the soft skin just below her belly button. "And other stuff." But talking was definitely on his agenda. They got along great at work now that he trusted her to make sound decisions for the resort. They got along beautifully when Ben was around because she was better with him than anyone he knew besides his immediate family. They got along spectacularly when they were bare-assed naked.

But he still didn't know much about Lily, and she never talked about her life before moving to the island.

He figured her past must be painful.

He understood painful because of the tragic way his mother had passed. Hell, it'd been almost twenty years, and the Remingtons rarely spoke of it.

So maybe it was time he and Lily both opened up about the unpleasantness of their pasts. As great as the sex was between them, he wanted more than just a superficial relationship. Been there, done that, and no thank you. If he and Lily were in, then he wanted them to be *all* in. The great sex was a bonus.

He traced a finger from her belly button down to the soft center he was looking for.

Correction. Their incredible sex wasn't just a bonus. It was like they'd hit the Powerball.

Her knee angled to the side to give him access, and one of her hands found its way up his neck and into his hair. "'Bout what?" Her voice went low and raspy.

"About you."

She tensed, and her fingers stopped their playful romp through his hair. "I'm pretty boring and ordinary, really. Are you going to hold that against me?"

He nipped her earlobe. "You're a lot of things, Lily Barns, but boring and ordinary aren't on the list," he breathed against her ear. "The only thing I plan to hold against you is this." He pressed his hard-on against her firm ass, and she moaned.

When she opened her eyes again, she stared back at him in the mirror, worrying her bottom lip. The muscles in her slender neck moved as she swallowed, put the mascara down, and slowly turned in his arms so they were face-to-face.

"We do need to talk." She chewed her lip and stared at a button on his shirt. "Since I'm in a hurry to get to my office, can we talk tonight? Alone?"

Trace could swear her eyes grew moist.

"Hey." He molded a palm to her cheek and rubbed the soft skin under her bottom lashes. "Whatever it is, it'll be fine."

"I—" Her voice cracked, and she cleared her throat. "See, I work for this guy who is very special."

Unable to resist her lush mouth, he bent and nipped at the corner. "And really great in bed?"

She angled her head to the side. "He's okay."

Trace sank his teeth into the notch where her neck met her shoulder.

"Okay, I see stars when we're in bed," she said.

He released her flesh.

She fiddled with the same button on his shirt she'd been staring at. "He's a great guy and a great boss, and I don't want to disappoint him."

"I have it on good authority your boss will be much more disappointed if you leave for the office now." He buried his face in the hair just above her ear and breathed in the faint scent of flowery shampoo. "He might even fire you."

She stiffened into a plank of wood. He leaned back, and for a second something that looked like fear flashed in her eyes.

"Hey." He put a finger under her chin and turned her gaze to meet his. "Poor choice of words. I'm sorry." He pulled her into his arms, and her towel came loose, slipping to the floor.

"Fuck." He devoured her mouth in a hungry kiss.

"Yes, let's." Her voice was breathy with need, and she cupped his throbbing crotch.

He growled. "I thought you were in a hurry?"

"I guess I can spare a few minutes for the boss." Her eyes held a sultry glint that said he was about to get lucky.

God, he loved that glint.

She opened a drawer and pulled out a purple box that said SECOND SKIN in bold white letters. "They warm to the touch."

"I love that gifted mind of yours, always thinking ahead." He carried her to the bedroom and gave her a playful toss onto the bed.

She squealed, all fear and moisture gone from her eyes. He liked this look on her much better.

His prick strained against the rough fabric of his jeans. "I can't start my day anymore until I hear you moan."

"Lose the clothes and you will." She sat up and reached for his zipper.

When she slipped her hand inside to grasp his length, he groaned.

"Who's moaning now?" She ran her hand along his length again, and he had to agree that his moans were just as intense as hers.

Suddenly he felt very overdressed and shucked his clothes like it was a race. When he was naked, he climbed up her lush body and braced his hands on either side of her head.

"Just be still for a sec and let me enjoy the view." She ran both dainty hands up his flexed arms, over his shoulders, and down his chest, lifting to place a kiss in the valley between his pecs. She explored him with her hands, softly running a fingernail along the muscles of his abs.

Her lips and her fingertips were velvety soft against his taut skin, skin that hummed with desire.

He reached for a condom.

"Uh-uh." She encircled his wrist with her slender fingers. And before he knew it, she flipped him onto his back and straddled him.

Nice.

"Remember your naughty text?" Wickedness gleamed in her eyes.

"Every dirty word." He cupped both of her breasts in the palms of his hands.

"Well, you've fulfilled your promise." Her fiery gaze dropped to his mouth like she was remembering how he'd pleasured her with it. Several times. She bent, kissing a smoldering trail down his neck to his chest. Then lower. "I want to return the favor," she whispered against his stomach, then moved farther down to close those perfect pouty lips around his throbbing flesh.

He forgot his fucking name.

Her clever hands moved over his skin, and that mouth . . . *Christ.* That mouth was a gift from heaven.

He buried both sets of fingers in her silky hair.

His entire body tightened, and he grasped her shoulders, drawing her up to roll her onto her back. He had himself covered before she could protest, not that she would, and filled her in one swift stroke.

Her body arched toward him. *"Trace!"*

It was the most beautiful sound he could remember.

Another deep stroke and her hot flesh undulated around his prick. The first glimmer of an orgasm sprouted deep inside him.

They rode the wave of ecstasy fast and hard until they were both spent and well satisfied.

By the time Charley's horn beeped in front of the cottage, the workday had been long since underway. And their talk that had been interrupted by the crazy undeniable attraction between them had long since been forgotten. But neither one of them was going anywhere, and when she was ready to open up, he wanted to know everything.

Maybe it was the warm, sunny weather so unusual in the Pacific Northwest. Maybe it was the incredible sex. Maybe it was the way Trace, Lily, and Ben had settled into a routine that was so comfortable and family-ish. Whatever the case, Trace found himself whistling again as he left Lily's cottage and followed the path to the main lodge in search of his dad.

It was time to solicit some fatherly advice about several things.

On his way, he dialed Megan's number. He'd tried to call several times since inviting her to the island, but she'd ignored every one of them. Today was no different, and it went straight to voice mail.

As Trace circled around the side of the resort, he lifted a hand to greet Spence, who was replacing rotted two-by-fours over the covered activities area. Trace stopped to take in the transformation. New sparkling-white sand filled the volleyball pit, and a new net was strung across its width. Fresh paint gave the Adirondack chairs around the fire pit an inviting look, and Spence had sawed logs into small stumps and varnished them so they served as stools.

The game room renovation was under way too. Ben and Lily had scoured furniture and electronics catalogues every night over dinner, Ben getting more excited with each passing day.

All Lily's doing. If she could pour so much heart into his family's business . . . into his *family*, then Megan could damn well take a second to talk about their son's future.

Sick and damned tired of jacking around, he tapped Megan's number again. When her phone went to voice mail, he sharpened the edge to his tone and left a clear message.

"Megan, I've tried to be reasonable, but since you won't discuss this like an adult, you're leaving me no choice. Ben doesn't deserve to be dragged through a nasty court battle, but if you want a fight, you've got one." He hesitated, then decided to pull off the gloves. "If you think I'm going to let you take our son away and use him as a publicity stunt, you've miscalculated. I'll make sure every detail of your absence from Ben's life goes public. Every doctor's appointment you've missed, every school function, every birthday party." He pinched the bridge of his nose because of what he was about to say. It had caused Ben so much pain that Trace didn't want him to have to relive it. "Every time Ben cried himself to sleep because you didn't show up after promising him you would. I've swept things under the rug for Ben's sake, but the damn rug is level with the ceiling by now. The choice is yours, Megan. Choose wisely."

He hung up and pushed through the front doors of the main lodge.

Trace made his way to the family den, which had become his father's workspace the past few years. He and Elliott sat at the round table with Elliott's laptop open and a stack of bills next to it.

Elliott greeted Trace with the usual. "Hey, asshat." He kept pecking at the keyboard.

Trace flicked an imaginary speck of dirt from his cheek with a middle finger. "Right back at ya, little brother. What're you guys doing?"

His dad drew in a frustrated breath. "Elliott and Lily insist it's time to automate. I don't see why. Writing checks the good old-fashioned way works just fine."

Elliott rolled his eyes. "It's not just about paying bills, Dad. I need to be able to run financial reports, project our annual budget, and a lot of other number crunching without having to calculate everything by hand." Elliott's financial wizardry kicked in, and his body seemed to inflate as he leaned forward and launched into a numbers spiel that had his dad's eyes glazing over. "I can even run incremental profit-and-loss projections to correlate with anticipated expenses of new programs or equip—"

His dad held up a hand. "Don't bother. I'm too old to learn spreadsheets."

Elliott tapped the stack of bills. "We've gone through our monthly expenses, and some of these prices from our regular vendors seem exorbitant." His voice turned to that shrewd all-business tone he only used from his high-rise corner office overlooking San Francisco Bay. Now that he was back on the island, it rarely came out unless he was talking numbers for the resort. "I'll start checking around." And if Trace knew his little brother, that translated to "I'll cut our overhead by a large percentage."

Elliott flipped the screen of his laptop down and gathered up the bills. He glanced at Trace. "With you as our new delivery source, we'll have more flexibility to haggle with vendors." The vendors didn't stand a chance with Elliott taking over the resort's financial management. He looked at his dad. "I'll keep you posted."

His dad shook his head. "You can keep me in the loop, but I want you three boys to keep each other posted. I'm planning to ease out of the management responsibilities now that the resort is on the rise again."

Elliott's expression blanked. "You're—"

"Retiring?" Trace finished.

His dad pushed back from the table. "It's time. This place didn't deteriorate for no reason."

Trace leaned against the back of the sofa. "Still, Dad. This place is *yours*."

"That's where you're wrong, son. The resort belongs to you three now. I'm having the paperwork drawn up." Lawrence scratched his head. "I planned to have this conversation with all three of you at once, but I'll bring Spence up to speed later." He chuckled. "Lily's got him working nonstop with repairs and renovations. The only time I've seen him lately, he's either on a ladder or has a power tool in his hand." His dad sobered. "Which is why it's time for me to step aside. The resort will benefit if I pass the reins to you kids, especially with the dynamite hospitality manager I hired." He gave Trace an I-told-you-so look. "You're welcome, by the way."

Lily did approach everything with a take-no-prisoners attitude. And by everything, Trace really meant *everything*. He couldn't stop a smile.

"But what'll you do?" Elliott rubbed the back of his neck. "Where will you go? Giving us ownership is kind of extreme."

"I'm staying right here, dummy," his dad teased. "I'll be around if you need anything, but I plan to spend a lot of time with my grandson and grandniece." He gave Trace a shrug. "Now that Charley's taking over the restaurant and you're starting a delivery service, you both could use a hand with the kids."

Trace wasn't ready for his brothers to know his delivery service might already be in jeopardy because of Megan. He rubbed the back of his neck and gave his dad a look that said, "Yeah, we need to talk in private."

His dad studied Trace for a moment, then turned his attention to Elliott. "With any luck, I'll have more grandkids on the way eventually."

"Spence needs my help." Elliott practically burned a path in the floor on his way out the door.

His dad nodded. "Knew that would get rid of him. What's on your mind?"

Trace chuckled. "If I've got to hire an attorney, it might mess with my plans to buy a plane."

"So lease one," his dad said. "We can wait to buy one later when the custody thing is over. Ben comes first, no matter what."

And that's why Trace loved and admired his dad. He'd always been a great family man, always putting his sons first. Which was why the resort had declined. Because of their mother's tragic accident right there on resort property and the pain it caused all of them, his dad had pushed them out of the nest after high school. Encouraged them to go out into the world and find themselves. Once they were gone, his dad couldn't bring the resort back to its former glory on his own, but no way would he have asked his sons to come home and help. Returning to the island was something his father wanted them to decide to do on their own, not out of a sense of obligation.

Trace gave his dad a nod. "You're pretty smart for an old guy, you know that?"

"Yeah, I do know it," his dad said. "What else is bothering you?"

"It's that obvious?" Trace took a seat across the table.

"A father's instinct." His dad shrugged. "Plus, your shirt's inside out."

Trace looked down at his plaid shirt. *Shit.* No wonder buttoning it had been so difficult after his morning romp with Lily.

"I assume that has something to do with the budding romance between you and Lily?" His dad's expression grew dark with concern.

Trace was so busted. "Dad . . ." Trace hesitated, not sure where to begin. "Do you think getting romantically involved could hurt my case if Megan really follows through with this?"

His dad drew in a deep breath. "I never went through a divorce or a custody battle, so I don't know for sure. Seems to me that a stable relationship with a woman as solid as Lily would help your case, though."

"Do you think it's unprofessional to get involved with an employee?" Trace knew it was, but he couldn't stop the way he felt about Lily any more than he could stop the storms that rolled over the island.

"Yes." His father didn't mince words. "It's unprofessional and puts everyone in an awkward situation. Me, you, Lily, your brothers, and the resort." He stared across the room at a watercolor painting of the resort that hung over one of the sofas.

One of Trace's earliest memories was of his mother hiring an artist to paint the resort and the island landscapes so that she could hang the canvases around the Remington.

"It's also how I met your mother." A wistful smile curled his dad's lips. "You know the story."

Trace knew it well. She didn't have a formal culinary education, so the only cooking jobs she could land in a big city were line-cook positions. So she applied for the chef's position at the Remington when Dad first opened the resort. She was a city mouse who didn't slide right into small-town life, but she fell madly in love with a country mouse named Lawrence Remington and stayed on the island for good.

"I took a chance on Lily because she reminded me so much of your mom. Brave, determined, ready to take on the world." His dad scratched his chin. "I figured a city girl looking for a change of pace had worked out so well the first time, why not give it another try." He leaned forward. "I'm not sure that helps, but it's the truth."

"Thanks, Dad. It does help."

Lily's body language, the fact that she only opened up a little at a time, leaving him to slowly peel back layers one by one . . . it led Trace to believe that she didn't trust easily. That she'd been hurt badly.

He wanted her to trust him. He wanted her to believe that he would never take advantage of her just because she was his employee. And more than anything, he wanted to show her that he'd never let her down.

Chapter Eighteen

Late Friday morning, Lily hustled to set up tables and chairs under the covered activities area before Ben's class arrived for a field trip. That was how Lily had enticed Ben's teacher not only to help develop the summer children's program but also to be in charge of it as a summer employee at the resort.

Lily was late getting everything ready. Starting her workday late was becoming a habit because of the covert bedroom games she and Trace played every morning after Ben left for school.

She stilled, holding a folding chair in her hands, and stared into the overcast sky. Getting involved with her employer was a big risk. Risks of that nature hadn't worked out so well for her in the past. But Trace was genuine. His devotion to his son and his family was proof that he had integrity and cared about others more than himself. It was still a risk, but maybe this time she'd chosen wisely.

And he definitely made her moan louder than her masseuse, so technically, she was only breaking half of life lesson number one—*never date a man who can't make you moan louder than your masseuse can.*

Unfortunately, this time Lily was the one with weak spots in her integrity. Both times her conscience had prodded her to tell Trace the whole truth, they'd been interrupted. Her mom's impeccable timing had stopped her on the front porch of her cottage the night they'd almost had storage-room sex. Trace's joke about firing her when she was wearing nothing but a towel had thrown up the second roadblock.

Just in case he did hold the truth against her, she didn't want to leave her job until her obligations to the resort, to the Remingtons, and to the businesses she'd made bartering agreements with were fulfilled. If she didn't stay around long enough to lend those businesses her expertise, they might pull the plug on their agreement with the Remington.

So she'd slipped in little nuggets about her pre–Angel Fire Falls life when she and Trace spent time together, but she'd shared little else.

To make matters worse, her work ethic was slipping. She'd never been late to work a day in her life. This morning's massage with heated oil and then their subsequent long, hot shower for two to wash it off had been too tempting. Her fingertips were still wrinkled from the amount of time they'd spent under the steamy water.

Meow.

The folding chair slipped through her fingers and clattered against the concrete floor. The loud sound jarred her back to the present, and she hurried to finish setting up.

"Need help, Lily?"

She whirled to find Elliott walking toward her. She'd been so intent on her mission and her waning job performance—and the massage and the shower for two—that she hadn't heard him approach.

She took several deep breaths to calm her racing heart. "Yes. *Please* help me." She pointed to several more tables that were stacked to the side. "Line those up in rows and put six chairs around each. We're giving the children's summer program a trial run this morning on Ben's class. I thought this would be a good place to serve them lunch after they do a nature walk along the hiking trails. Ben's teacher has a craft planned too, so this spot is perfect."

Elliott followed her instructions and set up tables and chairs. "Where's Trace?"

She busied herself even more. "Um, no idea. How would I know?"

"Because he spends more time at your place than his own?" Elliott said.

She moved at warp speed, covering the tables with butcher paper. "Ben spends a lot of time with the ducks. It's his science project."

Elliott unfolded another table. "I don't think Trace's constant whistling and good mood is caused by Ben's science project."

Obviously, their bedroom games weren't as covert as Lily thought.

"He's picking up new guests on the Cape." She used disinfectant to wipe down the chairs.

"Ah." Elliott pulled out his phone. "Let me check to see when they'll be back so I can meet them at the dock to help with luggage." Of all the Remingtons, Elliott's aggressive business personality had embraced the changes at the resort the fastest. He tapped on the screen.

She was glad someone was utilizing the app she'd been so hell-bent on implementing because *she* certainly hadn't checked the bookings lately. Between massage oil and showers and the late morning arrivals to work, she couldn't suck much more as a hospitality manager if she tried.

"Two new couples are coming in for the weekend." Elliott swiped across the screen a few times like he was studying the reservations calendar. He frowned. "Remember that Parker guy Trace didn't like?"

She stopped wiping a table and straightened. "Yes." She drew out the word, dreading whatever was coming next.

"He's booked a room week after next," Elliott said.

Not all that strange if Parker was an undercover reporter sniffing around for a story. She put on a brave face and smiled. "Maybe he's just that impressed by the Remington."

And snowballs existed in hell. Because if Lily believed her own pep talk, uncertainty wouldn't be winding around her stomach and cinching it tightly enough that she'd want to toss the warm doughnut she'd eaten for breakfast.

With measured, mechanical movements, Lily set down the cleaning rag and bottle of disinfectant and pulled her phone from her hiking pants. Pants she'd never have worn as Scarlett Devereaux. But as Lily Barns, they'd grown comfortable, just like her life at the Remington. A life she was going to have to put on the line soon by telling Trace about her past.

If Ronald Parker didn't screw her over first.

She refocused on her phone and pulled up the app. And yep. She'd totally missed Mr. Ronald Parker's name on the reservations list, even though the system had flagged him. Obviously, Trace had missed it too, or he likely would've mentioned it.

Something niggled at the back of Lily's mind. Try as she might, she couldn't ignore it. It was the clickity-clack of guilt against her conscience. The rap-tap-tap of remorse against her soul. The tick-tock of her inner clock that was running out, because Karma was coming for her.

That witch.

Except Lily had no one to blame but herself. When she left NOLA, she'd thought starting over with a new name sounded like an exciting adventure.

Now she thought it sounded about as smart as, say, moving across the country to work for a boss who could pass for a Mr. July centerfold pinup, then showing up the first day on the job riding a tricycle and carting a flock of ducks.

A yellow school bus turned into the Remington and rumbled down the long drive.

"I'll show 'em where to park, then I've got more vendors to yell at." Elliott winked. "I mean reason with. I'll be in my office if you need help." He started toward the lane but stopped. "By the way, I'm process-ing payroll. I noticed you still haven't cashed your paycheck."

She was still rationing the cash she'd brought with her from New Orleans. "Um, I've been so busy." She gave him the brightest smile she could muster. "I'll get to it." As soon as she figured out how to cash a paycheck written to Lily Barns using an ID for Scarlett Devereaux.

At the rate she was going, she might end up in the cell next to her father. Which would suck, because she looked terrible in orange.

She laughed out loud, only to clamp a hand over her mouth. Because hell, she was back to either laughing or crying, just like that first day on the island when she'd tried to pedal her way to a new life on a giant tricycle.

She started toward the parking lot where Elliott had directed the bus. Purple was more her color. Maybe purple could be the new orange so at least she'd look good behind bars.

Before Ben was born, Trace had maneuvered through some of the most terrifying weather conditions a pilot could face. He'd landed tem-peramental billionaires on airstrips the size of a yardstick. He'd flown the rich and famous to movie shoots in war-torn countries where the chances of his plane returning to Los Angeles riddled with bullet holes was almost a given.

But damned if showing up at the resort with his ex-wife where Lily would be hard at work wasn't about to bring on his first panic attack.

Imagine his surprise when he was loading up the new guests at the Cape Celeste commuter airport and a call came in from Megan inform-ing him she'd just landed and needed a lift. He'd had half a mind to tell her he'd already left the ground and she'd need to take the ferry. Megan got a bad case of motion sickness on boats and small planes. A little nausea might serve her right, but his goal was to kill her with kindness no matter how nasty she got and let her screw the visit up on her own.

Could he help it if they'd hit some wicked pockets of turbulence while crossing the channel? Or if the landing was much bumpier than normal?

Trace flipped his headset off and hopped out of his plane as soon as Elliott had it tied to the dock.

"Why so late?" Elliott asked as he opened the door for the passengers. The color drained from his face as the new and improved Megan, who'd apparently been through an image makeover, stepped into the doorway. She held a perfectly wrapped gift, and instead of her usual runway-model clothing, she was dressed in a conservative suit like she was going to church on a Sunday morning. The only thing missing were little white gloves and a matching hat. Never mind that her pale-yellow jacket and skirt clashed horribly with the pale-green color of her face.

Trace gave his brother a bland stare. "Look who I found."

"Megan," Elliott said, his tone blasé. "So nice to see you."

"Oh, cut the crap, Elliott." Megan covered her mouth and swallowed like she was trying to hold back the effects the bumpy ride had had on her stomach. "I know you never liked me." She marched down the airplane steps and started toward the path that led to the lodge without waiting for Trace.

"Can you take care of the guests?" Trace asked Elliott through clenched teeth. "They've paid good money to stay here. It would be so unfair for them to have to spend another minute with her."

"Of course." Elliott stepped up to the passenger door.

"Where's Lily? I've been trying to get ahold of her to warn her," Trace said.

A middle-aged woman appeared in the doorway of the plane, so Elliott dropped his voice. "She's had her hands full with Ben's class. They're here for a field trip." Elliott held out his hand to the guest and guided her down the steps.

Field trip? At the resort? Neither she nor Ben had mentioned it to Trace. Of course, Ben had been preoccupied with the ducks, who were growing feathers and getting bigger. And louder. And Trace had kept Lily preoccupied with, well . . . just being loud.

He pinched the bridge of his nose, because this was about to get very awkward.

He started up the path, lengthening his strides to catch up with the clicking of Megan's kitten heels against the path. Really, who wore clothes like that to a vacation island?

A twinge in his chest made his breath hitch.

Lily's clothing had been out of place when he first ran into her at the masseuse station. Very different than what she'd been wearing when he found her on the road that first day. Since then, her wardrobe had vacillated back and forth, almost like she was two different people. He knew there were things she hadn't told him. Things that were probably too painful to talk about. He'd made some progress and peeled back a few of her layers. The rest of the layers could come off when she was ready.

He shook it off. He was a guy, so what did he know about women's fashion anyway. He preferred to focus on what was underneath Lily's clothes.

Before he caught up to Megan, she stopped and turned around. "Where's Ben?"

Trace ground his teeth into dust. "I just got here too. I'll have to find him."

"He doesn't have a phone so we can keep track of him?"

"He's eight and is rarely out of my sight unless I know exactly where he is and who he's with. And I don't want him getting addicted to a phone and all the bad things it can open him up to." Trace glanced at his watch. "It's twelve thirty. On a Friday." He brushed past her, and she hurried to keep up.

"So? What's that got to do with anything?"

Trace's jaw went on lockdown. The click, click, click of her inappropriate heels was almost as annoying as her disregard for showing up unannounced in the middle of Ben's school day. "It's got to do with the fact that he'd normally be in school."

"Oh," Megan whispered, clicking along behind him.

"But lucky for you"—because the situation didn't feel especially lucky for Trace—"his class might be here at the resort on a field trip." Trace veered to the right and took the path around the main lodge.

"*Might* be here?" Megan said it like she'd caught him making a mistake.

Trace came to an abrupt halt, and Megan nearly collided with his back. "For God's sake, Megan. Stop. Just stop. This isn't a war." If it was, he'd won the second she'd signed over full custody. He just hoped his new battle strategy would get her to surrender before the new war she'd declared broke out for real. "You're here. Let's make it a pleasant experience for Ben."

Her lips pinched. Which was much better than the constant whining he'd been subjected to since the minute he picked her up on the Cape. So he led her around the lodge in blissful silence.

Until they rounded the corner to find twenty or so second graders chattering with so much excitement they might as well have been jacked up on espresso. They were on the far side of the circular entrance, sitting at tables under the covered portico. Lily, Ben's teacher, and all the kids were covered in what looked like paint. There were a lot of bright colors to splash around, but the blue matched Miss Etheridge's blue-tipped hair perfectly. And the best part was, Lily and the teacher were letting the kids smear the paint onto large white sheets with their . . . *fingers*.

It took amazing willpower to hold back the smile Trace felt from the top of his head, where his aviators sat, all the way to his suede hiking boots. Because Megan didn't do noisy kids or finger paint. And she especially didn't do them at the same time.

Guess this wouldn't be her day.

He didn't know whether to give Lily a raise or kiss the hell out of her.

When Lily saw him walking toward the group, she waved, and her entire countenance brightened. Then she went back to helping the kids. She laughed when Ben walked over and dabbed her nose with yellow paint as radiant as a sunflower in full bloom. She dabbed Ben's right back, and they both belly-laughed.

He stopped just before he reached the cement slab and watched.

Megan took up a spot next to him, stiff as a board, impatience pouring off her in waves.

Miss Etheridge bounced over. "Hi, Mr. Remington. Thanks for letting us do this field trip on such short notice."

News to him, but sure. "Anytime. Looks like the kids are having fun."

"We hiked some of the trails, and now they're painting something from the natural landscape," Miss Etheridge said. "It was Lily's idea."

Of course it was. Every good idea at the resort belonged to Lily.

"Lily and I came up with some great summer activities." Miss Etheridge had a blue glob of paint across her shirt. "I'm so excited to be the Remington's kids' camp director over the summer."

Another surprise, but he put on a smile because recruiting Ben's teacher to work at the Remington was damn smart. Plus, Miss Etheridge was being friendly, so hiring her seemed to have earned a few brownie points. Something Trace hadn't been able to do the entire school year, try as he might. Lily was getting both a raise and a kiss. "Glad to have you on board."

He glanced at Lily across the covered area. She was helping other kids like a pro. It didn't seem at all like a chore. She was obviously having fun by the way she smiled at the kids, laughed with them, and ruffled their hair or patted their shoulders.

Ben's back was to them, and he still hadn't noticed his mom's arrival.

"Lily was thinking I might need help once in a while since the resort is so booked up over the summer with families." Miss Etheridge's voice drew his attention away from the two people he'd come to care most about—Ben and Lily.

A thrill swept through him. He did care about Lily. She and Ben occupied his every thought. It wasn't just the intimacy with Lily, although that was incredible. It was the time they spent together when they were fully clothed that encircled his heart and made it thump with happiness and contentment. For the first time in his life. The three of them seemed like a package deal now.

Like a family.

He glanced at the woman at his side. Megan couldn't have been more different from Lily if she'd come from another planet. They'd never functioned as a family, even when they were married. And now that he'd finally found someone who seemed to really want to be a part of Ben's life, Megan was here to try to take it all away.

Miss Etheridge kept talking, the most personable she'd been the entire school year. "Lily spoke to the third-grade teacher about working here over the summer too." The young Miss Etheridge actually blushed like she was embarrassed. "It would give her a chance to get to know Ben before school starts. Maybe they can bond quicker and make his transition smoother than it was in second grade."

This time Trace's smile was warm and genuine and full of gratitude. "That's a brilliant idea." And he knew exactly who to thank for it. His gaze wandered back to Lily and stayed locked there even as he spoke to Ben's teacher. "Thank you. For all you've done for Ben this year—"

"*Ahem.*" Megan's fake throat clearing was so thick with irritation he doubted he could've cut it with a chainsaw.

"Miss Etheridge, this is Ben's mom, Meg—"

"Megan Remington."

Since when? Megan had stopped using Trace's last name before the ink dried on their divorce papers. Using it now must've been another pathetic attempt to present an imaginary connection between her and Ben.

Miss Etheridge's surprise was obvious. She didn't know the details, only that Ben's mom was never around for parent-teacher conferences, open houses, school plays, or classroom parties, which spoke for itself. "Nice to finally meet you." Miss Etheridge obviously didn't intend the insult she'd just delivered.

But Megan took it as a slight anyway and sniffed.

"You look familiar," Miss Etheridge said, giving Megan a quizzical look.

And that's all it took for Megan to welcome Ben's teacher back into her good graces with a dazzling smile. "I've got a new television series coming out this fall." Megan's accent shifted from a high-pitched whine to Hollywood-chic.

Trace fought off an eye roll. "I'll go tell Ben you're here." He headed to Lily first, hoping to give her a heads-up before Ben caught sight of Megan.

"Hey," Lily said when he approached. The tender smile she gave him showed in her glittering eyes, and it slayed him on the spot.

"Hey yourself," he said softly. He did not want to dim that beautiful smile she wore by explaining who their unexpected visitor was. He'd rather wrap her up in his arms and kiss her with so much passion that she'd go weak in the knees.

Trace stepped closer. Besides the yellow dab of paint on her nose, a splotch of purple streaked her jaw and chin. It was cute and loveable and sexy as hell. He swiped at a purple speck with his thumb, completely forgetting they weren't alone. "You wear purple well."

Lily's beautiful smile disappeared, and she drew in a sharp breath.

Maybe she thought he was talking about her sexy purple lace number that drove him wild. He glanced around at the chatty second graders, then hurried to explain. "You've got paint on your face." He held up his finger to show her the smudge of purple finger paint.

She let out the heavy breath she'd been holding.

"Listen, I've been trying to reach you." He scratched the back of his neck.

"Sorry, I haven't checked my phone." She waved a hand at the crowd of kids. "They've kept me busy, but I think Miss Etheridge will do just fine for our summer kids' camp director. Today was a test run."

"So I hear." His voice softened again. "Miss Etheridge told me you've recruited the third-grade teacher too. Thank you." No one had ever gone to such lengths for Ben, and the realization of what Trace and Ben had been missing churned in his stomach and bubbled up to catch in his throat. He'd planned to do all the parenting on his own, and he could do a good job at it alone if he had to. But with Lily sharing his life, he'd be so, so much better. Because he was so much more as a man and as a person with her in his life.

Lily glanced over his shoulder. "New guests?"

"Not exactly." He shoved both hands in his pockets and sighed. How could he explain that Lily was the kind of mom Ben deserved, and Megan was nothing more than an egg donor? The woman he'd married out of obligation because she'd been carrying his child but who'd never contributed a thing since. Yet here Megan was trying to ruin their lives, and Lily would have to take it for Ben's sake.

He hadn't realized until now how much Lily had come to mean to him. How much he wanted her in his future. If she still wanted him after she met Megan and the nastiness his ex could dish out. "She's—"

Ben squealed. He jumped from his chair so fast it fell backward and skidded across the cement floor. His footsteps thundered across the concrete toward Megan, and he hollered, "Mom!"

Lily's lips parted. "Oh," was all she said. Her usual fearless, unflappable tone was gone, replaced by a small, wavering voice.

What he saw in her expression made his teeth grind and his heart beat against his chest. The little bit of openness he'd been able to coax out of her had just taken a hit.

Chapter Nineteen

LILY'S LIFE LESSON #19
Don't get mad. Put them on every spam email list in existence.

Lily watched Ben thunder toward his mother. Instinct told Lily this wasn't going to end well, and the wheels of her problem-solving skills were already spinning in her mind. Damage control was imminent.

She had to get over the fact that Trace's ex-wife was gorgeous. And that Ben obviously adored her, even though he didn't have much reason to. Lily couldn't exactly throw stones.

"Oh shit," Trace whispered under his breath and started in the same direction as Ben. Before he got very far, Ben launched himself at Megan.

She let out a strangled scream as the beautifully wrapped package she had in her hand crashed to the ground. She pushed Ben away, stumbled back, and looked down in shocked horror at the paint smeared across her custom-designed Italian suit.

Lily could spot Dolce & Gabbana at a hundred paces, thanks to her mom.

What broke Lily's heart was Ben's puckered lip and the way he rubbed his thighs with both hands.

"Goddamn it," Megan seethed, still surveying the damage to her pale-yellow suit.

All the kids quieted and looked in that direction. Miss Etheridge took a step back and shot looks between Ben, Trace, and Megan.

When Trace reached his son, he put an arm around Ben's shoulder and pulled him close.

"Hospitality Lily" took over, and she hurried to the scene of the unfolding crime. "Miss Etheridge," Lily called out to the teacher as she walked toward them. "Would you mind having the kids finish their paintings? It'll be time to clean up and head back to school soon."

Miss Etheridge gave Lily a grateful look and hurried over to her class of staring children. If they understood any of what just happened, they were going to have quite a story to share with their parents as soon as the last bell rang to end the school day.

The moment Lily stepped into the fray, Ben pulled away from Trace and threw his arms around her waist.

She smoothed his hair. "Hello." She held out a hand to Megan. "I'm Lily, the hospitality manager here at the Remington. I'm so sorry about your clothes. Can I help you clean it in the lodge?"

Megan's eyes narrowed at Lily, and she ignored the outstretched hand.

Lily kept a smile on her face and glanced at Trace.

His expression said he couldn't be more sorry if he'd introduced her to Attila the Hun.

Pffst. Lily had dealt with wealthy, entitled women at the exclusive hotel she worked at before she moved to the island. She wasn't sure which was worse—the drunken male corporate execs, their wives, or their mistresses. Megan would probably seem like a Girl Scout compared to them.

Lily withdrew her hand and gently rubbed Ben's shoulder to soothe him.

Megan glared at Trace. "You planned this, didn't you?"

"Really?" He folded both hands over his chest and glanced at Ben. "You're really going to go there?"

"Lily, can I go to your house and check on the ducks?" Ben sniffed.

"I came all this way to see you, Ben," Megan insisted. "Don't you want to open the gift I brought you?" She bent to pick it up.

He shook his head and buried his face in Lily's side.

The gesture and Trace's expression made Lily's heart thump against her rib cage. She wanted nothing more than to see both of them happy. To erase the disappointment they both were experiencing.

And it killed her that she was going to have to deliver the same disappointment soon.

"Come on, Ben," Megan said. "Open your gift."

He shook his head again. "No!"

She turned a huffy look on Trace. "You've already worked on him so he won't want to come live with me in Los Angeles."

Ben's little body trembled at Lily's side, and she rubbed his back.

"Megan." Trace shook his head and nodded to Ben in a gesture that said *Not in front of him*.

Ben dropped to his knees and rocked. "I'm not leaving my duckies! I'm not going to live in Los Angeles!"

"Megan, it's time for you to leave." Trace stepped between Ben and his mother.

"I'm not ready to leave. I came here to see my son," she said.

"Ben." Lily pulled her phone from her pocket and leaned down to whisper in his ear. "I'll see if I can fix it with your teacher so you don't have to go back to school on the bus." It was an overstep, but she doubted Trace would mind if it meant protecting Ben. Kids could be unkind when they sensed weakness, especially on a school bus. What if they'd understood enough to ask Ben questions about his mom? In his agitated state, it was the last thing he needed. But the ducks always soothed him, so she handed her phone to him. "Want to take today's pictures of the ducks?"

"Really?" His rocking slowed.

Megan and Trace's showdown wasn't over, but Trace was doing his best to shield Ben from the fireworks by staying firmly planted between his son and Megan.

Lily nodded and gave Ben a gentle hug. "The school day will be almost over by the time you get there. After you take pictures of the ducks, it might be a good idea to record them because their chirps are turning into squawks." She'd grow feathers and cackle herself if it meant keeping Ben from having a meltdown.

He snatched her phone and ran full-throttle toward the lane that led to the cottages.

"*Ben!*" Megan called after him.

He didn't slow.

Lily stood, but she didn't leave just in case Trace needed her. She turned and made a wrap-it-up gesture to Miss Etheridge. Better the kids head over to the bus in case things got even more out of hand.

Megan's knuckles turned white as chalk as she gripped the gift. "This isn't over."

"Damn straight it's not." There wasn't a morsel of sympathy in Trace's tone. "I knew you'd screw this up. I just didn't think you'd do it quite so publicly while stabbing Ben in the heart."

For the first time since she'd arrived, Megan looked contrite. "Fine." Her bottom lip quivered. "Take me back to the Cape."

Trace huffed out an exasperated laugh. "Take the ferry." He strolled in the same direction as Ben. "I'm not your chauffeur." He stopped long enough to turn to Lily and said, "I'll be with Ben."

Megan's eyes rounded, and she stared at Trace's retreating back. Obviously, she was used to Trace mediating between her and Ben instead of making a real effort as a mother.

"Megan, can I get you a cloth?" Lily kept her professional demeanor firmly in place. She knew from dealing with her friends-turned-mean-girls after her father was arrested that it was best to kill them with kindness. And if kindness didn't work, signing them up for every spam email list she could find made Lily feel better. She bit the inside of her lip and waited for an answer.

Megan turned glazed eyes on her. "Beg your pardon?"

"For the paint." Lily pointed to the bright smears on Megan's suit.

Megan shook her head and looked down at the gift. "It's ruined." She fingered the ribbon. "I guess I didn't handle that very well, did I?"

It wasn't Lily's place to say *Hell no, you didn't*. Megan stood there in her expensive clothes and nails, so perfect she'd probably walked out of LA's most posh salon and stepped right onto a plane bound for Angel Fire Falls. All Lily saw was a younger version of her mother. Perfectly put together on the outside, pathetically unhappy on the inside. And all Lily could do was pity her. So she said, "Parents make mistakes."

"You're very good with him. He seems to be very attached to you," Megan said.

Something prickled up Lily's spine. "I work here, so we see a lot of each other." Lily had a sudden urge to bolt just like Ben, but no way was she leaving Megan to roam the resort or the island alone so she could terrify the villagers and wreak more havoc on Trace and Ben. "Can I find you a ride to the ferry?" Maybe Charley would be willing to drop Megan at the terminal before picking Sophie up from school.

Megan studied her. "Of course," she finally said. "That would be lovely."

Wow. She sure was some actress to have switched her tone on a dime. No wonder she'd risen above the laxative commercials Trace mentioned.

"Great." Lily brightened. "I'll be right back with someone to drive you to the terminal." She started toward the lodge to find Charley but stopped. "Would you like me to give that to Ben?" She nodded to the gift in Megan's hand.

Megan hesitated, then handed it over. "Please do. Thank you. And tell him his mother loves him."

Maybe it was Lily's imagination, but Megan seemed to emphasize the word *mother* like she was trying to make a point.

◆ ◆ ◆

Trace did not want to adult today.

It seemed unfair that he had to be the grown-up when Megan got to act like a child.

He took a seat on the ground behind Lily's cottage, leaned against a tree, and watched Ben record the ducks. Some pecked at the new pellets he'd picked up at a livestock feed store on the mainland, and the others swam in the shallow pond Ben had created from an old plastic container Charley had marked for the trash. They'd gotten so big that the toddler swimming pool Trace'd bought a couple of weeks ago was now their inside home because they'd outgrown the plastic habitat.

Just like the ducks, Ben was growing up much faster than Trace cared to admit. Now that Megan had derailed her own ridiculous plan to gain custody, it was probably time to have a man-to-man talk with his son about the situation.

Ben lumbered over to sit on his knees next to Trace. "Guess what I learned about girl ducks and boy ducks?"

Trace chuckled. "Tell me."

Ben laid Lily's phone in the grass and bounced on his knees. "Girl ducks quack louder than boy ducks, and their beaks are different colors."

"Have you figured out the girls from the boys?" Trace plucked a blade of grass and fiddled with it.

His heart squeezed when Ben mimicked him with a piece of grass. His little head shook back and forth. "They all sound the same, but in a few weeks, we'll be able tell the difference."

"Will it bother you if we have to rename them?" Trace propped his forearms over his bent knees.

"Nope, because a boy should have a boy's name," Ben said as though he'd given the problem a lot of thought. "And a girl should have a girl's name."

Trace pursed his lips and nodded. "Good thinking." He gave the gray sky a once-over. "Ben, do you want to talk about what just happened with your mom?" Asking Ben to focus on the pain Megan inflicted was like driving a knife into Trace's own heart.

"I don't want to live in Los Angeles," Ben blurted.

"You don't have to." Megan was smart enough to know that twenty kids, their teacher, and the Remington's hospitality manager had just witnessed her theatrics, and she hadn't left a glowing impression on any of them. Trace drew in a sad breath. "Do you ever wonder what it would be like to live with your mom?"

Ben nodded, and he rubbed a hand against one thigh. "It would be boring."

"Why do you say that?" Trace was curious because Ben hadn't been around Megan enough to know what it would be like.

"Because Mom doesn't like me." Ben's tone was blunt.

Trace's heart broke. "She likes you." He doubted it, but how could he say so to an eight-year-old kid?

"No," Ben said, all serious and analytical. "She's the same as the kids at school who don't like me. They stay away from me and say I'm weird."

Dear God. Trace was a grown man, but damned if he didn't feel a sting behind his eyes. He didn't speak for fear his voice would crack.

Ben bounced on his knees. "And you're like my friends at school. They play with me all the time. They don't care if I'm weird."

"You're not weird," Trace managed to say with a steady voice.

"Dad," Ben drew out. "I am too. Just like Miss Etheridge's blue hair is weird. I think it's okay to be weird as long as you're a nice person." He pointed to the ducks. "See Waddles? He's different from the other ducks."

Waddles, with his slight limp and one wing a bit smaller than the other, was the only duck Trace could pick out of the bunch. The others looked exactly alike to him. Still, he wasn't going to let such shallow things form his son's perception of what normal should look like.

"A limp and a lame wing doesn't make him weird, Ben."

Ben shook his head impatiently. "*No.* That's not what I mean. When the rest of them play follow-the-leader in a circle, he walks a circle in the opposite direction. It's funny, and he's not hurting the other ducks, so it's okay."

Trace's intake of breath was sharp. The ducks were teaching Ben so many things, including life skills. Lily's instincts had been spot-on about keeping the ducks, just like everything else. And Trace hadn't seen it.

"If I lived in Los Angeles, Mom wouldn't want to be around me there either because I'm different." When the ducks started a game of follow-the-leader, he lifted the phone and hit record. And sure enough, the duck with the slight limp went in the opposite direction, lapping the others with a squawk. "And you and Lily and Grandpa and Uncle Spence and Uncle Elliott and Charley and Sophie and all the ducks live here." He let it all tumble out at once. "So it would be boring if I lived with Mom."

Made perfect sense to Trace. What amazed him was that Ben had figured it out on his own.

Trace picked at a clover. "Does it bother you . . ." *That your mom doesn't like you? Doesn't want to be around you? Thinks you're weird?* "That your mom isn't around much?"

Ben kept recording the ducks. "Not anymore."

Huh. Not the answer Trace expected. "Why not?"

Ben rolled his eyes as though Trace should've been the one to figure that out already. Ben kept recording the ducks. "Because Lily's sorta my mom now."

Trace's pulse kicked up a notch. Lily *had* developed a special bond with Ben. With Trace too, and she was slowly opening up to him. He hadn't wanted to hire her, but she'd upended his world in the best way possible. He didn't know how or even if it would all work out. She was the real deal, though. A future with Lily may not be a sure thing yet, but he wanted to take the chance and find out because she was worth the risk.

If she'd have him. Megan probably wouldn't vanish completely. She'd likely always be an issue to deal with, at least to some degree.

"Hey, you two." Lily appeared from the side of the cottage.

The splotch of paint on her nose made Trace want to pull her into his arms.

"Everything okay?" She sat on the grass next to Trace and cut her eyes at her left hand, which was hidden at her side. She had the gift Megan brought Ben, only it was a little more tattered since Megan had dropped it.

He nodded and gave her a warm smile at the thoughtful gesture. That's what made Lily so different. When most people, including Ben's own mother, ran away from the difficulties of Ben's condition, Lily ran toward them. And then tried to make things better for him.

"Hey, Ben." She held out her hand. "Can I have my phone back?"

He stopped recording and handed it to her.

She immediately started texting, and Trace's phone dinged.

He drew his brows together and gave her a quizzical look.

She raised an eyebrow and nodded to the phone in his pocket.

So he took it out and read the text.

Charley's taking her to the
ferry.

Trace didn't have to ask which *her* Lily meant. The less they spoke of she-who-should-not-be-named, the better. He typed back.

Thank you.

228

Her smile was tender when she read his response. She typed, and his phone dinged.

You're welcome.

She winked. "The kids left to go back to school, but Miss Etheridge said Ben could stay here."

Lily thought of everything. Trace couldn't help it. They hadn't shown a lot of PDA in front of Ben, but he reached up and caught a wisp of her hair, tucking it behind an ear. Then he let his eyes roam her beautiful face.

She returned his affectionate stare in spades.

"Are you guys gonna kiss?" Ben snickered. "Cuz I want to record it and show it to everyone!" He lunged across Trace's lap and grabbed for Lily's phone.

Trace could swear fear flared in her eyes, and she held it out of reach.

"Hey, we need to print the pictures of the ducks for your project, right?" Lily asked.

Ben righted himself and bounced on his knees. "Can you come watch my presentation at school?"

"Of course," Lily said.

"Uh," Trace said like he was shocked. "You want me to go too, right?" Because he was beginning to think Ben preferred Lily over everyone else on the planet.

"Dad," Ben drew out again, clearly exasperated.

Trace ruffled his hair. "If you move the ducks inside, I'll spring for ice cream in town."

"Can Lily go too?" Ben asked.

Trace lifted both brows at her so she could answer for herself.

She rubbed her chin thoughtfully. "You know, I think I like ice cream almost as much as doughnuts. Of course I'll go, especially if your dad is buying."

Ben cheered.

Trace felt like doing a little cheer of his own, because it was Friday afternoon, and they were going for ice cream. Like a real family should. He slipped her hand inside his and nodded to the gift. "Ben, do you want to open the gift your mom brought?"

Ben nodded but wasn't all that excited.

Trace took the gift from Lily and gave it to Ben. He tore off the wrapping paper. He studied the mechanical duck robot on the box with no emotion. "Do I have to go live with Mom if I accept it?"

Jesus. Ben really did know the score with his mother much better than Trace thought. "No, buddy. You're staying right here with me."

"And with Lily?" Ben asked.

Trace glanced at her. Her lips had parted, and a light shimmer of wetness glistened in her eyes. He wanted to blurt *Yes, with Lily,* and he was close to positive she felt the same way.

Before he could respond, her smile wavered. "Um, well." Her eyes darted away. "I want to stay here, but we'll see."

Um, well. What the hell? Obviously, they weren't on the same page, because that wasn't at all what he'd thought she would say.

And even more alarming—how did Megan know to get Ben a duck-themed gift? Trace was certain neither he nor Ben had mentioned the ducks to her before today. So was it a lucky guess? Or was someone feeding her information?

Chapter Twenty

Lily sat at her desk and clicked the red notification alert in the top corner of the resort's reservation calendar. The same notification she'd clicked on several times since Elliott had brought it to her attention last Friday.

Ronald Parker's upcoming stay mocked her.

She chewed her nail and stared at the screen.

She'd used her alone time the past few days to search the internet, social media, and online news sites for every Gulf Coast TV channel she could find. Nothing about her had surfaced. Neither had anything about Ronald Parker.

Still, her time was running out, and she needed to finish setting up the resort to run without her should it have to.

As promised, she added STATE-OF-THE-ART GAME ROOM AVAILABLE THIS SUMMER SEASON, COURTESY OF BUZZBEE ELECTRONICS & GAMING AND BILLIARDS & MORE! to the Remington website along with their links. The new game systems had already arrived, and the boxes were scattered around Lily's office. The game room renovations were underway, but there wasn't time to set up the electronics, so she organized the boxes and pushed them against the back wall.

As she finished up, her phone dinged.

The day is too beautiful to waste indoors. Pick you up in an hour. Dress comfortably.

Before she could respond, another text popped onto the screen.

Thing One & Thing Two are holding down the fort for a few hours.

She smiled at the screen. She didn't text back. Instead, she walked to her cottage to change. Exactly one hour later, a knock sounded at her door. When she opened it, Trace lounged against the frame, a sexy smile on his handsome face.

Lily's girl parts sighed.

He let a lazy gaze wander over her. It snagged on the frayed edge of her shorts. "Nice. An inch shorter and those would be Daisy Dukes."

She stepped outside and closed the door behind her. "How does a single guy who wears generic T-shirts that probably come in a plastic package know about Daisy Dukes?"

"Beautiful, every straight guy with a pulse knows about Daisy Dukes." He held up a backpack. "This one's yours. We're taking a scenic walk." He pulled out the aviators that were hooked at his neckline and slid them onto his nose. "Ready?"

"As I'll ever be." She took the backpack and slung it around her shoulders. "Now I'm intrigued." She'd assumed they'd be driving. Since it was shaping up to be a gorgeous, clear day, she lowered sunglasses from the top of her hair onto her nose.

He hitched his pack onto one shoulder and laced his fingers through hers as he led her off the porch. "Backpacking for a few hours is all it took to intrigue you? To think I've been wasting my time with the hot flyboy act and the great sex."

If he was going to be such a smart-ass, then she was going to give him a hefty sample of the same. "Who've you been having great sex with?"

He stopped dead in his tracks, pulled her back to him, and laid the sexiest, sultriest openmouthed kiss on her. With lots and lots of tongue. So *much* tongue that it was all she could do to keep her knees from buckling. A tiny noise came from somewhere deep inside her, and she melted into him.

He broke the kiss and let his mouth linger a fraction from hers. "Want to ask me that again?"

"Maybe later," she whispered.

He chuckled, laced his fingers with hers again, and they walked up the lane.

When he led her down to the dock, past the pier, and around the boathouse, Lily asked, "Where are we going?" She'd explored the grounds, but the map Lawrence had given her didn't show anything beyond that point.

The wood walkway ended just past the boathouse, and Trace stopped. "Ever wonder how Angel Fire Falls got its name?"

Now she was *really* intrigued. "Yes, actually. I have."

He took off his backpack and handed it to her. Then he turned his back to her and stooped. "Then climb on, and I'll show you."

"Um . . ." *Climb on?* "Riding on your back would be an awkward position at my age."

He glanced over his shoulder with smoky eyes. "Of all the positions we've been in, piggybacking you across a muddy trail is the least awkward."

She was sure she blushed.

"Come on," he said. "I'll carry you."

She caved and climbed on his back. He carried her as easily as a feather.

When they got to a yellow rope that had a Keep Out sign anchored in the center, he lifted the rope and handed it to her. "Flip this over our heads." He stooped, and she did what she was told.

"I didn't realize anything was down here," she said.

He ducked under a mass of overgrown vines and veered left. They cleared a copse of maple trees, and then the landscape opened up into a sandy beachhead that gently sloped to the water.

"This is a hidden treasure," she said as he set her down. She handed him his backpack. "Why isn't the resort using this as a swimming hole? It's close enough to the resort that it would be perfect. Families would love it." The cove was as smooth as glass, and sunshine reflected off the water.

"I secretly named it Camilla's Cove after my mom." He toed the wet sand with the tip of one hiking boot, sadness filling his expression. "No one comes this far anymore."

She angled her head to the side. "Why not?"

He shoved both hands in his pockets and scanned the expanse of the cove. "She . . . this is where we lost her."

She let out a soft gasp. "Oh, Trace." She walked over and slipped her arms around him.

"It was hard for all of us, but especially so for my brothers. They were with her that day." He swallowed. "I was with my dad on a campout with the Scouts."

"I'm so sorry," Lily whispered. She'd spent a lot of time feeling neglected by her parents. Losing one completely was beyond her imagination.

"Maybe that's why I'm so overprotective of Ben." Trace rested his chin against the top of her head. "I've felt like a parent since I was eleven. Spence and Elliott had a rough time after it happened, and I had to be strong for them. The responsibility has been like a weight around my shoulders for years."

She rested her cheek against his chest. The soft rhythmic beat of his heart lulled her.

He stroked the nape of her neck with his fingertips. "I guess I felt betrayed and abandoned by Mom's absence."

A feeling Lily knew well. "Sometimes we don't understand our parents' actions." Lily felt fortunate that her parents had still been around to explain why their lives had taken a turn for the worse, so she could finally start to heal. Trace didn't have that luxury because his mother was no longer alive. "But they usually do have an explanation for their mistakes. I'm just sorry you don't have the answers you're obviously looking for."

They stayed wrapped in each other's arms for a long time. Finally, he leaned back to look down into her eyes. "The last few weeks that weight has felt much lighter." His expression turned lazy and lustful. "Thank you."

His attraction, his need was raw and so apparent that Lily's heart squeezed.

He wanted her. And she wanted him. But she wanted him to have *all* of her. Not just the girl he'd found on the road one day trying like hell to pedal her way into a new life. She wanted him to know the person who'd been desperate to escape the abusive media coverage she and her mother had endured. The death threats in the form of a spray-painted message across her car, and the suspicious package that showed up on their doorstep, which had been the last straw that'd made up her mind to become someone else.

And she wanted him to love her in spite of all that.

Her pulse kicked through her veins.

She wasn't sure how it had happened so fast, but she was falling for him. Hard.

She fought off a shiver of guilt mixed with regret, both so powerful she wanted to blurt the whole truth right then.

"Come on." He crooked a finger at her. "This isn't what I wanted to show you." He notched his chin toward an overgrown trail that meandered up a steep hill on the far side of the cove. "The falls are up there."

When he held out his hand, she took it, determined to enjoy the moment with Trace while she still could.

Trace led Lily up the trail. He hadn't walked along the old boat launch or hiked to the falls in years. The last time had been in high school on the anniversary of his mother's death, and he'd kept it a secret. It was too painful, too personal for his brothers.

After the accident, his dad had shut down that part of the grounds. So when Trace moved back to the island, he'd forbidden Ben and Sophie from going past the boathouse. But Trace wanted to share this part of the resort, this part of the island with Lily because it *was* a treasure, just like her. Spence and Elliott may not ever be able to enjoy that part of the grounds again, but Trace was ready to move on. And he wanted to move on with Lily.

After his ex's disastrous trip to see Ben, Lily hadn't seemed sure about her future on the island. Today was about showing her how special she was, how much he wanted her to be there. With him.

Just before they reach the bluff, he stopped. "Close your eyes. I want it to be a surprise."

"You want me to climb the rest of the way with my eyes closed?" she protested.

"Do you trust me?" Waiting for an answer had every muscle in his body tied into knots. He didn't know many details of her last relationship. Didn't know anything about her family, but it couldn't be good. She wasn't very trusting, and she certainly wasn't into sharing information about herself. For some reason, gaining her trust with this small thing would give him hope that she'd eventually trust him with the big stuff too.

When he glanced over his shoulder, she had a plump bottom lip pulled between her teeth.

She nodded. "Yes." Her voice shook. "I trust you."

His heart pumped with relief. "Then take my hand and stay close." A sense of protectiveness and possessiveness filled him when she held tightly to his hand.

Just before he took the last step that would bring his grand surprise into view, he said, "Eyes closed?"

"Yep," she said. "Promise."

"Okay, keep 'em closed tight." As soon as he led her onto the bluff, the sound of rushing water filtered toward them. "Don't open them until I say." He stepped behind her and placed his hands over her eyes.

"I hear water." The excitement in her voice was palpable.

He walked her to the center of the bluff where the falls were visible to the right and an expansive view of the island swept left with the ocean beyond. "Ready?"

"Yes." She gripped his hands with hers. "I'm dying to see."

When he moved his hands, she gasped. She ran a few more steps and then stopped, her hands covering her cheeks.

God, but she was so damn gorgeous. Those itty-bitty shorts and her tight light-pink T-shirt that molded to every curve and showed enough skin that his prick had roared to life the second she'd opened the door were killing him.

"It has to be the most beautiful place on earth." Her tone was all full of awe and admiration.

Relief slammed through Trace. He hadn't realized how important her approval was. How much he'd wanted her to embrace his home instead of thinking of it as a resort. How much he wanted her to belong there with him instead of just existing as an employee.

She used a hand to shield her eyes as she looked up at the falls cascading over the tall cliff. The spray of water created a prism against the sun, and heavenly white clouds peeked over the top of the cliff, the combination setting the sky on fire. "It's breathtaking. I can see where the name came from."

He took her hand, his fingers lacing into hers. "See where the water pools at the base?" He pointed to the bottom of the falls. "There's a nice swimming hole there." He tugged her in that direction.

"I don't have a swimsuit handy."

"I know." Desire thickened in his tone.

"Wait a minute." She pulled up short, tugging on his hand for him to stop. "Are you saying all of this is resort land?"

"Yep." He started toward the waterfall again. "The land on the far side of the bluff is ours too."

"My God," she said. "I knew the resort was big, but I had no idea just how big."

He tugged her hand and gave her a quick kiss. "So you're impressed by the size? Because every guy knows size really does matter."

"You're doing just fine in that department," she teased. "I'm magnificently impressed."

He chuckled, pulling her against him to snake an arm around her slender waist as they walked toward the falls.

She snuggled into his side. "It's perfect for a wedding venue. Costly, though. The civil engineering alone for road access would be staggering. If we turned the flatter land on the other side of the bluff into a nine-hole golf course, we could recruit investors and combine it with the wedding venue. As long as the Remingtons maintain a controlling interest, we'd still be in charge."

Her mind clicked at a faster pace than most everyone he knew combined. She never stopped surprising him at how smart and creative she was. But what had his pulse racing with satisfaction was that she used the term *we*. As in her and him together as a team.

"Do you know how much it turns me on when you talk like a corporate shark?" He eased her up against the rock wall that created a half circle around the falls. From the pool of water where the falls landed, a spray of cool mist drifted up and coated them.

Her eyes smoldered with passion. "Funny how many of my ideas you actually like, even though you didn't want to hire me."

He nipped at her bottom lip. "Those shorts are very persuasive."

She pinched him.

"Ouch." He flinched.

She pinched him again.

"Ouch." He laughed. "I take it back."

"You better." Her finger caressed the sting from her pinch. "That's not the best strategy if you want me to go skinny-dipping with you."

He anchored one hand to the rock wall next to her head. "No? Then how about this?" He drew one of her legs up to circle his waist and pressed his throbbing prick into her center.

"Better." Her eyes floated shut, and she arched into him. "Much, much better." She wrapped her arms around his head. "Since we own the place, I say we turn it into our own private topless swimming hole." She bit his earlobe. "No swimsuits allowed."

He growled. "I hear nothing but good ideas out of you."

"Yeah?" she teased. "Does that mean my probationary period is over?"

"Babe, it was over the second you found a way to stop Mrs. Ferguson from cooking." He pressed into her again.

Her breath hitched, and her lusty gaze settled on his mouth like she wanted to feast on it.

"Hungry?" he teased. "'Cause lunch is in the backpacks."

Her lips parted, and a pretty pink tongue darted out to smooth across her bottom lip. She nodded. "Oh, I'm hungry." She lifted her chin like she was playing along.

He bent his head to take that sassy mouth in a kiss, but she slipped under his arm, and he fell forward, catching himself against the rock wall. "Hey." He glanced over a shoulder.

"We can have lunch later." She backed toward the water with a wicked smile on her lush lips. The backpack was the first thing to hit the ground. A tennis shoe came off with the next backward step, then the other.

He turned and leaned back to watch the show.

Her slender fingers went to work on the snap of those sexy shorts, and then the zipper made a quick whirring sound as it lowered. With one swift push, they dropped to the ground and she stepped out of them, still moving backward.

He shifted, his pants growing more uncomfortable with each step she took toward the water. He jammed his hands into his pockets to keep from acting like a caveman. This was just too damn good not to savor.

She flicked the T-shirt over her head and kept moving backward, slowly, in nothing but a matching set of lacy lingerie. She ran a fingertip over the top edge of one bra cup.

"Jesus, Lily," he rasped out, his voice nothing more than a gritty whisper.

A naughty smile spread over her beautiful mouth, and she lifted a brow. She reached around to her back and unhooked her bra. She tossed it onto the ground too, leaving a nice trail of clothes that taunted him to follow.

By the time she reached the edge of the pool, a thick sheen of spray from the falls glistened off her skin. She turned to dip a toe in.

He swallowed. Because *hello*. She was wearing another thong.

She shivered and wrapped both arms around her torso to peek over a shoulder. "The water's freezing. You said this was a swimming hole." Her eyes were wide with fear.

Her silky hair cascading down her bare, toned back and the creamy skin of her perfectly round ass cheeks were his undoing. He was on her before she could turn around again, shucking his clothes as he went. He wrapped her in his arms and molded himself around her.

He nuzzled her ear and whispered, "It's easiest if you plunge right in instead of easing in a little at a time."

Another shiver and shimmy against his cock made him groan. He pressed against her so they leaned toward the water.

"You wouldn't," she said.

"Let's jump together." He applied a little more pressure to her back. It seemed symbolic of their relationship, their connection, and there was no one else on earth he'd rather jump with than Lily.

"Trace." Her hands clamped on top of his, and she tried to push back. Did no good.

She squealed as he propelled them into the water, and she slipped from his grasp.

He broke the surface first, and then she popped up gasping from the frigid water.

"Oh . . . you . . . " She couldn't finish because of her chattering teeth. She splashed him.

He laughed and reached for her.

She pushed away and swam in the opposite direction.

"At least let me warm you up, babe." He said it with pure innocence.

She ignored him and disappeared through the falling water to lounge on the far side where a rock formation formed a shelf. Elbows behind her, she stretched her legs and kicked her feet.

He pushed off and swam to her, breaking through the falling water into the private cavelike alcove. His feet touched bottom, and he framed her with a hand on each side of her shoulders.

Her wet lashes batted at him. "This place is beautiful. You're very lucky."

"Maybe it can be yours too if you'll stay here with me and Ben."
He placed a soft kiss on each eye, then feathered kisses down her neck
and across her collarbone.

"Trace," she whispered. "I . . . maybe we should . . ."

He bent lower and grasped one of her granite nipples between his
teeth.

She hissed in a breath.

There was plenty of time for talk. Maybe a lifetime, if things
between them kept going so well. His lips closed around the nipple
again, and he began to suckle.

She let out a loud moan.

God, he loved it when she moaned.

He covered her other firm breast with a palm and massaged. And
they spent the rest of the day doing exactly what he'd wanted—they
enjoyed the beauty of the resort that was his home, his future. And Lily
could be part of it if she wanted.

Chapter Twenty-One

The next few days passed in a blur, with Lily firming up the new programs she'd implemented for the resort and setting up as much as she could to fulfill her obligations and the bartering promises she'd made. Trace's dangerous talk about the future during their skinny-dipping adventure stiffened Lily's resolve to get everything in order so she could come clean without leaving the Remington at risk.

She sat at her desk and finished up a list of instructions and contact numbers should a new person fill the hospitality manager's position in the near future.

Ronald Parker was scheduled to arrive—she glanced at the time on the screen—fifteen minutes ago.

The clock had run out on her conscience, and she planned to tell Trace the truth as soon as she could get him alone. Unfortunately, alone time had been in short supply between Lily's busy work schedule, Trace getting his delivery business ready to roll, Trace's endless argumentative phone calls with his ex-wife, who still hadn't dropped the custody suit, and Ben's science project.

She picked up her phone and sent Trace a text.

> Did you notice Ronald Parker on your manifest?

The dots did their dance.

> Yep. Running late. Guests' luggage didn't show yet.

Lily sighed. To keep busy, she flipped through the next few months on the reservations calendar, very few vacancies showing. Now fully staffed, the resort already buzzed with activity even though the official summer season didn't kick off until the following weekend. Her hard work was already paying off for the Remington family. They deserved it.

Even though her stay on the island also marked the biggest personal failure of her life, Lily was proud of all she'd accomplished professionally in such a short amount of time. When it came to the job Lawrence had hired her to do, she'd kicked a lot of ass and taken more than a few names.

She planned to go big for the Remington. Unfortunately, she might also have to go home, which would suck.

"Lily!" Ben rambled through her office door with his usual unfiltered zeal. A pumpkin-shaped candy basket dangled from one of his fists, and squawking came from inside.

"Hey, Ben," she said. "Home from school?"

"Yeah!" He tumbled around the desk to stand next to her. "I brought Waddles to see you!" He barely took a breath.

She peeked inside the basket. "Hi, Waddles."

The bird cackled in response and pecked at the cushion of duck-food pellets around his feet.

"Can we print the pictures of the ducks? I have to start the poster for my science project." He bounced with excitement. "I have to stand up in front of the whole class and give a presentation."

Such a big word for a small kid. Then again, Ben was mature beyond his age. She often had to remind herself he was eight.

"My turn to give the presentation is next week. Are you still coming?"

She chewed her lip because she didn't want to let Ben down the way his mother had. "If I'm on the island, I'll be there." With a few swipes on the screen of her phone, the printer spurred to life and spit out several pictures of the ducklings. "Wow. Look how much they've grown." She flipped through the shots on the screen. "They've gotten huge since we found them."

"*You* found 'em," Ben corrected.

She angled her head to the side. "Yes, but they're *our* ducks. You've done a great job taking care of them, kiddo."

"Can you help me right now?" Ben asked.

"Sure." She laced her fingers on top of the desk.

"Then come on!" He grabbed her hand and pulled her out of the chair, still holding on tight to the orange basket that had been converted into a pet carrier.

"Wait," she said with a laugh and grabbed the stack of printouts. "We can't forget the pictures." She let Ben drag her outside. The sky was darkening, and the wind had picked up, making the trees shift and dance in that ominous way before a storm. "Should we bring Waddles home?"

Ben shook his head and kept pulling her along. "Waddles needs to come with us."

When they reached the dock, Ben stopped and frowned.

She looked up at the dark thunderclouds rolling in from the mainland. "I'm not sure your dad wants you down here with a storm coming."

"I need to find a new place for the ducks to swim," Ben said. "The pond I made for them isn't big enough anymore."

"Sweetie, I didn't bring my phone. Maybe we should go back to my office and call your dad. Or we could wait here for him. He should be flying in soon."

"No," Ben insisted and rubbed his thigh with his free hand. "Dad said he'd be home by now, but he isn't. This is part of my project. I need you to help me with it *now*."

She looked off into the distance. Trace hadn't said how long he'd be, and she didn't want Ben to get upset. His insistent demeanor usually meant he'd set his mind on something and wasn't going to give up. She weighed the situation, finally sighing. She'd rather help Ben with his project than risk him wandering off to find the ducks a place to swim on his own.

She pointed to the pier. "How about there? When they're ready, we can let them swim by the pier."

He shook his head. "It's too close to where Dad lands. I learned in science class that birds are dangerous to airplanes."

"You're such a smart kid. Sweet too." How many eight-year-olds thought of their parents' safety? "Not to mention cute."

"Dad says guys aren't supposed to be cute."

"Too late," she teased. "Because you are, and so is your dad." She took in the gloomy sky. "Your dad showed me a place. If we hurry, we can get back to my cottage before it starts raining." She bent to slide the printed pages under a heavy rock. "Let's leave the pictures of the ducks here. I'll have to piggyback you because the trail's muddy."

It took some doing, but Ben was finally on her back with one arm around her neck and the other clutching the pet carrier for dear life.

"Hold on tight to me and Waddles." She picked her way through mud until they reached the yellow rope. She maneuvered them under it and kept going until they cleared the trees and stood in the sandy cove. "What about here?"

"*Whoa.*" His voice was pure wonderment. He ran to the water's edge.

She ran after him. "Ben, maybe you shouldn't let Waddles—"

Ben scooped the bird out of the carrier and set him in the water before Lily could finish.

The bird darted out to the center of the cove.

"Waddles!" Ben yelled. "Come back!" He tried to run into the water.

"Ben! No!" Lily captured him in her arms. She had no idea how deep the water was.

Ben's arms flailed to get loose, and he hollered.

Waddles swam in circles. He preened and made new noises Lily hadn't heard from the ducks yet, like he was speaking a new language now that he'd been introduced to his natural habitat. He dove under the water.

Ben struggled to get free. "Waddles!"

Tears stung Lily's eyes as she held Ben back. She'd never seen him have a full-on meltdown, and it stabbed at her heart. Even worse, it was her fault for giving in to him to begin with instead of waiting for Trace.

The gathering storm and windy conditions didn't make for a smooth landing when Trace set the plane down in the inlet. Farther down the dock, sheets of paper littered the pier as he hopped out of his plane. Grinding his teeth, he opened the door for the passengers, one of whom was Ronald Parker.

The guy seemed to watch Trace's every move, and his gut told him Parker wasn't just a guest who enjoyed the Remington.

Trace had been preoccupied with work, Ben, Lily, and the new family routine they were settling into. Megan calling him every night with veiled threats if he didn't agree to at least partial custody hadn't helped. Apparently, someone had convinced her that she still had a chance of winning a custody battle, even after showing up at the resort during a field trip and acting like the mommy from hell.

He'd had it and had been interviewing lawyers over the phone to narrow down his search before he set up face-to-face appointments on the mainland. All things considered, he wasn't surprised he'd let the notification of Parker's unwanted reservation slip through the cracks.

Elliott stepped up to help the guests from the plane.

"Need help with the luggage?" Spence asked, walking up. "I ran out of drywall for the game room, so I'm free at the moment."

Trace nodded. "This is my last run for the day too."

Spence and Elliott shot Trace a glance when Ronald Parker stepped out of the plane.

Trace scratched his left temple with his right thumb, which was Remington brothers' code for *This joker can't be trusted.*

A harsh gust of wind sent several sheets of paper tumbling around their feet. Trace picked one up and turned it over. His forehead wrinkled as he looked down at a picture of the ducks.

Just then he heard muffled shouts in the distance. His head popped up, and he stared down the narrow trail behind the boathouse.

Something odd slithered up his spine.

The guests milled around the dock as his brothers unloaded the luggage.

Trace held up a hand. "Shhh."

As soon as the shuffling feet stopped moving and everyone went quiet, another shout came from the direction of the cove. Made no sense because that area was off-limits to everyone.

He cocked his head and listened, still holding up his hand to keep everyone quiet. The next shout sounded an awful lot like *Ben.*

Trace dropped the paper and took off at a dead run. When he reached the muddy trail, he didn't slow. The soft ground shifted under his feet, sending him tumbling into the thick brush. He jumped up, ignoring the sting of cuts and bruises, and kept running. He vaulted over the yellow rope like an Olympic track star and kept running until he broke through the clearing.

They stood in water just below their knees, and Lily had her arms anchored around Ben like a straitjacket. Tears streaked her cheeks.

Ben was hysterical. "Waddles!" He twisted and thrashed.

One of the ducks—presumably Waddles—floated in the center of the cove.

Trace reached them in a few long, powerful strides. He grasped Ben's arms. "Ben, calm down."

Did no good.

Ben sobbed. "We have to get Waddles."

Spence and Elliott both splashed into the water alongside Trace.

"Elliott, go take care of the guests at the dock," Trace said. "The last thing we need is an incident ruining our summer season."

As he turned to watch Elliott trudge back to the trailhead, Trace's anger flared.

Ronald Parker stood in the clearing with his phone pointing right at them. He didn't ask if anyone was hurt. Didn't ask if he could help. Just kept recording.

"Spence, stay here with Lily?" Trace asked because his son was still bawling and fighting to get loose.

Spence nodded, and Trace stalked over to Parker. "Who are you, and why are you here?"

"Trace," Lily said from behind him. "I think he's here because of me."

Parker's lips curved up into a self-satisfied smile.

He wasn't sure what Lily had to do with any of this, but he was damn sure going to get answers. "Start talking, Parker." Trace's tone had gone low and lethal, and he took a step toward Parker.

Parker's face paled, but he kept recording. "Megan's agent hired me. I came here to gather information on you, but *Ms. Barns* fell into my lap like a gift. Or do you call her by her real name?"

Her real name? Trace turned to stare at Lily.

"Trace, I can explain," Lily said, glancing at Ben. "Can we talk alone?"

Trace pinched the corners of his eyes. "So that's how Megan knew to get Ben a duck-themed gift." Trace drew in a breath and clamped his hands to his side to keep from wringing this clown's neck. "You've been spying on me to help my ex-wife win custody of our son?"

"No!" Ben yelled. "I'm not moving to Los Angeles! I live here!" He tore free from Lily's grasp, and before Spence could grab him, he plunged into the water.

"Ben!" Lily screamed.

Spence went after him.

Trace hit the water running and didn't stop. He dove in, passed Spence, and caught Ben just as the water reached his neck. "Ben," he growled. "Stop it. We'll get the duck, but you have to stop fighting me."

Ben shrieked hysterically in the throes of the worst autistic melt-down he'd ever had.

Spence swam out and tucked the quacking duck under one arm.

When they were close enough to shore to stand, Spence handed the duck to Ben, who stopped wailing and fighting for the first time since the whole mess began.

Trace knew from Spence's tortured look how difficult the situation was for him. "Thanks, little brother. I owe you."

Spence's face was pale, but he shook his head. "That's what families do."

Trace carried Ben onto dry land and loosened his hold on him. Ben ran to Lily and burrowed into her side as she stroked his hair.

When Trace looked up and saw Parker still recording, he'd had enough. "Want to record something? How about this." Trace stalked over to him again. "You're really going to help a woman gain custody who hasn't shown a morsel of interest in her son since he was born? You'd actually help take a special-needs child away from his stable home to dump him in an environment that's uncertain at best? You're that much of a scumbag?"

"You gave your ex-wife the leverage she was looking for when you let *Ms. Barns* into your life," Parker said, looking past him to Lily. "It wasn't hard to track down information about you because of your accent. All it took was a little snooping and some googling."

"Trace." Lily lowered her voice. "I'll explain everything when we're alone."

His hair prickled on the back of his neck. He'd had the same sensation the first night she'd arrived on the island, and he'd ignored it. Now something told him that had been a decision he'd live to regret.

"Ben, can you and Uncle Spence take Waddles home?" Trace asked.

Spence got the message. "Come on, buddy. Let's go."

Parker turned to leave behind Spence and Ben.

"Hold up." Trace drew himself up to tower over Parker. "Tell Megan and her agent I'll take my chances in court. I'm guessing the autistic charity that pays Megan won't care much for a spokesperson who doesn't want to be around her own autistic child." Trace folded his arms in a don't-fuck-with-me gesture. "And I'm guessing you have a few secrets you'd rather keep buried too, Mr. Parker. When I find out what they are, I'll bet a judge won't like the fact that my ex-wife is responsible for sending you here to spend time around my son. I'd also wager the authorities will be interested in your secrets. So get off my property," Trace said. "Better yet, get off my island, or I'll throw you off myself."

Parker turned and sped up the trail.

As soon as they were alone, Trace turned to Lily. "Care to tell me what he was talking about?" And for the first time in weeks, there was no softness to his tone when he spoke to her.

Chapter Twenty-Two

LILY'S LIFE LESSON #22
If you've heard the words *you're fired* more than once,
then it's probably your fault.

The thorny look on Trace's face made Lily want to sink into the ground, but she couldn't blame him. Today could've been catastrophic for Ben, and Parker had outed her before she could tell Trace the truth herself.

Parker had come looking for ammunition that Megan could use against Trace. Lily had given it to him. And now Trace wanted an explanation. An explanation that was well deserved and long overdue.

She nodded. "First, let me say I'm so, so sorry about this."

His cast-iron expression speared her in the heart.

"I wanted to call, but I left my phone in my office, and Ben was adamant about looking for a place for the ducks to swim right then." Lily hugged herself against the chilled wind. Suddenly, she felt so very, very cold. "It was thoughtless of me to bring him to the cove."

"I didn't want those damn ducks to stay at the resort because I knew they'd be trouble." Trace's voice was gruff. "And no, you shouldn't have brought Ben here." Trace pinched the bridge of his nose. "Hell, Lily. *You* shouldn't be here without me or someone else. It's dangerous, and you knew why it would bother me. But that's not the only reason I'm so damn upset."

The first crack of thunder echoed around them.

"I know." She felt her throat closing. "We should've already had this conversation."

Trace stopped pacing and gave her a look as dark and cloudy as the sky. "There is no *we*. Not unless you can explain what Parker meant. Please tell me you didn't give my ex-wife leverage she can use against me. Please tell me the years I've spent trying to protect my son weren't for nothing." His voice was strangled, and he ran his fingers through his hair. "Please tell me I didn't open myself up to the wrong woman again."

Lily's chickens—or ducks, if she wanted to put a fine point on it—were coming home to roost. A sting started behind her eyes, and not just because she was guilty. Tears threatened because of the pain her dishonesty was about to inflict.

She was definitely her father's daughter.

She drew in a breath, squared her shoulders.

"Lily's my middle name. The only person who called me that was my grandmother. *Her* name was Lily Barns. My name is Scarlett Devereaux."

His brows drew together as he stared at her. *"Scarlett?"* he whispered.

She laced her fingers in front of her chest and did some pacing of her own to keep her nerve up. "I lied to your father so he'd hire me." She let out a hollow chuckle. "My work experience was all true. In fact, I actually left things off my résumé so I wouldn't seem overqualified, but I used a false name and signed my own letters of recommendation."

"You told me your ex was your boss, and your last job didn't end well. Why?" Trace's voice was low, like he was stunned and trying to process everything.

"Andrew . . ." She chewed her lip. "My ex-fiancé fired me because my father went to prison. Andrew didn't want that blemish on his career, so he broke up with me. And he fired me too." She swallowed back the burn in her throat.

"But why?" Trace spread his arms wide. "Why go to such extremes to be deceitful?"

Ouch. That shouldn't hurt because Lily *had* been deceitful. But it did hurt. Cut her to the bone, in fact. "The press stalked my family for months. I thought it would get better after my father was convicted. It didn't. It got much worse, and no one would hire me to do what I do best because of the constant media coverage. And because of Andrew ruining my career to cover his ass."

"Why here? Why Angel Fire Falls?" He started to pace again.

She shrugged. "It seemed so remote, so far removed, I figured no one would find me here. I lost my job, lost my fiancé, lost all my friends. My father will be in prison for a very long time, and my mother was drowning in denial and booze. There was no reason for me *not* to move far away. I thought Angel Fire Falls would be the perfect place to start over." The thunder growled, and Lily looked up. "Your dad didn't do a background check. Obviously, that should be a requirement in the future, but I figured I'd do a kick-ass job for your dad and earn my place here." How wrong she'd been. "Caring about your family wasn't part of my plan. I didn't see that coming. I wasn't expecting to fall in love with you either."

Trace's expression morphed from dazed to confused. When he finally worked through his emotions to settle on just one, it stole her breath. She'd expected anger. Anger she could've handled much better than the pain she saw in his eyes, as though she'd just stabbed him in the heart with a rusty icepick.

So she made it easier for him. Took some of the burden because he didn't deserve to carry it all.

She gave him a reason to fire her.

"My father embezzled millions from FEMA and homeowners who'd lost everything. He defrauded businesspeople who'd invested into rebuilding hotels and casinos along the Gulf Coast. He's got a lot of enemies who've made threats and hate me by association." She let her eyes close for a beat. "I suppose Ben's mom could use it against you, especially since I spent so much time with Ben."

Trace's eyes were as hollow as his tone. *"Scarlett."* His voice was dull, resonating with the sound of brokenness and betrayal. So very different from the Voice that had turned her heart and her body into mush when its very first syllable licked over her. "You're fired."

She swallowed. Tried to stop the quiver of her lip and the bile welling up from her churning stomach. "I . . . I understand. I'd . . . like to tell Lawrence myself." Despite her best effort, her voice still cracked.

"You've done enough. I'll take care of it. Be ready to leave as soon as the storm blows over."

She nodded. "For what it's worth, I planned to tell you everything after I fulfilled my responsibilities to the resort and the other businesses who are working with us." She turned to trek up the path.

She'd expected as much. Deserved it, even.

Still, nothing prepared her for the pain that knifed through her chest as she made her way to her cottage, knowing she'd never see the resort, the island, or the Remington family again. Most of all, knowing she'd never see Trace, the man she'd fallen head over heels for even though he was her boss and the last person on earth she should've let herself love.

She hardly noticed the mud or the biting drops of rain as the sky opened up and the storm dumped on her.

Lily didn't see the sense in prolonging her painful and humiliating exit from the Remington. Instead of waiting for the storm to pass, she packed her bags and brought them to the front door.

She didn't want to bother the Remingtons any more than she already had by asking one of them for a ride. Instead, she made up her mind to rig her own transportation to the ferry crossing.

Where was Mabel McGill's giant tricycle when she needed it?

"Sorry, kiddos," she said to the ducks. "But I need your pool for my luggage." She dragged it onto the front porch, then went back inside for one last look.

She was going to miss her little cottage. Somewhere along the winding island road to her new life, the quaint cottage had become her home.

She knelt down in front of the larger habitat Ben and Trace had built a couple of weeks before to accommodate the growing ducks. "Promise you'll take care of Ben for me?"

They quacked and squawked, which brought a smile to her lips that didn't reflect her bone-deep sadness.

Fifteen minutes later, she had her luggage loaded into the toddler swimming pool and the pool secured to the back of the bicycle through a hole she'd punched in the pool's plastic side. She zipped her jacket and put the hood up to shield her from the rain.

No one was out and about at the resort because of the storm, so when she pedaled down the long drive and through the exit, dragging a plastic pool behind her, no one stopped her.

By the time she reached the ferry terminal, she was soaked.

"One ticket, please," she said as she stood in front of the scratched acrylic window.

Mabel McGill leaned forward to eye Lily's expensive French luggage. Which didn't look at all expensive anymore. The shape it was in said it'd been circling the globe since the day she disembarked from the ferry and asked to borrow a giant tricycle.

"Could you call the Remington after I'm gone and tell them the bicycle and pool are here? They belong to them."

Mabel lifted a penciled brow. "One-way ticket, then?"

"Um, yes." Lily handed her a few bills.

"You're just in time, hon. We're about to shut down the ferry because of the storm." She handed Lily a ticket. "Sorry it didn't work out. Those Remington men are heartbreakers."

Was it so obvious that Lily's heart was ripped in two?

She shook her head. "The Remingtons were great. This one's on me." She slung her alligator purse over a shoulder. "Thanks, Mabel. Take care."

Without a backward glance, Lily drew on every ounce of courage she could find and rolled her tattered luggage up the ramp to go . . . home.

Chapter Twenty-Three

Trace found Ben in the family den. He and Spence sat at the table, disinfecting a cut on Ben's hand he must've gotten during the chaotic mess at the cove.

"How's it going?" Trace ruffled Ben's hair.

Ben's lips puckered, and a crocodile tear slid down his cheek. "Did I get Lily in trouble?"

Trace drew in a breath, and he and Spence exchanged a look.

"I'm unhappy with both of you. Lily shouldn't have taken you to the cove without me, and you know better than to go past the boathouse. You ran into water way over your head."

"I can swim," he said bluntly.

Trace nodded. "Yes, but it'll take a few more summers of swimming lessons for you to swim well enough to go into deep water like you did. What if no one had been there to help you?"

Spence was still working on Ben's hand, and he stilled. His stare was vacant like he wasn't really seeing.

"You can't put yourself in danger like that again, Ben." The whole thing had almost cost Trace more than he could bear. "It's not fair to the rest of us. Imagine how sad we'd be if something happened to you."

"Like how sad I'd be if I'd let something happen to Waddles?"

Well, hell. For once, Trace hadn't put himself in his son's shoes. In Ben's eight-year-old mind, something bad happening to one of his ducks was horrifying.

"Yes. Only it would be much worse." Trace rubbed his jaw. "Promise me you won't do it again."

Ben nodded and sniffed. "I promise."

Spence finished putting a Band-Aid on Ben's hand. "Okay, little man." The paleness of his face mirrored his grim tone. "You're all set." He stood.

"Ben, you owe Uncle Spence an apology. It was very . . . difficult for him to have to be at the cove." Trace stumbled over his words, not knowing how much he could say before Spence lost his shit. "And then to have to go into the water to save Waddles was . . . a lot to ask."

"Sorry, Uncle Spence," Ben said.

Spence gave him a sad smile. "I'm just glad you're okay."

"Can you find Dad for me?" Trace asked with a knowing look. "We've got things to discuss."

Spence nodded, gave him the signal for *Let me know if you need me*, and left.

When they were alone, Trace pulled his chair closer to Ben. "Son, I'd really like to know what you were thinking. What would make you take a risk like that?"

Ben swiped at his nose with the back of his hand and sniffled. "I needed to find a bigger place for the ducks to swim because they've gotten so big and soon they'll be big enough to survive on their own, but Waddles still has a limp and his wing still isn't right so I thought maybe if they had more room he could heal in time to fly away with the other ducks." It all tumbled out at once.

Trace held up a finger. "I thought you were trying to *stop* Waddles from leaving."

"No." Ben's tone said he had a perfectly sound reason for his thinking, which Trace hadn't latched on to yet. "I didn't want Waddles to leave *today*. Not until all the ducks can fly away together. When I was doing research for my project on how to let the ducks go, I found out Waddles might have to stay here with us forever if his leg and wing don't heal." He paused just long enough to take a breath. "Wouldn't it be sad if he couldn't live with his family?" Ben's eyes glistened again. "Like if I had to leave you and everybody else to go live in Los Angeles. It would be horrible, so I asked Lily to help me."

Ah, shit. Trace had been hard on Lily about the cove. The adrenaline rush from Ben rushing into deep water had still been pounding in his veins. But he knew his son better than anyone, and Ben could be a handful. He might've gone to find a swimming spot for the ducks even if Lily hadn't agreed to go. Trace could see that now that he wasn't crazy with fear.

Even if she'd lied about everything else, thank God she'd been with him.

"So you're planning for the ducks to leave?" Trace asked, because all along he'd thought Ben would be upset over letting them go.

"Of course, Dad," Ben said with an eye roll in his voice. "It's part of my project. They'll be happier in the wild because it's where they belong." He rubbed one thigh. "Like I'm happier here than in Los Angeles because this is where I belong. Can I go apologize to Lily now?"

Trace pinched the bridge of his nose. "Why don't you go to the kitchen and see if Charley has a doughnut for you. I'll walk you to Lily's after I talk to Grandpa." Because Trace and Ben both owed Lily an apology for what had happened at the cove, if nothing else.

Ben hopped off the chair. "I'm sorry, Dad."

Trace squeezed his son tight. "Just promise me it won't happen again, and we're good."

"Promise," Ben said, and skipped away.

As he reached the door, Trace's dad came in holding a file. He tweaked Ben's nose. "You okay, pard'ner?"

"I'm going to get a doughnut." He kept on skipping toward the kitchen.

Trace's dad chuckled and took a seat at the table. "I just heard what happened." His expression turned solemn. Worried.

Trace did not want to tell his father about Lily. Because of the fantastic job she'd done at the resort, he practically believed she could walk across the water that separated the island from the mainland without getting more than the soles of her shoes wet.

"Dad." Trace didn't know where to begin. So he started with her name. "Does the name Scarlett Devereaux mean anything to you?"

His dad thrummed his fingers against the table. "As a matter of fact, it does. Lily listed her as a reference."

Trace leaned forward. There was no way to put it delicately, so he decided to blurt out the truth. "Lily is Scarlett Devereaux. She lied to you. To me. To all of us. She pretended to be someone she's not, and apparently, her father has a lot of enemies. The press has been after her. If they find out she worked here, Megan might even be able to use it. I just don't know." He drew in a breath to deliver the last of the story. The worst of it that would likely be a blow to his dad. "She targeted the Remington because we didn't do a background check." Trace hesitated. "I let her go. She'll be leaving the island as soon as the storm blows over."

His dad went silent, nothing but his finger-thrumming filling the room.

"Say something," Trace insisted.

Finally, his dad leveled a stare at him. "What makes you think I didn't do a background check on Lily?"

Trace stared at his dad. Cleared his throat but couldn't speak.

He had nothing.

"You know the story about how I met your mother," his dad said.

By heart. Trace waited because he had no idea where his dad was going with this.

"What I never told you boys is your mother lied on her résumé to get me to hire her."

Trace got up and paced across the room.

"She couldn't get a high-caliber restaurant to hire her, even though she was the best chef on the West Coast at the time. No one would give her a second glance except greasy-spoon restaurants who paid minimum wage."

"Why didn't you tell us?" Trace asked, pacing back to the table.

"Because you never needed to hear it until now." His dad shrugged. "When I ran a background check on your mother . . . because I *do* run background checks . . . I found out she didn't have the formal culinary education she'd listed on her résumé." He chuckled, staring at the floor like he was reminiscing. "What she did have was grit, and I liked that. It's what this place needed. It's what *I* needed. So I didn't tell her I knew the truth. Instead, I gave her a second interview in the kitchen. A second chance to prove herself. I let her cook for me."

"There's a big difference between Mom lying about culinary school and Lily—" Or whatever the hell her name was. "And someone lying about her name . . ." Trace threw his hands up. "Lying about her entire history. Hell, Dad. I don't even know who I'm in lo—" He bit off the last words. He was not in love with Lily Barns *or* Scarlett Devereaux.

Except that he was.

His dad smiled. "Desperate situations make us do desperate things." His dad told him everything he'd found out about Lily and what she'd been through because of her father. When his dad got to the death threats, Trace's protective instincts surged.

Lily had grit all right. She'd left her home, left her family, and came to a strange place alone. Had to have been scary. But she'd poured everything she had into the resort, opened herself up to Trace and his son and the rest of the Remington yahoos.

And Trace had fired her for it.

He knew exactly who he was in love with, and her name didn't matter. Yes, she should've told him everything, but he'd seen who she really was in the rest of her actions. The way she'd loved Ben. The way she'd loved Trace.

His dad's expression was solemn. "Our biggest strengths are often our biggest weaknesses. If Lily had it to do over again, she might make different choices. I know your mother would've so she could've seen you boys grow up." His dad gave him a thoughtful look. "You know, you're a lot like your mom. Nothing was more important to her than being a parent."

Trace's throat grew thick.

"She went out in the boat that day to spend quality time with your little brothers while you and I were away for the weekend."

And Trace had held it against her ever since, thinking it had been thoughtless and selfish of her to put herself at risk with no one home to come to her rescue. Trace had obviously been the selfish one, moping over the fact that he'd felt the obligation to take on her parenting role once she was gone.

Grief had swallowed him because he'd missed her, missed growing up with a mother, and didn't know how to deal with the private pain he knew his brothers carried inside. So it had been easier to blame Mom for dying instead of being thankful for the years they'd had a mother who'd loved them so wholeheartedly.

Trace blew out a breath. "If *you* had it to do over again, would you make different choices?"

His dad didn't hesitate. He shook his head with confidence. "Nope. I'd hire your mom, I'd fall in love with her, and I'd marry her because even though she died far too young, my life was still so much better having had her in it."

That made Trace stop breathing for a second as he tried to picture his life without Lily. Because he *couldn't* picture a life without her.

"So you followed your heart and took the same chance on Lily that you'd taken with Mom."

His dad nodded. "Your mom's grit is what this place has been missing since she's been gone. I figured Lily could bring it back."

Trace rubbed his eyes. If he'd expected honesty from Lily, he needed to do a little fessing up himself. He'd made his share of mistakes as a parent. Lily had never been a parent, yet she'd outshined just about everyone he knew when it came to bonding with Ben. Giving her another chance hadn't entered Trace's mind at the cove, but she deserved one.

He, on the other hand, wasn't so sure *he* deserved one.

"Having her at the resort could blow back on us and hurt my custody case." Trace was thinking out loud because there was no one he trusted more for advice than his father. "But she's important to me, and she's important to Ben. What kind of person would I be"—what kind of example would he set for his son?—"if I'm not willing to fight for someone we care about?" Someone he loved.

"We'll deal with it like we always do," his dad said.

Yes, each of the Remingtons had been through hell, but they'd always had each other to lean on.

Instead of being there for Lily, Trace had let her down as much as everyone else in her life.

He shot toward the door. "Gotta go. Thanks, Dad," he said over a shoulder. He widened his stride to reach the kitchen. He and Ben had to beat it to Lily's cottage because they both had some apologizing to do.

He blew through the kitchen door to find Ben gobbling up a doughnut.

Charley had the landline handset to her ear. "Trace is right here." She shoved the phone in his chest. "It's Mabel McGill."

He refused to grab the handset. "I don't have time."

Charley covered the receiver. "It's about Lily."

Trace wrinkled his forehead and took the phone. "Ms. McGill?"

"Yes, hon." Her scratchy voice came through the line. "Lily wanted me to let you know you can pick up your bicycle and swimming pool at the terminal."

WTH? This had to be a bad dream. "I don't understand."

Her laugh was interrupted by a smoky cough. "She rode a bicycle here and dragged her luggage in the pool."

Trace's heart raced like the howling wind brought on by the storm. "Lily was at the ferry crossing?"

"Yes, dear, but she's gone now. She caught the last ferry before we shut it down. So you can come get the bike and pool." Ms. McGill didn't seem to think it was the least bit strange. "She said they belong to you. Although, the pool isn't in the greatest shape."

Trace bet it wasn't. "Thanks for calling, Ms. McGill." He slammed down the phone.

He stopped to give Ben a kiss on top of his head, then looked at Charley. "I have to find a way to the Cape. Take care of him while I'm gone?"

Charley nodded. "Be careful."

Trace didn't just walk, he ran. He was going to get to Lily, come hail or stormy waters.

"Ooooh. God." Lily's moan echoed through the face rest of the massage chair at the Cape Celeste commuter airport. Why not go out the same way she'd come in? It was the first time she'd left the island since she'd arrived and had plenty of time to let Yin, her favorite airport masseuse, work out the knots in her back and shoulders. The storm had shut down the airport, and the next flight out wouldn't leave for at least a few hours.

Yin used the base of her palm to dig into a wicked spasm between Lily's shoulder blades, and she nearly whimpered. But then the pain melted away along with the spasm, and she moaned, *"Ooooh. Yes."* Who cared what people thought? The airport was virtually empty because of the storm, anyway.

She was a woman who'd just rolled the dice and lost at love. Big. She was going to treat herself right before leaving with her tail between her legs. Anyone who didn't like her moaning, well, they could bite her.

Yin's magical fingers distracted Lily enough to keep her tears in check. She would not let the dam she'd held back since Trace fired her at the cove burst. She'd known he'd be hurt. Known his reaction wouldn't be good. Known getting fired was a distinct possibility.

It still sucked.

"Ahhhh," she moaned again as Yin went to work on a spasm in her neck.

She didn't ask Trace to forgive her because she had no right to. She'd hoped he'd offer his forgiveness anyway because that's what she'd do for someone she loved desperately. Loved madly. Loved with her whole heart. She loved him enough to let him go, though. Chasing him, begging him, asking him for anything would've only added to her humiliation, since he'd obviously had no intention of accepting her apology.

She made a mental note to add *Never chase a man unless he's driving an ice cream truck* to her list of life lessons.

But then, she hadn't paid much attention to her life lessons, had she?

Obviously, she sucked at picking the right guy to fall in love with. Getting fired by her boss the first time wasn't enough for her to learn the lesson. She had to go and do it all over again.

She let out a heavy sigh that whistled through the headrest.

"You tight," Yin said. "Lot of stress."

Lily had heard that before, not so long ago.

"Need vacation," Yin said.

Ha! Actually, Lily needed a job so she could *pay* for the vacation. And it was a bummer that the only job she really wanted was the one she'd just lost in the most beautiful vacation spot on the continent.

Well, at least her mother would be happy that her baby girl, Scarlett, was coming home.

Yin pressed her enchanted thumbs into Lily's shoulders, and she moaned loudly. So loud, in fact, that Lin said, "Need boyfriend too."

A sting started behind Lily's eyes at the thought.

But then her phone dinged with a text. Probably her mother, because no one else on earth would be texting Lily at the moment.

She ignored it and let Yin work her magic.

Another ding had one of Lily's eyes cracking open. Her purse was on the floor next to her chair, so she searched without looking and found her phone. She slid it under the headrest to read the text, and her breath caught.

We need to talk.

A hairline crack formed in Lily's dam. Her thumbs flew over the keys, and she sniffed the tears back.

There's nothing left to say.

I have a lot to say.

She was sure he did, and none of it would be good.

Not now. Maybe soon.

If he wanted to vent his pain and anger toward her, she'd let him, but she needed to put some time and distance between them first.

Her phone didn't ding again.

Yin used her forearm to work the muscles in Lily's lower back.

"That feels better than—"

"I'll pay quadruple, plus a big tip for what she's getting," a familiar fluid voice said, just as a pair of suede hiking boots appeared under her headrest.

The deep masculine sound swelled and swirled inside her, making her insides tingle and her toes curl. Lily's voice caught in her throat, and she couldn't move without losing it.

"Wait your turn," Yin said to him. "No other masseuse here today. Not enough customers."

The boots disappeared, but the chair next to Lily creaked under the Voice's weight. Because, oh yes, that beautiful silky voice couldn't belong to anyone else.

"Enjoy your trip to this part of the country?" the Voice asked.

Lily could not look up. She couldn't. Not without knocking a hole in that dam of tears the size of a cannonball. "Um," her voice cracked. "Yes. Very much. Until today."

"Meet any interesting people?"

"Yes. Some were more than interesting." Her voice got croakier.

"Any worth sticking around for?" the Voice asked.

Lily's head popped up.

Trace sat on the edge of the chair next to her, leaning in her direction with his elbows propped on his knees. "Because I know a few people who really want you to stay. For good, if you still want to."

The dam broke, and Lily let the tears flow. "I'm so sorry."

Trace reached over and took her hand in his, stroking her fingers. "I'm the one who's sorry, babe. When you love someone, you don't ask them to leave just because they made a mistake."

She sat up and wiped her eyes.

Yin looked from Lily to Trace then back to Lily. "I take break." She disappeared.

He kept stroking the length of her fingers with his. One swipe, then another, his calloused fingers warming her soul. "You're willing to give me another chance?" she asked.

"If you're willing to give me one. But I do have one condition." A smile curved onto his lips. "Promise you'll give up your obsession with transportation that ends with *cycle*," he teased.

She threw her head back and laughed.

Trace pulled her into his lap and caressed her cheek. "I love you." He smoothed a stray lock of hair from her forehead. "And so does Ben." His eyes were as soft and silky as his tone.

Joy pushed out the sadness in her heart. "I love you too." She leaned her forehead against his. "And Ben too. But I don't want to stay if it's going to hurt either one of you."

"You were barely gone from the island an hour, and I felt like part of me had been torn away. I can't imagine living a lifetime without you, and Ben would never forgive me." He brought her hand to his lips and placed a gentle kiss on the inside of her wrist. "I want you to stay at the Remington. Make it your home. Make it your job." He placed another feathery kiss on her wrist that sent a tingle skating up her arm.

"What about the media?" she asked. "It's only a matter of time before they find out where I've been. It could hurt your custody case, and it could hurt the resort."

"I've watched you solve every problem in your path. We'll figure this one out together." He placed a soft, slow kiss on her lips. "I'm yours, Lily . . ."

Her breath caught.

"Or, uh, Scarlett?" he corrected.

"I'd love it if you'd keep calling me Lily." She smiled and placed a kiss on his lips. "My grandmother called me Lily, and I loved it."

He pressed another sweet kiss to her lips. "I'm hoping you could change your name one more time."

A wrinkle appeared across her forehead.

"I like Lily Remington." He smiled. "It has a special ring to it."

"*You* make me feel special," she breathed against his mouth.

His eyes dilated. "Let's get your luggage and go so I can make you feel *really* special."

"There'll be no making me feel special until tomorrow when Ben's at school," she scolded.

Trace shook his head. "We're getting a hotel room because my plane is at the resort, and the ferry is shut down until the storm passes."

She leaned back to give him a questioning look. "How did you get here?"

He winked, and the sexy pilot she'd met right there in the same spot the day she'd arrived was back. "I have a friend in the coast guard. He owed me."

Lily threw her arms around Trace's neck and kissed him until neither one of them could breathe. Because only a man desperately in love would hitch a ride with the coast guard to stop his woman from leaving.

Chapter Twenty-Four

LILY'S LIFE LESSON #24
When life gets tough, keep on pedaling.

Trace and Lily sat in the back row of Ben's classroom waiting for his turn to present his science project. Trace's cell phone vibrated in his pocket. When he took it out and saw the number on the screen, he leaned over to whisper in Lily's ear. "Be right back."

She nodded without looking at him. Instead, she gave Ben a thumbs-up for the hundredth time because he kept turning around to make sure she was still there.

Trace stepped into the hallway for privacy and answered the call. "Megan." He kept his voice flat.

"Trace." There was already a tremor in her tone. "Just so you know, I didn't know anything about Ronald Parker until after he'd already visited the island the first time, and I didn't know my agent was going to send him back to the island again." She hesitated. "I'm looking for another agent."

Hopefully, a more ethical one, if there was such a thing in Hollywood.

Trace responded with silence.

"I . . . I got the recording you sent," she said. "I'm not going any further with the custody suit."

"Good." He went quiet and waited. Just waited.

She caved within seconds. "You didn't have to have your girlfriend call the autistic foundation. I was planning to step down as their spokesperson after I heard what Ben had to say."

Since Megan was so hell-bent to use Ben to get her face on television, Trace had decided to show her what her son really thought of her. Trace had recorded Ben with the ducks that day, talking about how his mother didn't like him, thought he was weird, and how he'd compared his situation to the ducks, just like he had after Megan's field trip—mommy drama. An Oscar-worthy motion picture couldn't have been a bigger tearjerker, but it was time for Megan to see herself through Ben's eyes.

"I didn't have anyone call the autistic foundation," he said. "But I should've called them myself."

"Well, someone did." Her voice cracked. "They knew all about my last visit."

"Ben's teacher and twenty kids were present. Kids do go home and tell their parents things, especially when there's drama," Trace said. "Any one of them could have made the call. You wanted to be on television, and now you've put a target on your own back."

"Well, they let me go before I could quit." She sniffed. "I suppose that makes you happy."

"None of this makes me happy, Megan." He crossed an arm over his chest.

"I . . . I'm sorry. I just wanted to catch a break for once in my career. I'm not getting any younger." She sniffed. "I'm never going to be good with Ben. Not like you, Trace."

"You don't have to be like me," Trace said. "But you do at least have to make an effort with him. If you can't do that, then leave him alone completely because he doesn't deserve the heartache."

"Do you think Ben will ever forgive me?"

"He's a great kid. I'm sure he will, but he's already caught on to a lot. You're going to have to do much better if you want him to *want* you in his life."

After he allowed Megan more time for blubbering than she deserved, he ended the call. Only time would tell if she could change, but Trace wasn't going to hold his breath. He had too much to look forward to with his new life with Lily. And so did Ben.

◆　◆　◆

Lily was getting restless waiting for Trace to finish up his phone call in the hallway. Miss Etheridge introduced each of the kids who were presenting their science projects. Trace slipped back into the seat next to her just in time. It was the last week of school before summer break, and the class of second graders was jittery with excitement.

"Lily!" Everyone in the room heard Ben's loud whisper.

You've got this, Lily mouthed at him and gave the thumbs-up again.

Trace slid an arm around the back of her chair, and his fingers gently caressed her shoulder. "Thank you," he said low enough so only she could hear. "This project won Ben a lot of favor with the other kids." The tenderness in his eyes said how much that meant to him as a father of a child who didn't always fit in. "It wouldn't have been possible without you and your tricycle," he teased.

She elbowed him. "Careful. I have a new driver's license." Trace had brought her to the Cape the day before to get an in-state license. She needed to be mobile with the crazy busy summer ahead and the resort kicking off a record season in a few days. "If you think I was daring on a bike or trike, wait until you see me behind the wheel of a four-wheel-drive Jeep. No telling what type of animals I might bring to the resort now that we have a new pet-friendly policy."

His expression blanked. "I think I'm scared."

The rest of the Remingtons filtered in, squeezing Lily's shoulder as they walked by, and sat on the far end of the row to take the last empty seats. They hadn't blinked when she and Trace had walked into the resort several days before and he'd announced that she was staying and would eventually become an official member of the family.

After Lawrence made several lengthy telephone calls to animal-rights groups, environmentalist groups, and a Portland news station, the press had turned her into an overnight hero, robbing the haters back in NOLA of their juicy story. Her future father-in-law explained to everyone who'd taken his calls how Lily hadn't let her tumultuous circumstances hold her back. Instead, she chose to start over, and in the process, she'd rescued a brood of baby ducklings that wouldn't have survived on their own.

Donations were already pouring in to several bird sanctuaries up and down the West Coast, and they'd even invited Ben to bring the ducks there when he was ready.

But the thing that brought tears to Lily's eyes and joy to her heart was her father. He'd called Lily, and they'd had the best conversation she could remember since she was a kid. Then he'd called Trace and thanked him for taking care of his baby girl.

"Next we have Ben Remington," Miss Etheridge said. "And he's brought an extra-special treat for us."

Lily couldn't contain her excitement any longer, and she clapped.

Several of the ladies turned around to glare at her. Probably PTA moms. Charley had warned her that PTA moms could be even more vicious than hockey moms. Now that Lily was going to be one of Ben's parents, she'd have to volunteer and show them a thing or two about overseeing an event and running an organization. If that didn't put them in their places, then maybe pepper spray would work because their glares were terrifying.

Ben set up his poster on the chalkboard, then went to the large covered pet crate in the corner that Lily and Trace had delivered to the classroom while the kids were at recess. Ben had learned that covering a birdcage quieted the ducks down. Besides a few low squawks and quacks, this brood had done pretty well. He pulled the blanket off to reveal the ducks, and they tuned up.

The kids cheered and chattered.

When Miss Etheridge finally got everyone quieted down, she said, "Okay, Ben. Continue."

"This is Daisy, Sir Walter Raleigh"—he pointed to each and held up a different color Velcro foot band for each name—"Roxy, Oscar, Squeaks, Bandit, Oreo, Scooter, and Belle." Ben named every duck except one. Then he pointed to the one with a slightly smaller wing. "And this one's Waddles. He's different, like me."

He launched into an explanation of their growth, their food, and his plan to let them go back into the wild from the cove behind the resort. "If Waddles can't fly off with his family, then we'll take care of him, and he can be part of our family, and the other ducks can fly back and visit him." Ben's little body thrummed with excitement. "Just like Lily is going to be part of our family from now on. And her mom and dad can come visit anytime they want."

Lily got choked up that Ben had thought of her parents, and she covered Trace's hand with hers.

She and Trace hadn't explained the whole prison thing to Ben just yet, but soon they'd tell him why her father couldn't visit the island. Lily's mom was a different story, though. Lily had told her everything and introduced her to Trace and Ben through a live video call. As soon as the summer season was over, Trace and Lily promised to fly out and pick her mom up for a visit.

Trace stroked her shoulder and gave her a sexy wink.

When Ben was done, he passed out chocolate eggs to everyone, and Miss Etheridge let the class come forward to get a closer look at the ducks.

While they chattered and aahed over the ducks, Trace pulled his phone from his pocket and sent a text.

Lily's phone dinged, and she chuckled. Without looking at Trace, she retrieved her phone from her purse on the floor.

Did I mention how much I
love you?

Lily's thumbs flew over the screen.

Several times, but I never get
tired of hearing it.

"Good." He leaned over and whispered in her ear. "Because I plan to tell you every morning." He lowered his voice even more. "And show you every night."

A shiver lanced through her. She lifted both brows at him as a warning. "We're at Ben's school," she whispered.

He chuckled. "By the way, I just got good news. Megan dropped the custody suit."

Lily gasped and slid a hand to his thigh to grip it.

He waggled his brows at her. "We're at Ben's school," he mocked her. Then he sobered. "Megan's field trip drama at the resort got back to the autistic charity, and they dropped her as their spokesperson. Know anyone who might've called them?"

Lily shrugged. "Wasn't me." She hitched her chin over a shoulder at Charley. "I've been told the Remingtons stick together, though."

He laughed. "I've got a surprise." His fingers worked the keyboard of his phone as he sent her another text.

A picture of a cargo plane popped onto her screen. On the side of it the words TAKE FLIGHT DELIVERY SERVICE were painted, and ten yellow ducklings trailed behind the big letters.

"I had it custom painted. It'll be ready tomorrow," he said. "Just in time for the kickoff weekend."

Perfect.

"Oh," she said thoughtfully. "I almost forgot." She tapped the screen of her cell. "I have a little surprise for you too, but you better wait until we're alone to look at it. Now that I can drive, I did a little shopping." Jezebel's, Angel Fire Falls's only lingerie boutique, was Lily's new favorite place to shop. The old affinity for Saks her mom had drilled into her while growing up could suck it.

His cell dinged, and he tensed like it was killing him not to look. Finally, he cupped his hands around the screen and opened the text.

Slowly, he slid his phone into his pocket, took her hand, and pulled her to her feet.

The look of pure love mixed with a lot of lust must've shown on their faces, because Elliott leaned over and whispered, "Dude" as they left. Trace didn't stop. He tugged her out of the classroom and all the way to his Jeep.

And then he was kissing her right there in the parking lot of the elementary school, but she couldn't bring herself to stop him because his touch was pure heaven, and there was nothing else she'd rather do at that moment than have his lips on hers.

He was her future. Her family.

A man she admired.

The one who'd shown her a forever kind of love the day she'd left her problem-filled life behind and pedaled right into his heart.

Lily added one more lesson to her list, and it was the most important one of all. *When life gets tough, keep on pedaling.*

ACKNOWLEDGMENTS

I'm sending out a huge thank-you to Shelly Chalmers, my Golden Heart sister and critique partner extraordinaire, for her patience with the all-is-lost moment in every single book I write. You are a doll. I owe a debt of gratitude to Jill Marsal of the Marsal Lyon Literary Agency for her input into this story before I even started writing it. And of course, I'm grateful to my editors, Melody Guy, Megan Mulder, and Maria Gomez, and the entire Montlake team for the faith and support they've put behind my work.

Last but certainly not least, I'm extremely grateful to all my incorrigible readers who hang out with me over on my Facebook page. You make my day. A special thank-you goes out to Pamela Sayer for the "purse whore" idea for this book. You rock!

ABOUT THE AUTHOR

Photo © 2014 Frank Frost Photography

Shelly Alexander's first published novel was a 2014 Golden Heart final-ist. She is an Amazon #1 bestselling author in numerous categories, including contemporary romance, contemporary women's fiction, and romantic comedy. Shelly grew up traveling the world, earned a bach-elor's degree in marketing, and worked in business for twenty-five years. With four older brothers and three sons of her own, she decided to escape her male-dominated world by reading romance novels . . . and has been hooked ever since. Now Shelly spends her days writing novels that are sometimes sweet, sometimes sizzling, and always sassy. She lives in the beautiful Southwest with her husband and toy poodle named Mozart. Visit her at www.shellyalexander.net.